MAGGIE'S HOUSE

David Turnbull

MAGGIE'S HOUSE

GRAVESTONE PRESS

Chapter One

Our lives are often built on lies. They come in all shapes and sizes. Big lies and small lies. Lies told out of compassion to protect someone we care for. Lies told out of malice to hurt someone we despise. Lies which cover up dark secrets. Lies are the mechanisms by which we compensate for our faults and our regrets. The bad things we wish we'd never done. Sometimes lies are simply the things that are never spoken out loud.

I've had it with lies.

I'm going to come clean about what happened in Maggie's house.

It started with the three of us walking along an old railway track one sun scorched morning. The story I'm about to tell had furrowed its foul, creeping roots deep into the soil of the past long before that. But that day in the summer of 1973 is as good a place as any for me start.

Back then the track was a dark scar that slashed its way across a long swathe of countryside. A scar that reeked of its past industrial history, surface so black that you could smell the decades of soot and dust that had been ground into the dirt. Ragged shards of coal fallen from long ago steam trains that crunched under foot like fine gravel, releasing a sulphurous stench when they cracked.

It was sometime in late July that we walked the track, side by side, like brothers from some dysfunctional family, dressed almost identically. Ben Sherman shirts, faded Levi's, held up by wide braces. Danno's blue, HC's red, mine yellow.

Tattered black baseball boots on our feet. Each one of us with shoulder length, feather cut hair, spiky on top, attempting to emulate the style favoured by Rod Stewart and Ronnie Wood from The Faces.

The track sat on the crest of an artificially raised embankment. Nettles and curling fern grew in abundance on the steep slopes to either side, interspersed with yellow flowering gorse and clusters of wild lilac. Here and there small trees and shrubs clung awkwardly to the sandy soil. The upper fringes were lined with dandelions, bramble briars and the occasional outcropping of wild strawberries.

When it had been operational it had been a branch line, an offshoot of the main Edinburgh to Carlisle route. Trains hushed and hissed and rattled along its iron tracks, carrying goods and passengers. But its heyday had already faded and died before our parents were born. In 1973 it had been a good two decades since the iron tracks were lifted.

Now it was just a place to wander and squander away a summer day. The three of us had traversed it hundreds of times. It was one of half a dozen places in a compressed map of our little town that we seemed to frequently find ourselves aimlessly and predictably drawn to. That day, however, we were walking the track with a definite purpose in mind.

"So, are you going to make the *run,* or what?" asked Danno.

The three of us stopped as HC contemplated his answer.

He hesitated a moment, and then nodded his head sheepishly.

That settled, we set off again.

Just ahead of us I could see a week-old copy of the Daily Record, lying face up on the ground. With not so much as a hint of breeze to blow it away it just sat there in perfect stillness, pages slowly baking yellow from the attentions of the sun. As the three of us sauntered past it I glanced down.

'Scorcher!' blared the headline, in huge block capitals.

The picture beneath showed a kid in swimming trunks on the packed beach at Portobello near Edinburgh. He was squinting up at the camera, frozen in a moment of time. He had an ice cream cone in his left hand and a plastic bucket in his right. The ice cream was melting like streams of white lava over his fingers.

I'd seen that front cover umpteen times the previous week as I pushed the morning newspapers through people's letter boxes. The mini heat wave we were enjoying had lasted for almost over a fortnight now and the Record had carried several other front covers of a similar ilk. Most memorable was the picture of two teenagers frying an egg on the pavement in a Glasgow suburb.

HC claimed he knew one of the kids. Danno said that was balls, the picture had obviously been set up by the photographer who'd given the kids an egg and asked them to do it. I pointed out that it didn't matter if it was a set up, because anyone could see that the picture was real. It was so bloody hot that you could fry an egg on the pavement.

Nine days in and the heat wave showed no signs of breaking.

It was only just gone half past eleven in the morning but already I could feel the sweat soaking through my Ben Sherman. The red chequered material was sticking to my back. I wondered if it would leave a stain. I loved that shirt. I thought it made me look hard and edgy, like one of the guys on the front cover of the cheap skinhead novels that seemed to be endlessly passed around between the pupils at our secondary school.

Farther along the track we could see the heat rising in a shimmering haze. The weed-lined embankments hummed to the sound of bees and bluebottles. A multicoloured host of butterflies flitted back and forth across the track. Swarms of hungry midges hung in teeming clouds in the air.

An old man we knew from one of the bungalows near our housing scheme came along the track from the other direction. He was dressed in a polo shirt, khaki slacks, and a pair of brown sandals with accompanying brown socks. His Alsatian dog was padding along the track in front of him, tongue lolling to one side. As it approached HC crouched down and mussed it ears. "Good boy, *Captain,*" he told it. "Who's a good boy them." The Alsatian wagged its tail and slobbered over HC hands.

"Hope you boys are not up to mischief," said the old man.

"You know us, Mr Renton," said HC. "Good as gold."

"And I'm a monkey's uncle," scoffed Renton.

"We'll give you regard to Cheetah, then," said Danno, referencing Tarzan's pet chimp in the TV series.

Renton narrowed his eyes. "Less of your damned cheek."

Danno tried to stare him down. When I saw his fists clenching, I intervened with my impression of Shaggy from Scooby Doo. *"You think your dog would like a Scooby snack?"*

Renton chuckled. "You're that kid who does all the voices. I've no idea who that was supposed to be though."

HC ruffled the dog's head again and stood up. "I swear we're not up to mischief," he said.

"That'll be the day," laughed Renton and threw a chewed up old tennis ball for his dog to chase. *Captain* didn't seem too keen. But when the old man urged him on, he trotted ahead and grudgingly retrieved the ball.

Once they'd gone HC wiped his hands on the front of his jeans. "Why do you always have to try and make trouble?" he said to Danno.

Danno gave a shrug of his shoulders and kicked at the path, scuffing the rubber soles of his baseball boots along the surface, and sending up a little billowing cloud of dry dirt and old coal dust. "It's turning like the desert," he said, changing the subject.

I chopped at some wilting nettles with the stick I was carrying. "More like the jungle." A pollen heavy bee, striped in orange and black, flew blindly at my head, buzzing noisily. I ducked to dodge it.

"It's like that film, Bridge over the River Kwai," said HC. "We're like prisoners of war, getting force marched to build that bridge in the jungle."

9

"Nobody's forcing you to do anything," said Danno.

HC ignored him and turned to me instead "Do your Alec Guinness, Ranks. Do Alec Guinness, in Bridge Over the River Kwai."

I turned to face him, narrowing my eyes a bit against the glare from the sun. HC bit his lip. I could tell he was trying not to laugh too soon. I wedged my stick under my armpit and put on my best upper crust accent.

"One day the war will be over," I said, jutting my chin forward. *"And I hope the people that use this bridge in years to come will remember how it was built and who built it. Not a gang of slaves, but soldiers, British soldiers – even in captivity."*

"Brilliant," said HC. His face was so full of freckles he looked as if he'd come down with a bad dose of the measles. He grinned at me. "You're like Mike fucking Yarwood."

Danno punched me playfully on the arm. "Deserves an Oscar, so he does. One of these days he'll be on telly."

Mentally I gave myself a pat on the back. I'd found that the thing with impressions was that if you got the words down more or less perfectly it didn't really matter too much if you didn't sound exactly like the person you were attempting to impersonate. When people heard the words come out, they kind of filled the gaps and automatically imagined the voice, like it was the missing piece in an audible jigsaw.

"My granddad was a Japanese prisoner during the war," said HC.

Danno stopped to urinate into the nettles. A white butterfly landed on the back of his hand. "No, he wasn't."

"Was too," insisted HC. "He showed me the scars where they whipped him."

"More like the scars where he fell off the pavement when he was pissed," said Danno, shooing away the butterfly and pulling up his zip.

"Fuck you, Dalgetty," said HC.

Danno deliberately scuffed the soles of his baseball boots against the path again. This time HC walked right into the cloud of dirt and cold dust that drifted upward in the lazy heat. He coughed and spat, then turned and pushed Danno hard against the shoulders.

Danno balled his fists.

I got in between the two of them. We scuffled chaotically for a bit, in that stupid, almost comedic, Three Stooges manner we'd been endlessly descending into since we were six. Then, after a few punches and curses, the whole thing just fizzled out and we carried on as if nothing had happened.

"Look," I said, pointing down the track with my stick. "We're nearly there."

At the bottom of the steep embankment to the left of the track sat the dilapidated ruin of Maggie's house. The garden fence had been toppled and strangled by a rampant invasion of thorny brambles. Battalions of thistles and goldenrods stood like an unruly army in the garden itself.

Every window to the back of the house was smashed. All that remained were jagged fragments of glass that clung precariously to dry slithers of

11

putty. A huddle of filthy looking pigeons roosted lazily on the exposed attic beams, where part of the slate roof had collapsed. There were blades of grass growing out of what remained of the guttering. Raggedy bits of a dirty old net curtain hung in a limp tangle around a rusted drainpipe that yawed partially loose from the wall. Rust had bled into the curtain, making look suitably bloody and gruesome.

With its moss infested brickwork and its crumbling sills, the place looked like something out of a horror film. Locally it had a creepy reputation that fitted its image perfectly. Just looking down on it made my heart pound. Even the heat of the day couldn't defeat the cold shiver that suddenly ran through me.

"Are you actually going to do it this time?" asked Danno. "Or are you going to chicken out again?"

HC looked a little more sheepish. "The thing is," he said, "I've got something I need to tell you both. Something I'm not supposed to tell anyone. If I tell you now, you've got to swear straight on the holy bible, not to breathe a word."

I looked at Danno.

Danno raised his eyebrows and rolled his eyes.

"The thing is, I was born with this heart defect," explained HC. He looked so earnest and sincere that I might have started straight off to believe him. That is if I hadn't known full well what a relentlessly prolific lair he was. "The slightest shock might bring on a heart attack. I swear it's like a time bomb ticking in my chest. I could be gone like that." He clicked his fingers to demonstrate.

"Book him Danno," I said in my Steve McGarrett Hawaii Five O voice. It had become a thing now. Whenever HC told one of his whopping lies, I told Danno to book him. Danno started to laugh. And that set me off.

"That's utter crap, Anderson," said Danno. "You're talking out your arse again. That's what you do. You tell far-fetched stories all the time. That's how come you ended up getting called HC."

I was the one who'd given him the name in the first place. At the mention of it I danced a little jig and slipped seamlessly into my Danny Kaye. *"I'm Hans Christian Andersen. Andersen that's me."*

HC hawked up a gob of spit and expelled it noisily onto the path.

I could feel my cheek stinging from the heat of the sun.

"You two think you can take the piss out of me all the time?" he grunted. "Well, you've gone and shot yourselves in the feet this time. Because I had this little surprise that I was going to tell you about later. But now you can just go and fuck yourselves."

Danno heaved an exaggerated sigh. "Come on then," he said. "Tell us."

"We're doomed," I added, doing my Corporal Frazer from Dad's Army. *"Doomed, I tell ye."*

Danno laughed and play punched me again.

HC folded his arms over his chest and put on his serious face. The one we'd both come to associate with him preparing to tell yet another enormous whopper. Sure enough, out it came. "I was going to tell you that my uncle got us tickets to see Slade when they play in Edinburgh," he said.

"But now, because you're both such piss taking bastards, you can go and fuck yourselves. I'll find someone else to take."

Over the past few years HC's uncle had taken on a mythical persona. He'd apparently been everywhere, done everything, and met everyone. Danno and I had only ever seen him once. He was in the army at the time, and he came to HC's eleventh birthday dressed in the uniform of the King's Own Scottish Borderers. He hadn't been seen since. There was a rumour that he was serving a prison sentence for armed robbery. HC claimed this was a cover for secret work he was engaged in for the government and got really uptight if either of us suggested that this was bull.

"Your uncle hasn't got tickets to see Slade," sneered Danno.

"Oh, yes he has," HC shot back. "As part of his undercover work my uncle's been working a roadie for Slade. It's his job to set up Cozy Powell's drum kit."

I snorted loudly. "Cozy Powell isn't in Slade, HC. It's Don Powell. Don Powell is Slade's drummer. Cozy Powell played drums with Jeff Beck's band."

HC seemed to be caught on the hop. He scowled back at me. "Shows how much you know, Rankin. Cozy Powell and Don Powell are the same person. Cozy Powell is Don Powell's nickname. He used it when Slade lent him to Jeff Beck."

"Lent him to Jeff Beck?" I whooped at the notion. "You're having a laugh."

"I suppose your uncle told you that?" said Danno. "The same one who's been trying to infiltrate the IRA?"

"The same one who smuggled himself onboard Francis Chichester's yacht, so he could sail around the world?" I taunted.

"Come on, Ranks," said Danno, turning on the worn heels of his baseball boots. "Let's just leave him here. We're wasting our time. He's too chicken. He's just making up shite to cover how chicken he is."

"Guess that make it chicken shite then," I said.

Laughing at the joke the two of us started walking back along the track. Somewhere away in the distance I heard a workman's pneumatic drill, rattling relentlessly against concrete. A trickle of sweat ran down the side of my face. Another wasp buzzed at my head. I swiped it away.

"Wait," HC called after us. "I'll do it. I'm no chicken. But if something jumps out at me and I die of a heart attack you'll have to answer to my mum."

"If you die of a heart attack, I'll be so astounded that I'll have one myself," said Danno. "Your mum'll be the least of my worries."

I fell to the dusty track, clutching my chest and doing my impression of Jimmy Cagney in White Heat. *"Made it, Ma. Top of the world!"*

"Don't call my mum stupid," said HC.

He ran headlong at Danno. Still lying down I made a grab for his leg. As he toppled, he knocked Danno from his feet. For about a minute the three of wrestled in the dirt. Then it all fizzled out again. I looked at Danno. Out of the three of us he had the quickest temper. He was always getting into fights at school. He might have been a whole head shorter than both HC and me, but he was packed with muscle and aggression. If one of our little squabbles ever really got out of hand, both of us would probably come out the worst.

"So, are you going to do the *run*, or what?" asked Danno.

"I'm going to do it," said HC. "But if I die of fright, you'll be sorry.

Chapter Two

Maggie's house had stood empty since the mid-50s, slowly crumbling and collapsing in on itself. Everybody said that it was haunted. If you made the *run* the chances were that Maggie herself would be waiting for you behind one of the doors, all rotting flesh and bugged out eyes. Before you made your *run* you were obliged to confirm that you knew Maggie's *story*. Everyone who was about to make the *run* knew the story. You knew it by heart. You'd been making the *run* in your nightmares for weeks, the story rattling round in your head.

Especially the part about Maggie and how the police found her hanging behind one of the doors, the flex from her vacuum cleaner twisted around her neck, her tongue all black and swollen and poking through her lips. Her hospital gown still dripping from the rain. Hair hanging round her shoulders in rattails.

The *run* was legendary. It had become a rite of passage for teenagers from our housing scheme. By then it had been going on for years. Danno had made his *run* at the end of the Easter break. Once he did it there was huge pressure on HC and me to follow his lead. It had taken me till almost the start of the summer holidays to pluck up the courage. HC had managed to make excuses, till now.

"You know the story, don't you?" I asked HC. We stood at the top of the embankment, looking down through the weeds at the creepy, dilapidated property.

HC nodded his head. He looked pale and a bit fidgety.

"Maurice topped himself by putting his head in the gas oven," he said. "Maggie was so overcome with grief that she escaped from the hospital she'd been admitted to and hung herself with the chord from her hoover."

Everybody knew the story.

Maurice Henderson had owned a successful toy shop that stood on the High Street in the town centre. The exact spot where the Fine Fayre supermarket stood in 1973. Maggie had been his shop assistant, twenty years his junior. It caused a huge scandal when they announced their engagement. Maurice had doted on his young bride. Bought a plot of land that had belonged to the Railway Board. Built Maggie a house. Let her fill it with expensive furniture and all sorts of household gadgets that were fast becoming the rage in the early 1950s. Got himself into debt. Decided the only way to get out of it was to end it all.

"When you make the *run,* you have to go into every room," said Danno. "And you have to look behind every door, to see if Maggie's ghost is still hanging there on a mouldy length of rubber flex."

I swatted my hand back and forth at the cloud of midges that had drifted around me. My heart was fluttering in my chest. My mouth felt parched as the sun beat down on my neck. There was a sour feeling in my gut. I was remembering my own run. The experience had convinced me that there was something dreadful lurking inside the house. Something hidden in the shadows, lurking like some prowling predator, invisible to the eye, but with enough substance that it could make floorboards creak under its presence.

"Every single door," said Danno. "You got it?"

HC swallowed hard. "Jesus Christ. If I collapse from fright, you guys had better come and get me. You've got to swear you won't leave me in there with old Maggie hovering and slobbering over me."

I felt my nerves tingle, remembering the sheer terror I'd felt as the rusted hinges groaned when I looked behind each one of those old splintery doors. The pulses in my wrists had been pumping so fast at the possibility I might see her there, with her black tongue poking out, that I'd thought I was going to pass out.

"Just run as fast as you can," I told HC. "In through the kitchen. Look behind the door. Then up the stairs. Do the big bedroom first, then the bathroom, then the little room. Then back down the stairs to the dining room. Then the living room, and through the hall, and straight out the front door. We'll be waiting for you. It'll be over before you know it."

"But you have to look behind every single door," insisted Danno.

"Jesus, Mary and Joseph," said HC. He looked even paler now. I thought he might be about to puke. Hurriedly he made the sign of the cross against his chest.

"You got religion suddenly?" asked Danno.

"My uncle once had to pose a Catholic Priest," said HC, putting on his serious face. "He was on a secret mission."

19

"Is that the uncle who's trying to infiltrate the IRA?" asked Danno.

"Or the one who's a roadie for Slade?" I added.

"Fuck the two of you." HC looked as if he was about ready to walk off. "I warned you both."

"Book him, Danno," I said.

"Are you going to do it?" said Danno. "Or are you just too damned chicken?"

It looked like we were about to get into another scuffle. Then HC turned and began hurrying his way down the overgrown path that cut through the weeds and down the embankment to the collapsed fence of Maggie's garden.

Danno followed. I fell in behind. The situation put me in mind of a scene from Butch Cassidy and the Sundance Kid. The part in the storyline where this guy, played by Strother Martin, hires Butch and Sundance to act as his bodyguards.

"Morons!" I called out, doing my best to remember Strother Martin's lines. *"I've got morons on my team. Nobody is going to rob us going down the mountain. We've got no money going down the mountain. When we have got the money, on the way back, then you can sweat."*

I heard Danno laughing. *"We're just trying to spot an ambush,"* he called back.

"Would you two just shut up," said HC, arriving at the wreck of the garden fence. "I'm doing my best here not to shit in my pants."

Chapter Three

He turned to the side and rubbed his eyes with the heels of his hands. It looked like he was holding back the tears to stop himself from crying. I put my arm around his shoulder. "Just run as fast as you can. In and out of every room. Then out the front and it's over."

"But you look behind every door," insisted Danno.

"Holy shit," said HC. "Holy, holy shit."

I could feel him trembling.

We were standing by the hollow frame of the back door. The door itself had rotted and fallen from its hinges long ago. What was left of it was leaning against the listing ruin of an ivy-covered garden shed. You could see straight into the gutted remains of the old kitchen.

The heat pulsing out from the house was like the wall of heat that engulfs you when you open the oven on Christmas day to see how the roast is doing. I looked at the gap between the warped remains of the worktop and wondered if that was where Maggie's cooker used to sit. I thought about poor Maurice, down on his knees, head resting on the shelf of the oven, gas hissing him slowly and surely toward endless sleep.

I squeezed HC's shoulder again. "This is it," I told him. "We're going to start walking round to the front. You count to ten, then run like the fuckingest fucking fucker there ever fucking was."

Danno instantly doubled up with laughter. "Fuckingest fucking fucker there ever fucking was? Where did you come up with that one?"

I unwrapped my arm from HC's shoulder and shrugged.

"I don't know," I said. "It just came out."

Then I was laughing too.

HC started to laugh, quite maniacally, eyes bugged wide. It was as if all the stress that had built up inside him was coming out in one long stream of lunatic mirth. I thought I might want to try and remember that laugh for an impression. It sounded a bit like the Joker on Batman.

"We're going now," said Danno. "Every door, you hear?"

We began picking our way through the weeds and brambles to the side of the house. A little brown mouse shot out of a hole in the wall and disappeared into the tangled undergrowth. We could hear HC counting. "One, holy shit. Two, holy shit. Three, holy, holy shit."

"Stupid boy!" I said, in my Captain Manwaring voice.

Ahead of me Danno was manoeuvring his way through the debris that littered the little alleyway. It tended to be a dumping ground for people who couldn't be bothered to go to the town tip. We had to negotiate around an old pram, a rusted car wheel, several bags of hardened cement, what looked like a whole pile of rose pruning cut offs and a stack of broken floor planks.

It was normally cool to the side of the house. We'd often been there, daring each other to make

22

the *run*, but never plucking up the courage. That day though, even the shade couldn't dissipate the sultry heat.

We heard HC yell, "Ten!" and hurried to the front.

There had once been a gravel driveway to the front of Maggie's house. Now there were weeds poking up all over the place. It was littered with bits of shattered slate that had blown from the roof, interspersed with other stuff that people had dumped there. There was a rusted iron fence, all tangled up in weeds. There had once also been an ornate set of decorative iron gates. But these were gone. Rumour had it that the local scrap merchant had turned up in his flatbed lorry one night and spirited them away.

The front door of the house had also been removed. The doorway looked like the maw of some fiendish mouth, the hallway its long, narrow throat, just waiting to swallow you whole. We heard HC's feet thumping up the stairs. A moment later he leaned out through the empty window frame of the big bedroom. He was clutching his chest, freckled face contorted into a grimace. "My heart's giving out on me," he groaned. "See what you've done, you pair of bastards."

I looked at Danno.

Danno's mouth dropped open.

"Ha!" cried HC. "Got you!"

I gave him two fingers.

"Maggie's waiting for you behind the bathroom door," taunted Danno.

"Fucking hell, Danno," said HC, looking less smug. "What did you have to go and say that for?"

He stepped back and disappeared from our view. Danno and I waited in silence. Under my breath, I started counting down from a hundred, placing little bets with myself as to whether HC would reach the front door before I got down to zero.

I had just reached fifty HC let out a scream that turned the blood in my veins to slush. The pigeons roosting in the rafters rose in a noisy, chaotic mass and flew away in the direction of the old railway track. We heard HC clambering down the stairs and yelling. "Holy shit! Holy, holy shit!"

My heart started to pound an erratic tattoo inside my chest. I looked up at the window of the small bedroom, half expecting to see Maggie there, face all black, electrical flex hanging round her neck like a gruesome necklace. HC burst through the front doorway. He was running so fast he almost tripped on the undone lace of his left baseball boot.

"Run!" he screamed and shot straight past us out of the gate.

Danno and I stood there, frozen to the spot.

The moment broke. We fled, chasing HC headlong along the road and then down the tree lined dirt track that led to the river. The summer heat had taken its toll on the level of the water in the river. Whole swathes of its banks were exposed. We found ourselves on a long stretch of stones and pebbles, bleached white by the sun into a melancholy skeletal beach.

HC was crouched low, head bowed, hands on his knees, breathing heavily.

Danno was drenched in sweat.

There was a huge and painful stitch stabbing at my side.

"This better not be one of your games," said Danno, shaking his head like a wet dog and sending beads of sweat flying in every direction.

"Holy shit," mumbled HC. "Holy, holy shit."

I winced and rubbed at my side.

HC raised his head. Behind his freckles his face was as pale as the stones and pebbles we stood on. "Guys," he said. "There's a dead body in the little bedroom. A dead body. I swear to God."

Danno erupted. "That's crap, Anderson. That's utter crap, and you know it. You're always full of crap."

He punched HC so hard on the shoulder that HC staggered back a couple of feet. HC let out a yelp and ran at him. He wrapped his arms around Danno's waist and tried to drag him to the ground. Still suffering from the stitch, I yanked HC by the shoulders and hauled him off. When Danno tried to throw another punch, I got between the two of them and grabbed his wrist.

"Let go, Rankin," warned Danno, through gritted teeth. "I'm going to beat the lying little shit to a pulp. I swear, if you get in my way, I'll beat the shit out of you too."

"I don't think he's lying!" I yelled back.

I pointed to the dark, wet patch around the crotch of HC's jeans.

HC looked down. When he saw what I was pointing at he let out an embarrassed yell and ran straight into the river. After splashing around like crazy and scattering a huge shoal of minnows he came squelching back onto the stone covered bank, jeans well and truly drenched.

He looked as sick and sorry as a dog. "Holy shit," he said. "I pissed myself from fright and I didn't even know. Don't tell anyone. If we bump into anyone just say I fell in the river."

The stitch in my side was dissipating. Danno still had his fists clenched. He was staring at HC as if he was about to kick off again. I edged myself between the two of them. Across on the opposite bank of the river a crow settled in the branches of a tree. It cawed loudly, black beak opened wide, like some gothic portent.

Away the distance the pneumatic drill started in again.

"Just tell us what happened," I said to HC.

HC drew a deep breath. I saw a tear rolling down his cheek.

"I did like you told me, Ranks. I went in the kitchen, and I looked behind the door. Then I ran up the stairs and I looked behind the door in the big bedroom. Then I looked out the window at you guys. Then I went in the bathroom and looked behind the door. Then I went to the little bedroom, As soon as I walked through the door, I saw him. He was just sitting there in an old beat-up armchair. His eyes were open. They were looking straight at me. But they were all glassy, like. And I knew he was dead. Holy shit, Ranks, I've never seen a dead man before."

"Lair!" spat Danno. "There's no armchair in the little bedroom."

It was true - I hadn't seen one when I'd made my *run*.

I sensed Danno moving forward and edged myself sideways to block him.

"I swear I'm not lying this time, guys," said HC. "The thing is I know exactly whose body it is. I recognised him straight away."

I looked HC in the eye. "Who was it?" My mouth felt so dry, I thought my tongue would stick to my teeth.

"It was Catweazle," said HC. "It was old Catweazle himself, sitting there, stone fucking dead in Maggie's house."

"Catweazle?"

HC nodded.

Catweazle was a tramp who'd been hanging about town every summer since we were in primary school. Nobody knew where he went in the winter. Some said it was to a homeless hostel in Edinburgh. But every summer he'd be endlessly mooching around in the town centre.

You'd see him guzzling cans of Tennant's lager on the bench in the ornamental gardens, or picking up fag ends from the pavement, or rummaging around in the bins outside Fine Fare. If you were waiting for a bus, he'd been stinking up the waiting room in bus station. When we were little, he'd been called Stinky Jock. But when the Catweazle series started on TV he got his new

27

name. With his straggly hair and his wiry grey beard, it was the perfect name for him. I was tempted to try and lighten the tension between Danno and HC by saying something witty about *elec-trickery* in my Catweazle voice.

Instead, it was Danno who spoke first. For once he sounded conciliatory. "You sure?" he asked. HC nodded. "Fuck," said Danno. "I know," said HC.

Danno took out the pack of ten cigarettes we'd all chipped in to buy that morning at the local newsagents. "*Players No.6*," I said in a voice like a TV ad. "*The choice of discerning delinquents*." We all took one. Danno struck a match. HC's hand was trembling as he pressed the brown filter tip to his mouth.

"We need to phone an ambulance, or the police, or something," I said, twin streams of smoke gushing out of my nostrils.

HC nodded and drew on his cigarette.

"But the nearest phone box is on the housing scheme," I said.

HC shrugged. "Don't suppose it makes much difference to Catweazle if he has to wait a bit longer."

"We could go up to the road and flag down the next car that comes past," I suggested.

"The first thing we need to do is go back to Maggie's house and take a look," said Danno.

"You are joking, aren't you?"

"What if he's still alive?" asked Danno and flicked the remainder of his Player's No.6 into the river.

28

Chapter Four

The three of us cautiously entered Maggie's house through the front doorway. The hallway hung thick with the smell of dust and blown plaster. The floor was scattered with remnants of old dry leaves and bits of rubbish that had blown in during the spring. A fat beetle was feasting on the dried up remains inside an old Ski yoghurt tub.

"He's definitely dead," said HC for the umpteenth time.

He was lagging behind as usual, a good three paces behind me and Danno.

"We still need to check," insisted Danno.

As we passed the half open door to the living room my nerves began to tingle. I felt sure that Maggie was waiting there with the electrical flex tied tightly to her cold, dead neck, chuckling wickedly to herself. There was a cast iron fireplace cut into the wall, above it a wide mantelpiece, varnish peeling like horrible flakes of eczema. On its shelf sat a dirty jam jar. Above the mantle there was a faded stain on the wall where there had possibly once been a mirror. I wondered what terrors might have been revealed in the reflection had it still been there.

"If you think I'm lying, you're going to be in for one big shock," said HC, catching up a bit.

"And if you think we're leaving without checking, you're in for an even bigger shock," Danno shot back at him.

We reached the area where the hall formed an L shape at the foot of the stairwell. Ahead of us was the kitchen. You could see straight through to the overgrown garden at the back. I looked at the gap between the worktops and thought again of Maurice with his head in the oven, sucking gas and floating slowly away to oblivion. The image was so stark inside my head that I could almost believe there was a smell of seeping gas hanging in the stillness of the air.

"Shit," said HC. "What if you're right? What if Catweazle is still alive? What if he turns out to be some sort of crazy murderer, just waiting to jump out with a knife and stab us all to death? Holy shit. Holy, holy shit."

"Catweazle?" I huffed. "Waiting to jump out with a knife? There's three of us, HC. How exactly would he go about stabbing us all to death in one go?"

"Mad people have got super strength, Ranks," he said. "I should know. My uncle once worked in an insane asylum."

"No, he didn't," I snapped back at him.

"If Catweazle is waiting to jump out, you two are giving him plenty of notice that we're on the way," said Danno. "Now shut up and let's just get this over with."

He began to climb the stairs. HC managed to get in between the two of us. I brought up the rear. I could hear HC whispering under his breath. *Holy shit. Holy shit. Holy, holy shit.*

The old stairs cricked and cracked beneath our feet. As he walked HC jeans dripped river water, leaving fat, wet splats in the dust. There was another black beetle crawling over the crevices of the flaked paint on the banister. I pinged it away with my index finger.

We all congregated at the top of the stairs. Dry dust was falling like fine snow from a gap in the ceiling where a big chunk of plaster had dropped away. Scraps of faded wallpaper still clung here and there in patches on the dirty walls.

The big bedroom was to the left of the landing and the small bedroom to the right. In the middle, directly facing the top of the stair was the bathroom. Though the open door of the big bedroom I could see the graffiti that was scrawled onto the wall in red paint. I remembered it from when I had made my *run*.

It had originally read – *Eric Clapton is God!* But someone had crossed through the word *God* and replaced it. It now read *Eric Clapton is Dog!* The first time I'd seen it I had been too scared to even crack a smile. This time wasn't any different. A hellish image of Eric Clapton as some sort of grotesque half human / half canine hybrid monstrosity shuddered to life in the dark recesses of my subconscious.

Danno held his finger up to his mouth and leaned his head in the direction of the open door to the little bedroom, cocking his ear to one side. HC chewed his lip and danced nervously from his left foot to his right.

"Can't hear anything," whispered Danno.

"What were you expecting to hear?" I whispered back.

Danno shrugged. "Breathing maybe?"

He took an unsteady step forward.

31

HC and I shuffled behind him.

A fly came buzzing around us.

Far away the pneumatic drill kicked in once again.

Danno turned. "Let's just stop pissing about and get it done with. I'm going to count to three and we're going to go right into that room and see what's what."

"Holy shit," said HC. "Holy, holy shit."

My mouth began to feel dry again.

"One – Two – Three," counted Danno.

We kind of advanced in small steps along the corridor, brushing shoulders and knocking each other against the blown plaster on the walls, till we literally fell like some multi limbed creature into the little bedroom. And there, just as HC had described, was Catweazle, seated in a battered old armchair with yellow foam stuffing poking through the torn-up patches of its faded floral-patterned upholstery.

"Told you," said HC. "Who's the liar now?"

"Never said you was a lair," said Danno, staring at the body. "I just said we should check to make sure he wasn't still alive."

Catweazle looked plenty dead to me. There was no animation at all in his rheumy looking eyes. They just stared emptily into the distance. Beneath his wild grey beard and his scruffy grey hair his skin looked almost bloodless. His chin was resting on his chest. There was a green tinge on his dirt caked neck that made me want to gag.

He was wearing a shirt that was so engrained in grime and disgusting looking stains it was impossible to tell what colour it had originally been.

He had a threadbare tartan travel rug draped over his legs. His left arm sat limply on his lap. His right was dangling over the armrest of the chair. His filthy, half chewed fingernails were almost touching the floorboards.

We were all looking at him in a mixture morbid awe and stunned silence. Flies were buzzing around his corpse, settling in the wiry briar of his hair and his beard, crawling up and down the bridge of his sunburned nose. In front of the armchair was an upturned Fyffes Banana box. On it sat a red flask and a badly scratched plastic tumbler. Beside them sat an apple core, probably his last meal. It had turned a dark shade of brown.

"Where do you reckon the chair came from?" It was the only thing I could think of to say to break the silence.

"Somebody probably dumped it in the driveway, and he dragged it up the stairs," said Danno. He sniffed the air. "He's starting to stink bit."

"Anyway, that's that." HC's voice had become high-pitched and charged with nervousness. He started to ramble, hardly drawing breath. "I mean that's it. He's stone-cold dead. Just like I said. Let's go to the phone box. You don't even need no money, nor nothing. You just dial 999. We have to say we want and ambulance and probably the police as well.

Do you think we might get in the papers? We might even get our picture on the front page. We might be heroes. Do you think he's got a next of kin? Maybe they'll give us some kind of reward for finding him and calling 999."

"Maybe we should look in his bag first?" suggested Danno, nodding his head to a tattered blue duffel bag that was resting against the wall.

I was starting to feel lightheaded. The heat was closing in on me. The smell of dead tramp filled my nostril with a rank odour. I could taste its sourness in my mouth. The buzzing of the flies was like some endless whispering in my ears. I half expected the door to slam shut and Maggie to be standing there.

"That would be disrespectful," said HC. "You can't just go round rummaging through a dead man's stuff."

Danno picked up the duffle bag. "Who'd ever know?" he asked.

He looked at me as if attempting to elicit my support.

"I'm not sure," I said.

HC was staring at the duffel bag. "Don't do it. We'll end up cursed or something."

"What if he's got money in here?" asked Danno. "We could live like kings for the whole summer, and no one would be any the wiser."

"Yes, but we might get a reward, or something," said HC.

"There's no reward," said Danno. "He's just an old tramp."

"An old tramp wouldn't have any money in his duffel bag," I pointed out.

I just wanted to get out of there. A fly was exploring the hollows of Catweazle's waxy nostrils. It made me want to gag again. I think if I had turned and walked straight out the two of them would have followed me. But somehow Danno had tweaked a strain of morbid curiosity deep within me.

"No harm in looking," he said, and pulled at the dirty string of the duffel bag.

The first thing he produced was a battered paperback.

He tossed it at me, and I caught it with two hands.

The pages were all frayed and dog-eared. It looked as if it had been drenched by the rain and dried out several times. The cover was chewed up and badly faded. It showed a colour drawing of someone who looked like a monk. He had a bald head and a beard. He was standing in front of some sort of Chinese temple. I thought it looked a bit like the Shaolin Monastery in the Kung Fu TV series.

The title read – *T. Lobsang Rampa – Wisdom of the Ancients*.

I just stood there with it in my hand as Danno dipped deeper into the grotty duffle bag. He produced a crumpled cheese and onion crisp bag. When he turned it over and shook it, dozens of crushed cigarette butts fell to the floor. A couple of matchsticks tumbled after them.

HC seemed didn't seem to be able to take his eyes off Catweazle's corpse. "This is bad," he said. "We're defiling his stuff. Once he's buried, he's going to claw his way back out of the ground and hunt us down."

The book felt like it was stuck to my sweaty hand. The buzzing of the flies felt like it was stuck inside my head. The far off pneumatic drill paused momentarily, then resumed. Danno produced a dirty handkerchief and dropped it to the ground, screwing up his nose. I wished that HC had chickened out and never made his *run*. I wished the summer holidays would just come to an end there and then. I wished it would rain and extinguish the oppressive heat that felt as if it was crushing me like a vice.

Danno kept producing items from the duffel bag, grinning as he held them up with a flourish. He was like some macabre magician. *And now for my next trick.* Another apple core, a dented and rusted tin of Heinz baked beans, a tattered pack of playing cards, a brass broach of some sort, which he tossed at HC and HC dodged, a ballpoint pen with its end chewed, a black wax crayon, a dirty golf ball and a pair of woollen gloves, with both thumbs missing.

Then Danno produced a little red Swiss Army knife. After examining it he slipped it into the pocket of his jeans and stared at HC and me, as if he was daring us to challenge him about his decision. Neither of us said a thing. I looked at the random items scattered on the floor around his dusty baseball boots.

"Imagine if that was all the belongings you had in the world?"

Danno upturned the duffel bag and shook it.

"No money, that's for sure."

The last thing to fall out was the dried-up husk of an acorn. It clattered across the floor and came a halt against one of Catweazle scuffed up boots. Danno dropped the duffel bag on the floor.

"You should pick all that stuff up and put it back in the bag," said HC, still staring at Catweazle's body.

"You should shut your mouth," said Danno.

It felt to me at that moment that there was something weird going on with Danno. He kept turning his head slightly to one side. It was like he was hearing something that neither HC nor I could hear.

"Well, if the cops start asking question after we phone them, you're going to be the one who has to come up with a good story," said HC.

"Who says we're going to call the cops?" asked Danno. He kicked the empty duffle bag. It went spinning across the splintery wooden floorboards.

Sweat was making my long hair stick to the side of my face. "What are you talking about?" I asked.

"Maybe we should just keep this to ourselves," he replied, and cocked his head to one side like he'd heard something again. From the corner of my eye, I could have sworn that I saw the flicker of a shadow moving behind the door. I bit down on my lower lip.

"What do you mean keep it to ourselves?" demanded HC. He began to pace around a little. "There's a dead body, Danno. You can't just say nothing to no one. We have to report it."

"He could be *our* corpse," said Danno.

It was so close and muggy I felt as if the walls were contracting in on me. The sound of the flies and pneumatic drill were merging into one long and terrible drone. The smell emitting from Catweazle grew fouler by the moment.

"Our corpse?" HC sounded incredulous. "Like a pet, or something?"

My fingers tightened around the grungy paperback.

"It might be interesting," said Danno. "Like an experiment. We could see how long it takes him to fester and rot. Like that thing we did with an orange back in Primary School. When all the white mould started growing on it."

I felt sickened - but somehow weirdly aroused by the notion.

HC stopped pacing. He looked at Catweazle. His head also cocked to the side. It was as if he too was now hearing what Danno had been listening to. He nodded his head, the way someone would do if they'd just been asked to agree to something.

When he spoke, he'd had a sudden change of heart. "Just for a few days." His voice sounded woozy and slightly slurred. I thought I saw that flicker of shadow behind the door again. I tried to convince myself it was just the heat getting to me and making me imagine things.

"Maybe we could keep him for a few days," HC was saying. "Maybe three at the most."

"Are you two mad?" I asked. "We can't keep a corpse just to watch it mouldering."

Danno blew air disparagingly through his teeth. "Who's to stop us?"

"We'll put it to a vote," he said. "All for one and one for all, and all that. If three of us vote yes, we'll keep the corpse. If one votes no, we'll go to the phone box."

"Do It!"

The voice that seemed to rasp in my ear was crisp and urgent, most definitely female. I even felt the hush of cold breath that came with it. I jumped as if I'd just been stung by a wasp. I tried to rationalise it by telling myself it had just been a fly buzzing past too close to me.

"All those in favour raise your right hand," said Danno.

I wanted so desperately to abstain. But something had me so deep within its thrall that I was hardly even conscious of my arm going up. The three of us stood there like some felonious Boy Scout troop, swearing a deathly oath.

Chapter Five

Danno and HC were oblivious to what appeared to be happening to us. We were like lambs to the slaughter, the delicate strands of our collective free will in the possession of something dark and malevolent. It seemed that only I had an inkling of what was happening, and I was helpless to do anything about it. I was like a falling man, plummeting over a precipice, arms hopelessly pummelling dead air as plunged deeper into some dark abyss.

After we took our vote, we fell into a kind of stunned silence again. Just standing there, staring at Catweazle's corpse, watching the fat black flies buzzing around him. The heat was still getting to me. The tattered paperback book remained in my hand. I couldn't seem to let it go. Behind Catweazle's armchair a floorboard cracked, as if someone had stepped on it. We all exchanged worried glances. An hour before and we would have taken fright and ran. Instead, we remained standing, trapped by a mutual, unspoken acceptance of the terrible deal we had unwittingly entered into.

"I wonder how he died," I said.

Danno and HC turned their heads slowly, like they were waking from a daydream. "Heart attack, I reckon," said Danno.

"Heart attack from sleeping in the dark in this creepy old house," said HC. His eyes wandered to the door. I thought I heard a groan emit form its rusted hinges. "What now?" I asked, half expecting some terrible suggestion to be coldly whispered in my ear. Danno looked at Catweazle. "He stinks. If we're going to keep him, we're going to have to do something about that."

"We could come back tomorrow with air fresheners and stuff," suggested HC.

A wave of relief washed over me. If we could get ourselves out of the house, we could surely talk this over. We'd be free from whatever dark influence had gotten its claws into us. Once we were out in the open, we could all just agree never to come back to Maggie's house. Eventually someone else would stumble across Catweazle's body. He would become their responsibility. We'd be clear and free.

"Good idea," I said, wiping sweat from my brow with the back of my hand.

Danno nodded, then bent down and picked up the wax crayon he'd taken from Catweazle's duffle bag. We left the room. Out in the hall Danno pulled the door firmly shut. "This'll make sure no one goes in there if they attempt the *run*." He scrawled the words *Maggie's Ghost Waits Behind This Door* onto one of the panels in fat block capitals, going over and over them till they stood out. From inside the room, I heard the cracking of another floorboard and wondered if Maggie ghost did indeed wait behind that door.

We left the old house in a subdued silence. We climbed the embankment to the old railway track in the same subdued silence. The silence hung heavy around us as we walked along the track. The afternoon sun burned down on our backs. The

41

midge clouds swarmed crazily around us. The heat haze shimmered ahead of us.

Danno stopped and brought out the pack of Players No.6. We took one each. Danno lit a match. We walked on, still in silence, blowing smoke to dissipate the midges, cutting down the embankment to the wooded path that led to the housing scheme. When we reached the scheme, we just kind of shuffled around on the pavement. It felt like we were suddenly complete strangers, embarrassed to be in each other's company.

That might have been my chance. If I'd said something, if I'd pointed out what a sick thing it was that we just agreed to do, if I'd even hinted at how I thought something dark and unnatural had managed to sway our decision, it would have just ended there and then. We'd have never gone back to Maggie's house and none of what happened that summer would ever have unfolded.

But before I could muster the courage to speak Danno got in first.

"Meet back here tomorrow. About half-past-nine. Bring air freshener and whatever else you can get your hands on."

HC nodded. His jeans had dried out completely. They looked crushed and wrinkled around his skinny frame. To my surprise, I nodded in agreement as well. "I should be finished my paper round by nine."

We drifted off in separate directions, each heading to our respective homes. The block of flats where I lived with my mother and sister was at the end of a street where there was a play area, with

42

swings, a slide, and a roundabout. As I approached the little park, I noticed that Deb and her best friend Shona were seated on one of the wooden benches by the wire fencing.

I'd been going out with Deb since around the time Danno had done his *run*. She had the blondest hair I'd ever seen. So perfectly blond it looked white in a certain light. Her skin was delicately pale, and her eyes were a piercing blue.

HC said that he'd heard from one of his relatives who'd worked at the hospital where she was born that she'd been diagnosed as being an albino, like that American rock guy, Edgar Winters. HC was a liar. Back then he wouldn't have known the truth if it jumped up and smacked him in the kisser. Deb was just intensely blond, and that's all.

I wanted to sit down and talk to her. Maybe even break down and confess to her. Force her to berate me into calling the police and telling them what we'd found in Maggie's house. But when I entered the gate to the play area it was Shona, and not Deb, who approached me.

Shona was the opposite of Deb. She had densely black hair. Her skin was nut brown from the attentions of the long, hot fortnight. Thick black eyebrows hung heavy over her brown eyes. She was wearing a pair of brushed denims and cheesecloth blouse, through which I could see the outlines of a pink bra. I did my best not to stare.

"Hi, Ranks," she said. "You want to sit on the swings for a minute?"

I glanced over to the bench where Deb was seated. When she saw me looking at her, she bowed

43

her head and made out she was studying her fingernails. Shona settled herself on one of the swings. I sat down on the one next to her. The plastic chair of the swing was roasting from the heat. I felt something bulky in the back pocket of my jeans. I reached around and touched the edge of the T. Lopsang Rampa paperback. I didn't even recall putting it there.

Shona rocked herself back and forth on the heels of her dusty white plimsolls. "Deb wanted me to ask you if you're still going out with her," she said.

I was a bit wrong footed by the question. I turned to her, hand on my brow to shield my eyes from the glare of the sun. "Of course, I am."

"We'll she doesn't feel you are," said Shona. "She's hardly seen you the whole summer."

"I've been kind of busy," I said.

"With HC and Danno?"

I nodded.

Shona adopted a kind of lecturing tone. "Well, that's point, Ranks. Friends are one thing. Girlfriends are another. You've got to get your priorities right. She feels neglected."

"That sounds like something you read in the Jackie," I said.

My sister read the Jackie and sometimes I'd flick through it if she left her latest copy lying around. They were always going on about stuff like that, especially on the letter's page.

"Thing is," said Shona, "Deb's cousin is coming down from Aberdeen next week and if it's not working out with you, she might get with him instead."

"Her cousin? That's sick. Isn't that illegal, or something?"

"He's not really her cousin," said Shona. "Deb's mum went to school with his mum. Deb calls her aunty. But they're not even related. You've met him. He was down that summer when we'd just left primary school."

"That kid with the buck teeth and braces?" I shook my head. "What would Deb see in him?"

"His teeth are sorted now," said Shona. "Deb showed me a picture. He looks a bit like David Cassidy."

"And Deb, fancies him?"

"Deb fancies you. But she's not going to hang around much longer if you carry on ignoring her."

I stood up.

"Where are you going?" asked Shona. "You just going to walk away?"

"Tell Deb I'll be back in five minutes," I replied.

"Maybe she won't still be here in five minutes," Shona called after me.

I went around the corner to the newsagent on the little precinct hat served the housing scheme. It was where I had my paperboy job. I still had some money left from the three-way split on the pack of Player's No.6. I used it to buy a Cadbury Raisin Bar. Raisin Bars were Deb's favourite thing. I was going to use it as a peace offering.

I walked up to the bench. Deb and Shona were in the depths of a hushed conversation, no doubt about me. Shona gave me a frown, thick black eyebrows knitting for emphasis. Deb threw me a thin smile. Her face was flushed red from the sun. It flushed deeper into a blush.

"Hey, Ranks," she said.

I produced the Cadbury Raisin Bar and held it out to her, singing the little jingle from the TV advert. *"It's amazin' what raisins can do."*

"Lots of chocolate and raisins for you," responded Deb.

It was a little private thing that had developed between us.

Shona rolled her eyes and rose to her feet. "I'm off for my tea," she said. "I'll leave you two lovebirds to talk."

Deb gave her a little wave.

I sat down on the bench beside her and passed her the Raisin Bar. She was dressed the same as Shona, brushed denims, cheesecloth blouse, white plimsolls. The outline of her bra beneath the blouse was light blue. Her white-blond hair hung in delicate wisps over the small bulge of her breasts. Again, I did my best not to stare.

She unwrapped the Raisin Bar, broke it in two and handed me half. This was another thing we did. The heat was already melting the chocolate around the raisins. We both ate our halves quickly, so they wouldn't melt even more. As well as melting the chocolate the heat had turned the raisins plump. They were both sweet and juicy. When I was finished, I licked the chocolaty residue from my fingers and turned to Deb.

"You ever been inside Maggie's house?" I asked.

"Is that where you've been?" she asked back.

"Walked past it on the railway track," I lied. "Just wondered if you and Shona ever went in there?"

Deb shook her head. "We're not that stupid. My dad says it's not safe. Says one day one of those idiots who dare each other to run through that place is going to fall right through the floorboards."

"You believe the place is haunted?"

Deb shook her head again. "My dad says there's no such thing as ghosts."

"You know what happened in there, don't you?"

"Maurice gassed himself in the oven," I said, before she had a chance to answer the question. "Maggie was overcome with grief and hung herself from the door with the flex from her hoover."

"Not the way I heard it," said Deb. "The way I heard it Maurice gassed himself because he found out that Maggie was having an affair and Maggie hung herself because she found out she was pregnant by her lover."

"Who told you that?"

"Shona. All the girls in our year know the story. Maggie couldn't live with the scandal."

"Trust girls to want to turn it into some sort of romantic drama."

Deb looked a little hurt.

I changed the subject. "I hear you and Shona have been having a good talk about me."

47

"She's my best friend," said Deb, as if this was an infallible defence.

I delivered my Winsor Davies, It Ain't Half Hot Mum, impersonation. "*I will not 'ave gossip in this jungle.*"

"When are you going to audition for Hughie Green?" teased Deb.

"Are you going to the Youth Club this Friday?" I asked.

There was always an under-sixteen's disco at the Youth Club on Fridays.

"You already know, Ranks. I'm always there."

"And we're going to dance?"

She blushed a little again and pretended to be looking for chocolate stains on her fingers.

"Well, I thought maybe you'd be too busy this week," I said. "Mooning over your cousin, who looks like David Cassidy?"

Deb turned to face me. A hint of hurt and anger flashed in her blue eyes.

"He's not my cousin," she said. "And I definitely do not fancy him. Shona should never have said that stuff. Sometimes she's a right interfering bitch. She's the one who fancies my cousin. We'll not my cousin. But you know what I mean."

I did my Fred Flintstone. "*Calm down Wilma, you're upsetting Dino.*"

Deb scowled. "Me and Shona are going to have words."

I laughed. I was feeling better. Deb was lifting my mood. The events in Maggie's house were

48

starting to seem like they'd happened a long time ago. I was beginning to see a way out of all of this.

I knew that no matter how bad I felt I was still going to turn up to meet HC and Danno in the morning. And I knew that we'd walk along the railway track to Maggie's house, and we'd go into that room where Catweazle sat mouldering in his battered armchair. And we'd get dawn deeper into our terrible pact. The floorboards would creak. There would be shadows behind the door and cold whispers in the ear. And despite it all we'd go back the next day, and it would be worse than ever. But Saturday would come, and Saturday would be my chance to break the cycle.

Deb was going to help me do that.

"What are you doing on Saturday?" I asked her.

"Nothing much," she replied. "Me and Shona were planning to go to the High Street."

"You want to go to the matinee at the Pavilion on Saturday afternoon?"

"Maybe. What's on?"

"They've been showing all these old Elvis films. I saw in the paper that it's something called 'Stay Away Joe' this week."

"What's it about?"

I shrugged and replied in an Elvis drawl. *"Who knows, ma'am. But there's sure to be a big hunk of singing."*

"I like Elvis in the films," said Deb. "Much better than the fat one you see in the papers these days."

"It's a date then?"

Deb nodded. "I'll tell Shona."

I tried to wrap my arm around her shoulder and lean in for a kiss. She jerked back. "Not here, Ranks. Somebody might see and tell my dad."

She stood up. "I need to go home for my tea."

I grinned and did my Humphrey Bogart impersonation. *"Here's lookin' at you, kid.*

Chapter Six

"You're late," said my sister as soon as I walked into the living room.

The clock on the wall showed it was just after five.

Where had the day gone?

How long had we spent in Maggie's house?

Libby was curled up on the sofa, watching an episode of the Tomorrow People. Her hair was done up in curlers. She still had her pyjamas on. The ashtray on the coffee table in front of her was overflowing with cigarette ends.

I remembered the squashed butts that had tumbled out of the cheese and onion crisp packet that Danno had produced from Catweazle's duffle bag. It occurred to me that an ashtray like that would have been like a treasure trove for someone like Catweazle.

The room was like a sauna. I started sweating more profusely than I already had been. "You could have opened the windows," I said.

"Couldn't be arsed," she replied.

Libby was two years older than me. She'd left school at the end of the last term but, other than the Saturday job she'd had at Woolworth's since she was fifteen, she hadn't found a permanent job to suit her. She said she wasn't going to bother looking properly till September, because, even if she had left school, she was still entitled to her summer holiday. The way I saw it, sleeping till midday and then lounging around on the sofa wasn't exactly what I'd call making good use of the hot weather.

"You ever been in Maggie's house?" I asked her.

"Did you make your *run*?" she asked, not looking up.

Sweat pricked at my brow. I almost blurted out the whole thing. Then I got cold feet. "I was going to," I lied. "Then I kind of chickened out."

Libby sat up. "Nothing to be scared of."

I felt my eyebrows arching. "Have you made the *run*?"

"Walk," she corrected. "I walked through the house. Went in every room. Calmly looked behind every door. Nothing at all to be scared about. No ghosts. Maggie wasn't dangling there on a rubber flex."

She wouldn't be saying that if she'd experienced what I'd just experienced. Floorboards cracking. Door hinges creaking. Cold whispers in the ear. I was tempted to tell her about Catweazle, just to wipe off the smug grin that had spread across her face.

"Do you know what happened in that house?" I asked.

"Do you?" she asked back.

I gave her the version Deb had just recounted to me. "Maurice topped himself because he found out Maggie was having an affair. Maggie topped herself because she found out she was pregnant."

Libby shook her head, laughing. "The way I heard it, Maggie murdered Maurice and stuck his head in the oven to make it look like suicide. Then she killed herself when the cops started closing in on her."

Did everyone tell the story differently?

My stomach started to rumble. "Is there anything to eat?" I asked.

"There's a fish finger sandwich on the table in the kitchen," she replied. "It'll be cold by now. And there's butterscotch Angel Delight in the fridge."

"What time's mum getting home?"

"About half six. But old Dougie four eyes is on duty today, so I'd bet my last 5p that she'll go for a drink with him first."

Mum worked as a cleaner at the local hospital. Dougie was a porter. They'd been going out for six months or so. She'd invited Dougie round a couple of times. Libby hated him. I didn't think he was that bad, even if he was half bald and wore glasses that had lenses as thick as the bottoms of milk bottles.

I mooched off to the kitchen. There was a fly crawling around on the sandwich, rubbing its hairy front legs together. I shooed it away. The bread had gone a bit stale from being left out without a cover. I smothered the cold fish fingers in tomato ketchup. Then I made up a glass of orange squash. The water that came out of the kitchen tap was tepid.

I was about to start eating when I remembered where I'd been for most of the afternoon. I squirted some *Fairy Liquid* onto my hands and washed them under the tap, singing the jingle from the advert to myself as I did. *"Now hands that do dishes can feel soft as you skin, with mild green Fairy Liquid."*

I sat down at the table and took a sip from the orange squash. The fly was back on the fish finger sandwich. I swatted it away and took a bite. The taste was mainly of soggy breadcrumbs and ketchup. The theme tune from the Wombles TV show drifted through from the living room.

Then I did something that kind of defeated the whole purpose of washing my hands in the first place. I eased the T. Lobsang Rampa book out of the back pocket of my jeans and began to flick through its dirty, rain-stained pages.

One of the first pages showed something that looked like a bizarre coat of arms. There were two Siamese cats, rampant on their hind legs, holding a huge wax candle between them with their front paws. Beneath them was a shield, divided into four sections. The first section showed a monastery, built high on a cliff edge. The second showed some sort of rattle, and the third a pile of books. The last section showed a crystal ball.

Beneath the shield ran the motto '*I lit a candle.*'

In took another bite of the fish finger sandwich and washed it down with a mouthful of orange squash. I heard the end titles of the Wombles and Libby getting up to change the channel. I turned the page. The next page had a dedication. *"To the Lady Ku'ei who taught me many Siamese cat words and always encouraged me."*

My eyebrows creased at the bizarre notion of learning Siamese cat words. The lyrics of Peggy Lee singing *We Are Siamese If You Please* from Disney's The Lady and The Tramp repeated half a dozen times in a little loop inside my head.

The rest of the book seemed to be some sort of dictionary, with loads of exotic and hard to pronounce words. Words like *Abhinivesha* and

Brahmachari, that meant absolutely nothing to me. I flicked forward till I was almost three quarters through the book. There was a section headed – *Supplement C – The Stuff We Eat*. There followed a few pages of entries about vitamins and minerals.

This was the kind of thing that Libby and mum always referred to as hippy-trippy shite. I wondered what Catweazle was doing with a book like that in his duffle bag. I finished the sandwich and drained the glass of orange squash. When I flicked right through to the back of the book, I could see that several pages had been torn out. My guess was that Catweazle had just fished the book out of someone's bin and had been using the pages for roll-ups or firelighters, rather than reading it.

I went to the fridge and fetched the little desert bowl that Libby had left for me. I wondered how many vitamins and minerals there were in fish finger sandwiches and Butterscotch Angel Delight. Not many was my guess. When I'd finished my meal, I decided to take a warm bath to try and freshen up. I took the *Fairy Liquid* with me. We often ran out of bubble bath and shampoo. *Fairy Liquid* was our trusty family fall back.

The bath cooled me down a little and made me feel a lot less tacky and sticky. I rinsed out my Ben Sherman shirt in the dirty water and left it hanging on a wire coat hanger from the arm of the bathroom window. I dumped my jeans on the chair in my bedroom and placed the T. Lobsang Rampa book on the bedside cabinet. Then I dressed in my school PE shorts and an old tee-shirt and down went barefooted to join Libby in the living room.

This Is Your Life was just starting. Eammon Andrews had surprised this old, doddery actress with the big red book. I had no idea who she was. Apparently, she'd been some huge star in the theatre, but had only made a few cameo appearances on TV.

Every time Eammon was about to introduce a new guest she couldn't recognise their voice or even guess who the hell they were from the clues they offered. Libby found this hilarious. I was studying Eammon, trying to figure out if I'd be able to do an impersonation of him.

Mum came home just as the credits went up. Eammon handed the befuddled actress her copy of the big red book. Mum looked a bit flushed and unsteady on her feet. Her curly perm was wilting from the heat. I could smell a faintly boozy reek on her breath. She pushed her hands deep into the pockets of her blue overall, as if she felt somehow this was going to steady her.

She leaned in toward me and squeezed the skin on my cheek with her thumb and forefinger. "How's my little soldier?" She'd first done this to wind me up on my fourteenth birthday. Now it had stuck. Grinning at her little joke she turned to Libby.

"You could have opened the windows," she said. "It's like an oven in here. You'll melt the bloody Formica on the coffee table."

"She said she couldn't be arsed," I cut in.

Libby rose from the sofa in an obvious huff and barged past the two of us. She went thumping up the stairs and slammed her bedroom door. It was getting so that mum and Libby hardly lasted five minutes in the same room as each other. They'd barely exchanged a civil word since she'd left school.

Mum winked at me. "Never mind old grumpy knickers." Her upbeat tone couldn't hide the hurt that underpinned it. "Go and make us a cup of tea, while I open the windows."

She reached into her handbag and produced four ginger snap biscuits, wrapped in clingfilm. "Managed to snaffle these after the tea round on the wards," she said, with another wink.

I brought two mugs of tea and laid them down on the coffee table beside Libby's squashed up mountain of dog ends. Then I went back to the kitchen and brought the ginger snaps laid out on a saucer. Mum had opened the windows and seated herself in her armchair. All that seemed be happening as a consequence was that more hot air was being dragged in from the outside.

I sipped my tea. "Is it true that Maggie Henderson murdered her husband?" I asked.

Mum narrowed her eyes. "You better not have been messing about in that old house. It's not safe. You could fall through the floorboards and break you bloody neck."

I dipped one of the ginger snaps into my tea. "Libby said she went in there once. She was the one that told me that Maggie murdered Maurice."

Mum shook her head. "You don't want to listen to the nonsense people talk about that house. And neither does Libby. Nobody knows for sure what happened. Anybody who claims they do is a liar. Only two people know the truth and they took it with them to the grave."

Mum bit down on a ginger snap without dunking it. "Flip the channels," she said. "See if there's anything good on."

I knelt before the TV and pressed the buttons, moving from BBC 1 to BBC 2 and then to ITV. Something called 'Man about the House' was just starting on ITV.

"That's that new thing they'd been advertising," said Mum, reaching over to pick up her mug of tea. "It's got that Richard O'Sullivan from Doctor at Large in it. Let's watch that, soldier. It'll be good for a laugh. I wouldn't kick old Richard O'Sullivan out of bed."

I cringed. I hated when she said stuff like that in front of me. I hated that I could still smell the booze on her breath. I sat down on the sofa and dunked the rest of my ginger nut into my tea. Upstairs Libby was playing something on her cassette player. It sounded like *The Slider* by T Rex. From what I could tell she'd wound the tape forward to *Ballrooms of Mars*, which was her favourite track.

Mum looked up but didn't say anything. Libby had kind of figured out through trial and error how loud she could have the volume without provoking a huge argument. Mum laughed at something that had just happened on the TV.

The plot of 'Man About the House' centred on this trainee chef, played by Richard O'Sullivan, who managed to wangle his way into sharing a flat with two extremely attractive women, based on his cooking skills. The women then had to convince their landlords, a cranky old couple called the Ropers, that Richard O'Sullivan was gay, so they wouldn't turf him out.

Mum loved sitcoms. I watched her chuckling away, feet curled up in the chair, mug of tea balancing on the armrest. When I was little, and I'd had a fight with HC or Danno I'd climb into that chair with her and tell her all about it. I wished I could do that at that very moment.

I wished I could tell her about Maggie's house and Catweazle's body and how the three of us had taken a stupid vote that we were definitely going to regret. I wished I could tell her that I suspected Maggie's ghost had driven us to our decision. She was my mum. She'd know what to do to make it right.

But I didn't feel I could burden her.

She'd had a hard day at work. She'd been for a drink with her boyfriend. Who could blame her for that? She was only thirty-seven, no age at all really. Now she'd come home, and her daughter didn't want to give her the time of day. But she was getting some enjoyment out of a TV show, sitting there with her son, dunking pilfered ginger nuts into his tea.

I didn't have it in me to spoil that for her.

I held my tongue. As I already said, I reckon a lie is still a lie, even if it isn't spoken out loud.

Chapter Seven

I lay on my bed, dressed only in my Y fronts. Darkness had fallen and my window was wide open. The heat was still stifling. From downstairs I could hear mum laughing at the Dave Allen Show. In the bedroom next to mine Libby was listening to *Ziggy Stardust*, David Bowie warning us that we had five years left to cry in.

I picked up the T. Lobsang Rampa book and began looking through the alphabetical entries for the letter *A*. The first word that I came to that I felt was anywhere close to something I might understand was the word *ASTRAL*. The entry said it was the place or condition that someone reached when they were out of the body. It said it was the place where you could meet dead people who were making plans for reincarnation.

The entry beneath it was for *ASTRAL TRAVELLING*.

This was apparently a process whereby the soul of a person could leave their body and going travelling freely in something called the astral plane. Using *Astral Travel,* you could apparently go anywhere in the world. You could even travel back through time to your past lives, or forward through time to the future. T. Lobsang Rampa even speculated that your soul could travel through space itself to other worlds.

According to the entry animals could also engage in *Astral Travel* and humans who were nearing death experienced it more intensely than others, because they were already much closer to something called the *Astral Plane*. The entry said that a *Silver Chord*, which made sure you always returned to the right place after your travels, attached everyone's soul to their physical body. It put me in mind of the kind of philosophical stuff that Blind Master Po would spout when he spoke to Kwai Chang Caine in the Kung Fu show.

Hippy-trippy shite, nonetheless, I thought.

From next door I heard the opening chords of Starman strumming in on Bowie's guitar. I heard Mum switch off the TV and come up stairs. I heard her knock on Libby's door and tell her to turn off the music. I heard Libby heave an exaggerated sigh. She waited till Starman was finished before she turned off her cassette player.

The heat was causing sweat to trickle from my scalp through my hair to my pillow. Slowly I fell asleep. I dreamed that my soul was rising out of my body on its *Silver Chord*. I saw myself lying half naked on the bed, eyes closed, T. Lobsang Rampa book open on my chest.

I rose again and found myself high above the block of flats. I passed over rooftops of the housing scheme and saw the streets illuminated by the orange glow of the lampposts. Above me the sky was clear and filled with the shimmer of summer stars. The crescent moon amongst them looked creepily like a smile hanging sideways in the night.

I came to land on the dirt track of the old railway. I passed along it, my *Silver Chord* wafting behind me like the gossamer thread of a spider web. I floated and bounced along the path like an astronaut on a spacewalk. I could see the watchful eyes of nocturnal creatures gleaming out at me from the undergrowth. Bats flitted and danced before me, swooping down to snap up ladybirds and cockchafers in flight.

I came to the section of the embankment that led down to Maggie's house. The hollow outline of the house looked ominous and foreboding in the darkness. My disembodied soul could somehow sense my physical body thrashing around on the bed. My soul descended the embankment and passed over the collapsed fence and through the overgrown garden into the kitchen.

I could hear voices whispering down the hall. I followed. My physical body carried on thrashing and groaning on the bed, pleading with my soul to turn and follow the *Silver Chord* back to the safety of home. My soul pressed stubbornly on. It came to the door to Maggie's dining room and somehow passed straight through it.

What I saw before me was like some nightmare fusion of Miss Haversham's wedding banquette and the Mad Hatter's Tea Party. Great mountains of food all draped in grey shrouds of cobweb, writhing with swarms of flies and hordes of maggots. And seated around the table like the Hatter, the Hare and the Dormouse were Maggie and Maurice, with Catweazle as guest of honour.

At the head of the table Maggie had the vacuum cleaner flex bound so tightly around her neck that it was cutting into her skin, congealed blood oozing slowly over black insulated rubber. Her hair was damp and matted. Her hospital nightgown was rain sodden and clinging to her wan, wet flesh. To her left sat a little grey-haired man, who I'd guessed straight away was Maurice. He was slouched sleepily on the table, twin trails of misty vapour hissing endlessly from both nostrils. He hiccupped and more vapour rose from his slack jawed mouth.

To Maggie's right sat Catweazle. Only it wasn't Catweazle the tramp who sat dead in that old armchair. It was Geoffrey Bayldon, the actor who played Catweazle in the TV show. He held out his bony fist to me. When he opened it up, there was a fat, green toad sitting on the palm of his hand. *Touchwood*, Catweazle's familiar in the TV show.

The toad lumbered from his hand to the table and waddled its way through the mouldy feast. Maggie grabbed the flex around her neck, held it high over her head. She tugged twice on the flex. "Woo-woo," she cried. "All aboard for the hangman's express."

Catweazle picked up a cracked teapot and dipped the spout to an equally cracked teacup. The amber liquid that came out fizzed to a white froth inside the cup. "Anyone for Tennant's lager?" he asked. His toad was devouring a fly. Its front leg had pinned down a squirming maggot.

Maurice turned to me, sleepy eyed, vapour hissing copiously from his flared nostrils. "Have you ever tas-s-s-s-s-ted gas-s-s-s-s-s before?" More of the vapour hissed out through his teeth. His eyes closed and he seemed to slump into unconsciousness. Maggie poked him with a rank looking turkey drumstick and he came awake, swathed in a heavy fog of vapour.

Catweazle downed his cup of Tennant's lager and poured some more. Somewhere far in the distance I could hear a noise. At first, I thought it was the sound of a pneumatic drill. Then it became clearer. It was like a bell, ringing and ringing, incessantly ringing.

"Would someone please answer the *telling bone*," said Catweazle.

Without warning the *Silver Chord* yanked back on me.

"Time to go home," sang Maggie, in a slightly off kilter mimicry of a voice I remembered from Watch with Mother. She began to sing. *"Time to go home. Maurie and Caty are waving goodbye."*

Maurice and Catweazle waved maliciously to me.

The Silver Chord yanked at me again and suddenly I was dragged violently back through the door, and along the hall, and out through the kitchen, and up the embankment to the railway track. Before I knew I was flying high above the housing scheme again. Then down I tumbled, head over heels, and my soul slammed forcefully back into my physical body.

I came awake sucking breath, eyes instantly wide.

The alarm on the bedside table was ringing.

It was six thirty in the morning.

I slammed my hand down on it. Not wanting to give myself a chance of drifting off again I rolled out of bed. I felt disorientated and unsettled by the dream. The T. Lopsang Rampa book fell to floor. Somewhat groggily I stepped over it and grabbed my jeans from the chair. I pulled them on and laced up my baseball boots, then washed my face with cold water in the bathroom and unravelled my Ben Sherman from the wire coat hanger.

Usually, before I set off for my paper round, I would fortify myself with a bowl of Sugar Puffs. But when I shook them into the bowl, they reminded me so much of a seething heap of flies and maggots that I just had to abandon the idea of breakfast. Instead, I grabbed my canvas paperboy's bag from the under-stair cupboard and headed out to the street.

A thick mist had fallen in the early hours. It was going to be another scorcher. I headed through the housing scheme toward the newsagent shop. As I turned a corner, I saw the outline of a figure ahead of me in the mist. It stooped down as if it was picking something up from the pavement. A chill ran through me. It looked like Catweazle, bending down to pick up cigarette butts. Images from my dream crashed around inside my head. I retraced my steps and took the long way to the newsagent.

Mrs Aitken was on the early turn. When her husband was on the early turn, he usually had the Times spread out across the counter and would be so engrossed in it that you could usually swipe a few Bazooka Joe bubble gum packs to see you through your round without him noticing. Mrs Aitken was a different kettle of fish. She had eyes like a hawk and a second pair in the back of her head. She wouldn't give you an inch. You just had to be in and out as quick as you like. No hanging around in the shop.

My deliveries were set out in neat pile on the floor. I crouched low and began loading them into my bag. I could sense Mrs Aitken glaring down at me over the rims of her glasses. The headlines on most of the front pages were about Zulfihar Ali Bhutto, who'd just been elected as the 9th Prime Minister of Pakistan. Even the Daily Record was carrying the story. But it also had a little graphic of mercury exploding out of a thermometer like lava from a volcano, accompanied by the strap line – Hot! Hot! Hot!

I hefted the bag onto my shoulder.

"Step on it, young man," said Mrs Aitken. "We don't want people complaining that they had to leave for work without their papers."

For the next hour and half, I wound my way in and out of the streets of the scheme, walking up garden paths, climbing flights of stairs in blocks of flats, folding newspapers, and inserting them into letter boxes. I knew the houses where there were dogs that would snap at your hand if you weren't quick enough. I knew the houses where there were people who'd complain to the Aitkens if you accidentally kicked over their milk bottles and woke them up. I knew the houses that were good tippers at Christmas and took special care that their papers wouldn't crumple or tear when I pushed them into the letterbox.

By about eight o'clock the mist was starting to dissipate a little. I was coming down the stairwell of one of the blocks of flats when I glanced out of the window on the landing. I saw the figure again, stooped in the distance, bending to pick something up. My heart began to pound. I sat down on the stone stairs and gave it a good five minutes before I dared to even consider looking out of the window again. From one of the flats, I could hear the breakfast show on Radio One. The harmonies of Peters and Lee singing *Welcome Home* drifted down from the landing.

When I went to the window the figure was gone.

I finished the last few doors of my round at sprint.

When I arrived back at the flat home Libby was still snoring in bed. Mum had left for work. On the table sat a tin of spaghetti hoops and propped up against it a sachet of banana flavoured Angel Delight. There was a note from mum to Libby, saying these were for our tea. I wondered if I was ready to stomach a bowl of Sugar Puffs. I thought about the horrible banquette that had been set on Maggie's table in my dream and decided against it.

Chapter Eight

It was twenty past nine.

I was waiting for HC and Danno. I'd rushed to get there first. I think half of me hoped that neither of them would show up. The other half harboured this notion that I might be able to slip away before either of them arrived. And then when they challenged me about it later, I'd just shrug and go, "Where were *you*? *I* hung around for ages."

The mist was gone completely now, and the heat was kicking in like a furnace, slowly building toward midday. A wad of old bubble-gum stuck to the rubber sole of my baseball boot when I stepped on it. I lifted my foot up and a long, pink strand stretched with it. It reminded me of the *Silver Chord* that had attached my wandering soul to my dreaming body.

I walked out onto the road and scraped it off.

Then I pulled out the tatty T. Lopsang Rampa book from where it had been stuffed once more into the back pocket of my jeans and sat down on the kerb. The aerosol can of *Silvikrin* hairspray that was poking up from my front pocket dug into my side. I'd taken it from mum's dresser. I hadn't been able to find any air freshener in the flat. I thought *Silvikrin* was the next best thing. It said on the label that it was slightly scented.

I flipped through the dog-eared pages of the book till I came to *Supplement B – Stones*. The first entry was for *Agate,* a type of stone I'd never heard of. According to the entry there was a form of brown *Agate* that could radiate a vibration so strong that it could give a person enough courage to enable him to win victory over his enemies.

I picked up a flat brown pebble from the gutter and rolled it about in the clammy palm of my hand, wondering, with a dumb kind of naivety, if it might be *Agate*. Wondering if it might imbue me with enough courage to put my foot down and tell HC and Danno that the whole stupid affair had to end right there. Under my breath, I mimicked Blind Master Po from Kung Fu. *"Grasshopper, when you can take this stone from my hand, then it will be time to go."*

From the corner of my eye, I caught a glimpse of someone approaching. I chewed nervously at my lip. I didn't want to look up in case it was that ghostly figure again, bending down to pick stubbed out cigarette butts from the pavement. Someone came and stood to my left. Their shadow fell over me.

"How come you got here so early?" asked HC. "Did you shit the bed, or something?"

I dropped the brown pebble between the pages of the book, closed it and slipped into my back pocket as I stood up. "I was out delivering papers while you were still dreaming your cock was as big as mine," I retorted.

"My cock's so big I could go on Record Breakers," boasted HC, huge grin breaking out on his freckled face.

"You just want Roy Castle to measure your cock so you can let him touch it."

"Fuck you, Rankin."

HC swung a playful fist at me.

69

I dodged it long before it even came close.

We both sat down on the kerb, heat from the sun roasting at our backs.

"You know that story of how Maurice and Maggie both committed suicide?" I said. "Turns out there's more than one version of what happened."

"No shit?" said HC.

"There's even a version where Maggie murders Maurice."

"Holy shit," said HC. "What if that's the real version?"

I repeated what my mum had said to me. "Only Maurice and Maggie know for sure what really happened in that house."

"What if Maggie murdered Catweazle?" asked HC.

"Maggie's dead," I pointed out. "She couldn't murder anyone."

"She could," insisted HC. "She could scare a person to death. It's the same thing."

Danno came jogging along the road. He had a split lip. There was dried blood on his chin. There were pink, puffy bags under his eyes. You could tell he'd been crying. HC looked at me and I looked back at HC. We both knew what this meant.

Danno's old man had come home drunk and beat him up again. We also knew that if we dared mention it, or even looked the wrong way at the gash on his lip, Danno would get so riled he'd pick a fight with whichever one of us he could get his hands on first.

"Who brought air freshener, then?" he asked, full of obviously fake joviality.

I pulled the can of *Silvikrin* from my jeans.

Danno laughed, wincing a little as his fingers reached absently up to touch his split lip. "Hairspray? Is that the best you could do?"

"It's slightly scented," I pointed out.

"I brought this," said HC and reached into the Fine Fare carrier bag, whose handles he had twisted around his wrist. He produced a long plastic bottle.

"*Shake 'n' Vac*?" asked Danno.

"Puts the freshness back," HC pointed out.

"You two are useless," said Danno. He dipped his hand into the pocket of his jeans and came out with a round cake of blue toilet flush. "Never mind slightly scented, this has got disinfectant in it."

I was tempted to point out the complete impracticality of what he'd brought along, but I knew he'd be so tightly wound from the beating he'd endured that the slightest thing might set him off. Any courage that might have emanated from the little brown pebble went swirling impotently down the metaphysical drain. I knew this wasn't the time to even hint at questioning our deal.

We headed down to the railway track. The bees and the midges were already out in force. A couple of dragonflies went flitting past us on rapidly beating wings. The copy of the Daily Record, with the picture of the kid and his melting ice cream cone, was still there, face up, unmoving, paper baking steadily more yellow.

I told HC and Danno about my dream and how I'd come along the railway track and stumbled into Maggie's grotesque tea party. How Maurice had hissed gas out of his nostrils and Catweazle had a fat toad in his hand.

"Holy fuckeroni," said HC, faced flushing pale beneath his freckles. "That's like a premonition, or something, Ranks. If you go to a tea party with dead people, it means they're just waiting for you to join them."

I did my Jimmy Cagney. *"You'll never take me alive, coppers."*

"I mean it, Ranks," he said solemnly. "That might be sign that your number is going to be up any day now. I should know - my grandma is psychic."

"Psychiatric, more like," said Danno.

"Fuck you," said HC.

"Fuck you back," said Danno.

The back-and-forth banter between the three of us brought a somewhat inappropriate sense of normality to the situation. I hardly noticed when we descended the embankment down to Maggie's overgrown back garden. It wasn't till we all stepped through the back doorway into the gutted kitchen that the knot began to twist in my belly.

"You guys have got to let me do something," said HC. "When we get in that room, you've got to let me do something."

"Piss your pants again?" I asked.

Danno chuckled and made a jab for HC's crotch.

HC jumped back.

"When we get in the room," he went on. "You've to let me put all of Catweazle's stuff back in his duffle bag. No messing around. I agreed to

72

this, and I'm not going to back out. But we have to at least show him some respect."

Me and Danno nodded our agreement.

We climbed the rickety stairs. There was a beetle on one of them. Danno crushed it under the sole of his baseball boot. When arrived at the landing I glanced into the big bedroom with its *Eric Clapton Is Dog* graffiti. I still couldn't laugh at the joke. In my mind, Eric Clapton scurried around on all fours, barking, and wagging his flesh coloured tail.

The door to the little bedroom had Danno's warning scrawled on it in black wax crayon. *Maggie's ghost waits behind this door*. I thought I saw a shadow pass swiftly along the gap beneath the door. My heart quickened. Danno grabbed the tainted brass door handle. The knot in my belly twisted tighter. I tried to make light of the situation by holding up the 5p piece I still had in left my pocket from when I'd bought the Raisin Bar for Deb. I started taking off Michael Miles, presenting *Take Your Pick*.

What should he do, ladies and gentlemen? Take the money, or open the box?"

"Take the money," responded HC, hands cupped around his mouth, so he'd sound like the studio audience.

"Open the box," said Danno, and pushed the door open.

Catweazle's skin had turned a whole shade darker overnight. Sunlight was falling on him from both the large window to the front of the room and the small window to the back. The green tinge on

73

his neck had spread to his face and kind of melded into a greyish hue that was streaked with jagged blue forks of veins. His eyes stared glassily ahead at some distantly fixed point.

The flies were getting busy all over him. More of them than there had been the day before, burrowing down into his hair and beard, wallowing in the gleaming seepages trickling from the blisters that were raised in little clustered rashes on the discoloured flesh of his face and hands.

I took out the *Silvekrin* and sprayed it liberally. The flies scattered and then lit down once more. Danno coughed and waved his hand back and forth against the scented mist. "Steady on," he said. "The old bugger is stiff enough as it is. No need to make him any stiffer with that stuff."

We both laughed. There was a weird kind of guilty elation in the fact we could laugh about that kind of dark humour. Meanwhile, HC was diligently picking up all the scattered items from the floor and dropping them back into Catweazle's duffle bag. Once he'd finished, he picked up the red flask, the plastic tumbler and the apple core from the Fyffes banana box and dropped them into the bag too. Then he set the bag in a corner of the room.

I put the *Silvikrin* tin down on top of the box.

Danno sniffed loudly.

"The old fucker still stinks to high heaven."

He brought out his cake of blue toilet flush.

"Open his mouth."

I looked aghast at Danno.

"You are joking?"

74

"Wedge his mouth open so I can stuff this in and disinfect the smelly old bastard."

Wincing and squeezing my eyes tightly shut I reached out with one hand and pinched some of Catweazle's moustache with my finger and thumb. Then I did the same with my other hand, pinching up some of the wiry strands of the beard on his chin. I could feel the tickle of flies scurrying along the backs of my hands. I could feel an odd sensation, like cold exhalations, breathing on the back of my neck.

Was Maggie showing an interest in what we were about to do?

Ignoring the sensation, I tugged my hands in opposite directions.

"That's no good," said Danno.

All I'd managed to do was reveal Catweazle's set of nicotine-stained teeth.

"You need to wedge you thumb under his lower set and pull down," said Danno.

"Holy shit," said HC, hovering by his back. "Do you have to?"

"Do it!"

Again, that unsettling gush as the disembodied voice seemed to whisper into my ear. Almost without realising I pushed my thumb into Catweazle's mouth. It felt cold and oily. His teeth were as lifeless as the ivory keys on a piano. I pulled down and his stiff jaw snapped open with an audible pop. Danno's hand shot in between mine and stuffed the toilet flush into the gap.

I stepped back, grabbed the *Silvekrin,* sprayed both sets of fingers liberally, wiped the sticky residue against my jeans, sniffed my fingers, and then repeated the whole process. Catweazle sat there with his mouth half open, toilet flush poking out, as if he was blowing blue bubble-gum.

HC went and retrieved his Fine Fare carrier bag from where he'd left it by the door. Instead of bringing out the bottle of *Shake'n'Vac* he brought out a comb and a pair of scissors.

"What are those for?" I asked.

"I'm going to give him a haircut," he replied, rapidly clicking the silvery arms of the scissors together.

"What the fuck for?" asked Danno.

"To show some respect," said HC. "It's what undertakers do with corpses. Besides I need to get in some practice."

I shook my head and heaved sigh. "Let's hear it then. Practice for what?"

"For when I go to Las Vegas to work in my auntie's salon. She's had all the big names in there – Elvis, Tom Jones, Sinatra – you name it."

This wasn't the first time an imaginary auntie had come into play. *"Book him, Danno,"* I said, as Steve McGarrett.

"Does she fuck cut hair for big names," sneered Danno.

I fell into my Danny Kaye routine. *"Hans Christian Andersen, Andersen that's me."*

"You'll be sorry when I'm singing Viva Las Vegas," said HC, clicking his scissors.

"You little ginger haired lair," spat Danno and pushed him hard against the shoulder.

76

HC stumbled back. "You want to watch what you're doing. You shouldn't go pushing a person when they've got a pair of scissors in their hand."

I saw Danno's hands ball instantly into tight fists. "Is that a threat?"

I got in between the two of them. "Come on, Danno. If he wants to cut Catweazle's hair, just let him get on with it."

Danno breathed heavily and glared past me at HC.

There came a tiny creak from the hinges of the door. It felt to me as if Maggie was there, full of malicious expectation, willing something truly violent to kick off. Danno relaxed a little. His fists unravelled. He reached up and touched his split lip. It was like he was remembering how he'd gotten it. Then he turned away and stared out of the front window.

HC took his comb and scissors and started snipping at Catweazle's hair. The flies swam around him. But he didn't seem to care. He worked with a fixed determination, snip-snip-sniping at the frizzy grey hair, catching up clumps with the comb. Catweazle just sat there staring into his glassy vacuum, hair piling up on his tartan travel rug.

I admit I was impressed. HC had the makings of quite a good barber. He seemed to move with a practiced grace from one side of Catweazle's head to the other. When he was satisfied with what he'd done he stepped back a little to admire his handiwork. The he came to the front of the armchair and crouched down to finish work on Catweazle's beard.

77

When I turned to see if Danno was watching I found he was still staring out of the window, shoulders stiff and tensed. I saw him reach up and rub his eyes. I thought he might have been crying. I was tempted to go over and put my hand on his shoulder. But I decided it wasn't worth the risk.

HC finished his cut and trim. "I wish I had a little mirror so I could show him the back of his head," he said.

"He's dead, you idiot," grunted Danno, still facing the window. "What difference would a mirror make?"

"I'd just like to finish the job the way a professional would," said HC, brushing away stray grey hairs from his tee shirt and jeans. He leaned in slightly and whispered in a conspiratorial tone to Catweazle. "Would sir like anything for the weekend?"

Me and HC started laughing at the innuendo of his joke.

Before we knew Danno had turned from the window and joined in.

"Imagine Catweazle's scabby old cock all squashed up in a rubber Johnny," he said. "It'd look like a mangy pork sausage."

The three of us laughed again. HC started dragging fallen clumps of grey hair across the floor with the side of his foot and piling them into a heap in the corner. He took the tartan blanket from Catweazle's lap and shook it out the back window. Then he folded it and lay it beside the duffel bag. Danno put the can of hairspray on the floor and sat down on the Fyffes box. HC dropped his scissors and comb into his Fine Fayre bag.

"I've got an idea," I said. "Let's do Catweazle on *This is Your Life*."

I pulled the T. Lopsang Rampa book from my back pocket and held it open before me, like it was the Big Red book. When the little brown pebble dropped from the pages, I picked it up and slipped it into my back pocket.

"*Catweazle Shitypants*," I said, making my pitch at a first attempt on Eammon Andrews' Irish brogue. "*You thought you'd come here to fester and rot. But that's not the case. Because, tonight, Catweazle Shitypants, formerly known as Stinky John, This is your life.*"

Danno and HC had a crack at the theme tune.

"*Daa! Daa! Da-da!*"

I turned to Catweazle. The flies were all over his new haircut and freshly trimmed beard. They were scuttling around on their little wiry feet in the gluey drool that oozed from his blisters. "*Catweazle,*" I said. "*You were born in a battered old dustbin in nineteen forgotten. And here's a voice you might recall from those days.*"

HC took my lead and snuck out into the hall.

"*He was a smelly little shit,*" he called back, in the voice of an old woman. "*Even in those days.*"

"*Do you recall that voice?*" I asked Catweazle. "*It's none other than your mother, the Wicked Bitch of the West.*"

HC shuffled into the room, comically half doubled over.

"Tell us about the time old Catweazle shit his pants," I said.

"That one?" said HC, in his old lady voice. *"He was forever shitting his pants. It got so bad he had more skid marks that Brands Hatch."*

Danno laughed so hard he nearly fell off the banana box. He stood up, looking like he'd come up with an idea and nodded at me to introduce him next. I turned over a page in the book, just like Eammon Andrews would have done.

"This next guest you haven't seen in almost fifty years," I said.

"Hey, Catweazle," said Danno from out in the hall. *"'Member when we used to eat mouldy meat pies out of the swill bins behind Crawford the Baker?"*

I could see where Danno was going with this character. *"Your old pal Malkie the Alci from Mary Hill,"* I announced.

Danno came in, weaving and stumbling like a drunk. He looked at me cross-eyed and held up a finger to his nose, swaying slightly. *"This man is a legend,"* he slurred, pointing at Catweazle. *"There's not another man alive that could shit his pants the way Catweazle does."*

"Do some famous guests," said HC.

I did Sean Connery. *"Catweazle, I always remember how you used to like your Tennant's shaken and not stirred."*

I did Michael Caine. *"You're only supposed to blow the bloody doors off, not shit your bloody pants."*

I did Dixon of Dock Green. *"Evening all. I doubt if anyone will ever solve the case of the mysterious shitty pants."*

Then I did Peter Falk as Columbo, fat pretend cigar between my fingers. *"And another thing, sir, have you just shit your pants?"*

I felt I was on a roll. I had Danno and HC enthralled. I imagined I was performing in some nightclub. Hand on hip I camped it up as John Inman in *Are You Being Served*. *"Catweazle, have you been interfering with Mrs Slocom's pussy again?"*

Danno and HC fell about. Catweazle just stared at me with his glassy eyes. The flies hummed about him like a plague. One of his arms still hung down to the floor. The other rested on his lap where HC had placed it. The sun was higher in the sky now and the heat was intensifying. The glare from the windows was casting our shadows across the floor in multiple patterns. I couldn't be sure, but there seemed to be one too many.

"Who's next, Eammon?" asked HC, grinning at me. "Who's the next guest?"

I went straight into my Mohammed Ali. *"I'll flip like a butterfly, sting like a bee. His arse can't shit what his eyes can't see."*

No sooner had I finished than Danno started dancing back and forth, kind of hop-skipping around the old armchair, jabbing punches at Catweazle. Jab-jab-jab he went. Left, left, right, right. Jab-jab-jab. He danced too close. His right fist made contact with Catweazle's jaw. Catweazle's slack head jerked violently to the side. The flies scattered.

"Holy shit!" cried HC.

Before we knew it Danno was laying into Catweazle, crazily pummelling his head and his chest and shoulders with both fists. "I hate you," he screamed. "I hate you. I hate your guts." I looked at HC and the way he looked back at me I knew he was thinking the same as me. Danno was imagining laying into his old man.

The flies were darting everywhere in complete panic and Danno was punching Catweazle so hard that the old armchair was skidding around the room on its rusted casters. Amidst this the floorboards seemed to creak, and an excited voice seemed to hiss. *"Yes! Yes! Yes, yes!"* As if it was urging him on.

The two of us grabbed Danno and pulled him away. His arms were still pummelling, spit was foaming through his teeth, bubbles of snot inflating out his nostrils. We pushed him against the wall, so hard that he made a dent in the old plaster.

"Enough, Danno," I yelled at him. "Enough."

Danno stared at me. There was so much hatred burning in his eyes that it didn't seem he even recognised me. If HC hadn't been holding his arm, I think he'd have punched me so hard it would have knocked out all of my teeth out. There was a smell in the room. And it wasn't just the smell Catweazle's festering reek.

It smelled like leaking gas.

The floorboards creaked behind me.

Danno's breathing began to slow.

"It's OK," he said. "You can let go now."

Slowly, cautiously, HC and I eased our grips on him.

I turned to look at Catweazle.

The armchair was halfway across the room. Its casters had gouged lines in the floorboards. Some of the orange stuffing had come away and lay by Catweazle's awkwardly twisted feet. The banana crate was overturned. Catweazle's head was resting to the side on his left shoulder. His neck looked grotesquely elongated. Blue veins were standing out on the green, discoloured flesh. The toilet flush had somehow dyed some of the discharge that had dribbled out of his mouth. Part of his beard had turned blue. The flies were settling back on him. But mercifully his eyes were closed at last.

Danno was staring wide-eyed at his fists. They were gleaming with traces of whatever viscous fluid had been seeping from Catweazle's blisters. "Shit," he said and dragged both fists down the wall. HC and I looked our own hands, realising that we'd both touched Catweazle as well. Me when Danno had stuffed the blue cake into his mouth and HC when he'd given him the haircut.

"We should go down to the river and wash our hands," said HC.

I nodded and sniffed at the air. The smell of gas seemed to be gone.

83

Chapter Nine

It felt like we were walking on eggshells. Neither of us wanted to mention how Danno had just completely lost it. We both avoided eye contact with him for fear that our gaze would be drawn to that red split that gashed his lip. I had the notion that this was what it would be like in Danno's house in the aftermath of one of his old man's violent, booze fuelled outburst. Danno and his mum, skirting round the edges, not wanting to provoke his old man, decorating a denial of their circumstance with their mutual silence.

After we'd thoroughly washed our hands and cleansed them of the guilty stains of dead tramp, we hung around on the white stone embankment. Danno passed around three more of the Player's No6. We stood watching a huge, undulating cloud of midges that hummed above the river. Down in the river itself minnows and sticklebacks darted around in the glassy stillness of the shallows, swooping up to harvest the abundance of spindly-legged water striders that were skimming the surface.

It was past noon now and the sun was blazing down. Not a single hint of a cloud in the sky. Over on the other bank there was another crow roosting on the branch of a tree. Its caw echoed across to us. I wondered if it was the same crow from the day before. I wondered too if it had been dispatched by Maggie to keep an eye on us.

HC started skimming stones, waffling on about how his granddad's cousin had been one of the dam busters in World War Two. Danno lay down on his back, clicking his jaw as he blew smoke rings, one arm folded across his forehead to shield his eyes. I sat down on a flat boulder and began to read from the T. Losang Rampa book.

If we hadn't stumbled on Catweazle's body this was the kind of thing we'd had been doing anyway. We just generally spent our days aimlessly loitering in one place or another, settling for a while, mooching about, then wandering on with no specific destination in mind.

I flipped through the stained pages of the book, till I came to an entry for the word *SAMADHI*. This was said to be special state of being when someone could be acutely aware of 'reality.' You could progress so far that you reached a *'super-conscious'* state in which you became aware of divine realities. You could apparently also receive spontaneous enlightenment and have a sudden flash of revelation, which would give you instant and unexpected insight into the whole meaning of a word that you had been pondering upon.

I pondered on the word *SAMADHI*.

The spontaneous enlightenment came in the cynical tones of Libby's voice.

Hippy-trippy shite!

Danno sat up and flicked the last of his cigarette end into the river.

"I'm famished," he said. "How much dosh have you guys got?"

I glanced up from the book. The split on Danno's lip was starting to scab over and the puffiness under his eyes had eased a little. "I've got

5p to my name till I get paid from my paper round on Saturday," I said. "I'm going to have to wangle something out of my mum to get into the youth club on Friday night."

HC skimmed another stone, then dug down into the pockets of his jeans. "23p," he said, holding out his palm to show a pile of brass coins.

Danno counted what he had. "37p."

I did my *Fiddler on the Roof* impersonation. "*If I was a rich man...*"

"It's enough to get us a 50p bag of chips and a pickled egg to share," said Danno.

"And 5p left over," I said, hoping they'd let me hang on to my solitary coin.

We walked into the town. There was a fresh patch of tar, surrounded by some orange traffic cones on a section of the road. That explained the pneumatic drill we'd been hearing the previous day. At the municipal toilets in the town centre, we washed our hands again, this time with soap and hot water.

HC and Danno split the cost of the chips and the pickled egg. But they made me use my 5p buy a pack of Spangles to share as afters. We sat in the ornamental gardens near the High Street. Danno broke the egg into three pieces. HC passed around the chips. They were liberally smothered in salt and brown sauce.

"You know what bench we're sitting on, don't you?" said Danno, swallowing down his portion of egg.

I shrugged and licked brown sauce from my fingers.

"Catweazle's bench," said Danno. "This is where he used to sit to guzzle his Tennent's lager."

HC almost choked on his chips. "Holy fuckeroni!"

I blew on a chip to cool it. "When do you think was the last time anyone saw him alive?"

"Maybe a week ago," suggested Danno. "Maybe less."

"You saw him in your dream," said HC.

"That wasn't him," I pointed out, "That was Geoffrey Bayldon, the actor who plays Catweazle."

"Maybe Geoffrey Bayldon died?" said HC.

"It would have been in the papers," I said. "I'd have seen it when I was pushing them through letter boxes. Today it was all about this guy who just got elected as prime minister in Pakistan."

"They've got a prime minister in Pakistan?" said Danno.

The notion seemed to genuinely surprise him.

We finished the chips and tossed the paper they'd been wrapped in into the bin. I passed around the Spangles. Danno lit up the last Player's No6. We shared it around, taking long puffs. The afternoon wore on. The heat didn't abate.

Danno took out the Swiss Army knife he'd pocketed from Catweazle's duffle bag. It had a long knife and a short knife, a corkscrew, a bottle opener, and a little screwdriver as attachments. Danno ran his thumb along the edge of the blade of the long knife. "Blunt," he said, and folded all the arms back into the scuffed red handle.

We saw Danno's dad coming out of the bookies. He worked in the butcher's shop on the

High Street. He was dressed in a white overall and a blue apron. There were dark patches of blood on the arms of the overall. Back when Danno's mum had first met him he'd been a teddy-boy. He still had the haircut, swept back, smothered in Brylcreme, wiry sideburns right down to the line of his jaw. He was short and stocky like Danno. He walked with an arrogant swagger that suggested he thought the entire pavement belonged to him.

He scrunched up the betting slip that was in his hand and tossed it angrily to the gutter. Then he took the half-smoked cigarette that was wedged behind his ear, lit it, huffed smoke fiercely down his nose, and proceeded aggressively along the street toward the butcher's, rubbing the knuckles on his right hand.

"He lost his bet," said Danno, touching his split lip. "He'll be pissed off when he comes home for his tea." I wondered if that meant he'd be *pissed off* enough to land another punch on his son. I could see from the look that HC gave me that he was thinking the same thing. Neither of us said anything.

We went for a walk along the High Street. We looked at the bin that we used to see Catweazle rummaging around in. Then we went into Fine Fayre. HC and I started acting suspicious to attract the attention of the duty manager. While he was watching us Danno stuffed something down his shirt.

I tried to picture what the place had looked like when it was Maurice's toy shop and, Maggie, his shop assistant and young bride to be, had stood behind the counter in her overall. I wondered how it started between them. Had he invited her out for a drink? Had he made a pass at her in the stock room? Maybe they spent their days exchanging cheeky innuendos, as if they were Sid James and Barbara Winsor in a Carry on Film. It was like my mum had said. Only two people knew the answer to such things. And neither of them was talking.

When we saw Danno rapidly leaving shop, we gave the anxious manager a grin and sly wink and hurried out ourselves. We went to the bus station to see what he'd snaffled. I was hoping it was a pack of *Tunnock's Caramel Wafers,* like the last time we'd done this. Instead, it was a pack of sticky flypapers. "We'll hang these on Catweazle," said Danno. "That'll put paid to the fucking flies."

I felt my heart sink. We were definitely going to go back to Maggie's house then.

We dawdled our way back to the housing scheme. HC tried to convince us that he had a distant relative who'd worked on the formula for the glue that was used on flypaper. I did my Danny Kaye routine. Danno called him a liar. We got into one of our scuffles. It fizzled out. "Same time, same place tomorrow," said Danno when we parted to go our separate ways.

When I got home to the flat Libby was in a foul mood.

All the windows were closed again. The living room felt like a steam bath. Libby was dressed in pink shorts and a white sleeveless blouse. A blue towel was wrapped around her head like a turban. She had her bare feet up on the coffee table. The chemical smell of nail varnish hung heavy in the muggy air. She was watching a re-run of *The Singing Ringing Tree,* with that creepy little dwarf that had scared the life out of me the first time I'd watched it. Her toenails gleamed darkly red.

"You can make the tea," she said. "If you think I'm going to run around after you the whole bloody summer, you've got another thing coming."

I tried to disarm her with my Kenneth Williams impersonation. *"Stop messing about."*

Libby wasn't impressed. "Just heat up the bloody spaghetti hoops and stop expecting everything to be set out for you on a bloody plate."

I decided to make spaghetti hoops on toast.

But I burnt the bread. And I put too much milk in the Angel Delight, so it wouldn't set and ended up too runny. When Libby came into the kitchen, I was using a butter knife to scrape the black from the toast into the sink. The electric ring on the cooker was up too high and the spaghetti hoops were sticking to the pan.

"This what comes of mum treating you like a baby," she yelled at me.

"Get lost," I yelled back. "She treats you like a princess."

Libby smacked the toast out of my hand and turned off the cooker.

"Cinderella, more like. And she's more like a wicked bloody stepmother, than a real mum."

We descended into a blazing row. She pushed me, stamped off upstairs, and slammed her bedroom door. Moments later she put on Alice Cooper's *School's Out* and turned the volume up full on her cassette player. Libby had an extensive collection of cassettes, courtesy of her staff discount at Woolworth's.

Mum came home and screamed up the stairs at her to turn down the music. She smelled of booze again. Libby came thumping down the stairs and went into a huge rant about me burning the toast and the spaghetti hoops.

"I'm working my fingers to the bone to put food in your mouths," said mum. "I don't need to come home to this."

"Fish fingers and spaghetti hoops is hardly a five-star bloody menu," said Libby.

"It's all I can afford," said mum. "Maybe if you got off your arse and got yourself a proper job, we could have sirloin steak for supper."

Libby rolled her eyes. "Maybe if you stopped spending so much on booze with old Dougie four eyes, we could have a decent meal every now and then."

Mum slapped her hard on the face. The echo of it retorted like a gunshot. Sobbing and cursing, Libby forced her feet into her flip-flops and stormed out of the house. I asked mum if she wanted a cup of tea. She said she had a migraine coming on and went upstairs to lie down. I thought about going out myself. There was usually a whole gang of teenagers who hung out in the park till about ten o'clock at night during the summer holidays. Deb and Shona would probably be there.

But then, maybe HC and Danno would too.

I worried that if the three of us were together we might get tempted to slip off to Maggie's house.

91

I didn't like the idea of us being in that place at night. Even if it was still going to be light until well past nine thirty.

I took the Lopsang Rampa book from my back pocket, opened the windows in the living room and lay down on the sofa. The cushions smelled of the Aqua Manda perfume that mum had bought for Libby' sixteenth. The book fell open on the page that had an entry for the word *SIN*.

The text had examples of all the different ways a person could commit a sin and ended by suggesting that everyone should do as they would be done by. It said that if you wouldn't like something done to you, then you shouldn't do it to someone else. It suggested that if you lived by that, you would be safe.

Safe from what? I wondered. I thought about Catweazle. If I'd died alone in some old house, I would have wanted someone to do better by me than we were doing by him. I guessed that through my own stupidly sinful actions it followed that I wasn't exactly *safe*.

The entry after *SIN* was for *SOUL*. I hoped I'd glean a bit more about *Astral Travel*. The entry said that the soul was a misunderstood word. It said it was something called our Ego, or our *Overself*. It was using our flesh body in order to learn things on Earth that it couldn't learn in the spirit world.

Hippy-trippy shite, crowed Libby's voice in my head.

But I read on.

The next entry was for another strange word that I'd never come across - *SPHOTA*. This was supposed to be a thought, or some special sound that could make the mind open like a blossom in the sunlight, something that could stimulate the mind to unexpected awareness. A cold shiver juddered through me. The sights and sounds I'd been seeing hearing in Maggie's house, the creaking floorboards, the cold whispering in my ear, the fleeting, and inexplicable shadows. Were they stimulating my mind to become more open to Maggie's supernatural presence?

Hippy-trippy shite.

Hippy-trippy shite.

I went back a bit in the book and found that the entry before *SIN* was for *SILVER CHORD*. Due to my experience with the dream the previous night my interest was tweaked. The entry said that when a person was engaged in *Astral Travel* the soul rose on the *Silver Chord* from outer sheath of the flesh to float like a kite on string.

It said that when a person died the *Silver Chord* was severed and something called the *Golden Bowl* became shattered. The *Golden Bowl* was apparently the *nimbus or higher etheric* force that surrounded a person's head during life, only to depart at the moment of death.

I hadn't the slightest clue what *nimbus* or *etheric* might mean. But I was pretty sure that Catweazle's *Golden Bowl* was well and truly shattered and departed. I placed the book on my chest and tried to get my head around these new concepts and ideas. Outside a thrush was singing on a nearby rooftop.

I drifted off to sleep.

I dreamed that my soul was rising out of my body on its *Silver Chord* once more. I saw the empty sheath of my flesh lying, with eyes closed on the sofa. My soul floated high above the housing scheme, like a kite on string. My soul bounced lightly again along the railway track and down the embankment into Maggie's kitchen. This time I found Maggie and Maurice sitting with Geoffrey Bayldon in the living room. They had dished out a pack of cards and were playing a grotesque version of strip poker, in which whoever turned over the lowest card had to pull off their ear or pluck out their eye.

"Join us," urged Maggie.

"It's a gas-s-s-s-s-s," said Maurice.

Geoffrey Bayldon held out his bony hand.

His toad familiar was feasting on an eyeball.

I awoke with a start to find that I was still on the sofa. When I looked at the time it was six fifteen in the morning. I went and washed my face from the tap in kitchen sink and shook some Sugar Puffs into a bowl.

This time I wasn't going to be put off. I hadn't eaten anything since the chips and picked egg. The spaghetti hoops were congealing in the pan on the stove. Two slices of burnt toast lay in the sink. There wasn't enough milk left, so I smothered the Sugar Puffs in the runny banana flavoured Angel Delight. The sugar boost it gave me brought me to full wakefulness.

When I reached the news agent it was Mr Aitken who was on the early turn. While he was engrossed in the Times, I managed to grab a handful of Bazooka Joe's and stuff them into my pocket. The headline in the Daily Record was, *Hosepipe Ban Immanent!*

There was no mist that morning, but once on my round I thought I saw an ill-defined figure at the far end of the street, stooping down to pick up something from the pavement. I hurried on through the rest of the round, knot tightening in my stomach at the thought that soon I would be back once more inside the oppressive belly of Maggie's house.

Chapter Ten

Catweazle had bloated grotesquely in the ongoing heat.

He looked hideously huge within the armchair. His face was purple and intensely puffed up. His eyelids had somehow been forced open once more. His eyeballs were bugged out and shot through with ruptured veins. His mouth hung wide. His black tongue had poked out and dislodging the toilet flush. It had fallen onto his chest, causing a ripple of blue dye to fan out across his dirty shirt.

He looked like one of the walking dead from Hammer Horror's Night of the Zombies. His belly was so round and swollen with noxious gases it had popped the buttons on the shirt. There were maggots crawling in the streams of putrid fluid that dribbled from his eyes and nostrils. The humming of the flies that swarmed around him was terrible.

"Holy fuckeroni!" cried HC.

He fetched his plastic bottle of *Shake 'n' Vac* from his Fine Fare carrier bag and started shaking the powder all over Catweazle. At first, he was just cautiously dusting the body. Then his head cocked to one side in that dreadful tell-tale manner I was becoming accustomed to. Suddenly he broke into the song from the *Shake 'n' Vac* TV advert, wiggling his bum as he sang. *"Do the shake and vac and put the freshness back. Do the shake and vac and put the freshness back."*

My pulse quickened.

I was as sure as I had ever been of anything that Maggie was right there in the room with us.

This wasn't the experiment that Danno had made it out to be. None of us were bothering with the courtesy of taking notes, mental or otherwise about the deteriorating condition of the corpse. We were being manipulated for some malevolent purpose. When HC had finished, Catweazle didn't smell any fresher. The rank stench emitting from him made me want to gag. Covered in white powder Catweazle looked like he'd been out in a snow blizzard.

"The fat bastard looks like Santa Claus," said Danno.

HC went and stood in front of the armchair.

"Dear *Thanta*," he said, in a little boy voice that sounded a bit like Elmer Fudd from the Bugs Bunny cartoons. "What I'd *wike* for *Cwithmath ith* – is Rachel Welch in a little bikini." He grabbed his crotch and made a lewd gesture.

"Sit on his knee," said Danno "I dare you to sit on Santa's knee."

"You sit on Santa's knee," said HC.

Danno gave him a playful push. "Go on, Anderson. Sit on Santa's knee."

"Fuck off," said HC and pushed him back. "You sit on Santa's knee."

Danno pushed a little harder. Somehow HC lost his footing and fell right down onto Catweazle's lap. Catweazle's swollen hand flopped onto HC's leg.

HC screamed and leapt to his feet.

Danno fell about laughing. HC launched a kick at him. Danno dodged the kick and grabbed HC by the hair. They both swung punches. I tried to get in amongst them to separate them. I twisted my hand into Danno's shirt. We kind of spun around the room in a chaotic rugby scrum. I hit something with my leg and felt myself falling. We all landed in a jumbled pile. The Fyffes banana box lay smashed to splinters beneath us.

"Yes!" came the whispering, disembodied voice. *"Yes, yes!"*

"Sphota," I said, quoting T. Lobsang Rampa, and not quite realising I'd spoken the thought out loud.

"What the fuck does that mean?" asked Danno, picking himself up.

"Nothing," I said and pulled a slither of wood out of my hair.

I felt to me as if I wasn't entirely in control of my own actions.

HC was sucking blood out of a graze on one of his knuckles.

"You shouldn't go around pushing people into dead men's laps," he said.

"I don't usually make a habit of it," said Danno, winking at me. "But it *was* funny. You should have seen your face when his hand fell on your leg."

HC spat blood onto the dusty floorboards. "Fuck you, Danno."

"Fuck you back with spots on," said Danno, and gave him the middle finger.

I tensed myself, expecting everything to kick off again.

From outside we heard the sound of an engine as some sort of vehicle had pulled into Maggie's

98

overgrown drive. We all froze. I snuck to the window and peaked out. A British Gas van was parking up inside the gateway. The door opened and an engineer in a blue boiler suit jumped out. He left the engine running and sprinted to the side of the house to take a leak. Then he jumped back in, reversed back into the road and was gone.

"That was close," I said.

Danno produced the pack of Fine Fayre flypapers that he had apparently been carrying stuffed down his shirt. "We need to get these on Catweazle before the flies take over place," he said.

HC examined his knuckle and sucked it to stop the bleeding. "We need string, or bits of wire to tie them on," he said.

I dug into my pocket and produced the handful of Bazooka Joe's I'd stolen from under Mr Aitken's nose. "We could chew these up and use the gum to stick the papers to his hair and stuff."

"Bags I the wrappers," said HC. "I love those little Bazooka Joe comic strips."

We chewed down. The taste of the bubble gum was sweet and sugary, but it couldn't mask the sour taste that Catweazle's festering stench left in my mouth. There were six strips of flypaper in the pack. We took two each and used wads of bubble gum to stick them in various positions on Catweazle's hair, beard, shoulders, and chest. They worked a treat. The flies started settling on them and getting fatally stuck in the gum.

Danno produced something else from inside his shirt. He was like the magician again - *and now for my next trick*. What he held up this time was a crumpled paper pack, purple in colour. He pulled something out of the pack and held up a long stick, coated in a hard, pink substance.

"Sparklers?" asked HC.

"Not sparklers," replied Danno. "Incense sticks. I found them under Roy's old bed. They'll take care of the smell."

Roy was Danno's cousin. There was ten years between them, so he was more like an older brother to him than a cousin. For as far back as any of us could remember he'd lived in Danno's house. But he'd moved out a couple of months earlier. That had been a terrible thing for Danno. Danno's dad was a bit scared of Roy. He was pretty muscular, and an amateur rugby player. When Roy was around Danno didn't get beat up.

Danno started poking the incense sticks into little cracks in the plaster on walls. HC and I picked up the broken wood from the Fyffes box and piled it up in the corner beside the duffel bag. By the time we'd finished Danno had inserted an incense stick into each of the four walls. He poked two more into the upholstery of the armchair and went round with a match and lit all six.

The little streamers of smoke that rose from them gave off an intensely spicy smell. Soon the room was filled with a thick and heady fug that began to mask rotten meat stench of Catweazle festering corpse. The flies that hadn't already been caught up in the flypaper departed through the window to escape the smoke.

"Job done," said Danno, looking proud.

"We should push the armchair back into the middle of the room," said HC.

We all got behind the armchair and pushed. The casters moved forward across the floorboards. Once they got over some initial stiffness they seemed to glide with a surprising ease. The flypapers stuck to Catweazle's bloated cadaver fluttered and flapped as we pushed the armchair in a full circuit around the room.

"It's like the Batmobile," said HC.

I did my Robin impersonation. *"Leaping lizards, Batman, looks like the Joker is on the rampage!"*

We pushed chair around another two circuits, doing the Batman theme.

"Da-da. Da-da. Da-da. Da-da. Batman!"

This then it somehow transformed into the Z Cars theme.

"Na-na-na. Na-na-na-na-na. Na-na, Na-na-na. Na-na-na-na."

Then I broke away and, as HC and Danno pushed the chair around the room, I commentated, as if it was the Grand Prix and Catweazle was a racing driver.

"Jackie Stewart takes the lead on the second bend..."

The heat and exertion soon tired us out. We position the armchair in the middle of the room and went and sat down on the floor with our backs resting against the crumbling wall. I was in the middle, Danno to my left, HC to my right. Sweat dripped into my eyes. My heart was thumping. I felt parched. I passed around the last of the pack of Spangles I'd bought the day before.

Catweazle sat there - decked out in his collection of dead flies, staring at us though hideously popped out eyes, tongue like a fat slug between his black lips, beard died blue, maggots squirming in the discharge from his nostrils, smoke from the incense sticks swirling around him.

Danno picked up a piece of broken brick that had fallen from beneath the rotten windowsill. He produced the Swiss Army knife from his pocket and began sharpening the longer of the blades. HC unfolded one of the Bazooka Joe wrappers and read the dialogue from the little comic strip out loud.

"Mort says, '*I can go steady with any girl I please.*'

Bazooka Joe says, '*Why don't you then?*'

Mort says, '*I don't please anybody.*'

He unfolded another.

"Janet says, '*I made this cake myself.*'

Bazooka Joe says, '*This cake tastes awful.*'

Janet says, "*Oh yeah, Smarty – the cookbook says its tastes delicious.*'"

HC looked at me.

"It says on along the top if you collect the wrappers, you can win a prize."

"You have to live in America," I replied.

"I'll take them with me when I go to Las Vegas," said HC.

I opened my mouth to rebuff him and then changed my mind.

It was too hot to start a stupid argument.

He unfolded another wrapper.

"Herman says, '*Dad, did you ever see a machine that can tell when a person is not telling the truth?*'

Dad says, '*Did I ever see one? I married one!*'"

HC looked at me.

"Sometimes I think we're like Bazooka Joe and his Gang. All the stuff we get up to."

"Bazooka Joe and his Gang never found a dead tramp in a haunted house," I pointed out.

Danno held up the blade of the Swiss Army knife and touched his thumb to its tip. "You think if I stabbed Catweazle in his fat belly he'd pop like a balloon?"

"Holy fuckeroni," cried HC. "You wouldn't do that, would you, Danno?"

I turned to Danno. "You wouldn't?"

Danno shook his head as if he thought we were both idiots. Then he went back to sharpening the blade. I looked back at HC. HC raised his eyebrows and grimaced a little, before turning his attention back the Bazooka Joe wrappers. He started reading them under his breath.

Danno went on sharpening the blade. He built up a rhythm - left side – scrape-scrape, right side – scrape – scrape. I big part of me wished he'd just stand up and try to stab Catweazle in the belly, because if he did, our whole sorry situation would surely come to an end. HC would just walk out in disgust, and I'd surely follow him. Neither of us would go anywhere near the house again. The bond that had formed between us since we started Primary School would be well and truly broken, and so too would the chilling hold that Maggie's house seemed to have seized over us.

I took out the T. Lobsang Rampa book.

I found an entry headed *DEVILS*.

It said that *Devils* were the negative of the positive of good. It said that without the negative the positive couldn't exist. It was like a battery. You needed a negative terminal as well as a positive terminal to complete a circuit. It said that *Devils* were necessary because they provided an incentive for people to be good.

Above us, in the exposed section of the attic, the pigeons were cooing as they roosted in the sun. They seemed to alternate with the sound of Danno sharpening the knife. Scrape-scrape. Droo-droo. Scrape-scrape. Droo-droo.

It felt weirdly like a lullaby.

The heat and the smell of the incense sticks began to make me feel drowsy. The words on the page started to swim around. I found it increasingly difficult to keep my eyes open. I looked round at HC. The Bazooka Joe wrappers were sliding out of his slackening hand as his head lolled to one side.

My eyes fell shut.

Then snapped open as something clattered on the floor. When I looked at Danno, he'd dropped the knife and the brick. His chin was resting on his chest and the sides of his feather cut hair were dangling down like curtains. I tried to focus back on the book. Droo-droo-droo, went the pigeons. The heat embraced me. The smell of the incense engulfed me. My eyes fell shut again. I felt myself drifting into sleep.

I dreamed that my soul was rising from my physical body on its *Silver Chord*. I tried to rouse myself. I didn't want to see what I might be waiting for me in that room. But my soul rose like an ascending balloon that I couldn't quite catch. I saw the three of us sitting there fast asleep, backs to the wall. I saw Catweazle, bloated in his armchair, dusted in white powder, and decked in tacky flypapers that were so crammed full of tiny, twitching corpses they looked like plague pits. I saw the swirling smoke trails rising from the incense sticks.

I saw Maggie come gliding in ghostly form from behind the door. The electrical flex was tight around her neck. Her eyes were as bugged out as Catweazle's. Her wet hair was steaming in the heat. Her wet hospital gown clung grotesquely to the decomposed contours of her body.

I saw my own body twitch as my legs kicked out. The *Silver Chord* went taut. My soul was almost snapped back into its rightful place. But it somehow resisted and rose again, till it was level with the ceiling. Maggie came prowling across the room. She crouched low, examining us one by one. She seemed to covet us, the way she had once allegedly coveted material items for her house.

She had Maurice and, by accident rather than design, she had Catweazle too. Now it seemed that she wanted us. She wanted to possess us. She wanted us to populate the forlorn hollows of her house. And it seemed too that she had a special interest in Danno. Her discoloured, claw-like hand reached down and stroked covetously at his hair.

105

She puckered her blackened lips and pressed a kiss to the top of his head, the way a mother would kiss a son.

Maurice appeared behind Catweazle's armchair, hands on his chin, elbows leaning on the headrest. Vapour hissed in a long, slow stream from his nostrils. Catweazle held out his hand. When he opened it, the toad was there, dead and bloated, squirming with maggots.

Maggie leaned in and whispered something into Danno's ear.

"Holy shit!" HC's voice snapped me out of the dream. "Holy, holy shit!"

I opened my eyes and shook my head to wake myself. "What is it?"

HC jumped to his feet. "The chair moved. When we sat down it was facing us. Now it's kind of facing to the side. Holy shit."

"No, it wasn't," said Danno, awake now too. "That's the way we left it."

Danno and I stood up. HC looked at me for confirmation. I shrugged. The chair was turned at an angle, so that Catweazle wasn't facing us straight on. But I honestly couldn't remember if it had been like that when we'd dozed off.

The dream, I thought to myself. *In the dream Maurice had been leaning on the back of the chair. Had he moved it? Had I been somehow witnessing real events? Had I really travelled into the Astral Plane?* "Maybe we should go," I said, picking up my book and then handing Danno the Swiss Army knife.

"Good idea," said HC.

He didn't bother collecting up the Bazooka Joe wrappers. We hurried out of the room. Danno pulled the door shut. I read the words scrawled there in black crayon. *Maggie's ghost waits behind this door.* They never seemed truer.

"Same time tomorrow then?" said Danno.

As we made our way down the stairs, I told them about my cinema date with Deb.

"Well, I'm definitely not coming if it's not the three of us," said HC.

At the bottom of the stairs, it looked for a moment as if Danno was going to lose it. I saw his fists clench. Then his head cocked to one side as if he'd heard something. His fists slowly unravelled. "Sunday then," he said. "Same time on Sunday. Old Catweazle can have the day off tomorrow."

HC nodded. We were as helpless as flies drawn to something enticingly foul that seemed impossibly and improbably sweet. No matter what we couldn't so much as hope to stop ourselves from going back to it. We were caught in the fly paper of Maggie's house. And no matter how we writhed and struggled it seemed as if we were never going to be able to free ourselves.

Chapter Eleven

All the way back to the housing scheme I kept my silence, going back to the dream I'd had over and over in my head, trying to rationalise it, but never once mentioning it. And so, another lie got piled up on top of the others that were fast building the foundations of a house of lies that would eventually become as delipidated and dangerous as Maggie's.

I arrived back at the flat to find that mum and Libby had made up.

Mum was in a better mood than she had been in ages. She'd gotten her fortnightly pay packet and the overtime she'd been fighting to get paid for had been included. They'd let her leave work early. She and Libby had gone shopping to Fine Fayre. The two of them were sitting gossiping at the kitchen table, both wearing summer dresses, looking a bit like sisters. There was sliced ham, with lettuce and tomatoes set out on plates. In the middle of the table there was a big jug of orange squash. Next of it was a glass bottle of Heinz salad cream.

I sat down.

Mum pinched my cheek. "How's my little soldier?"

I elbowed her hand away. "You have to stop doing that."

She pinched my cheek again. "It's just a joke. Don't be so touchy."

Libby cut into her ham and forked up a piece to her mouth, with a slice of tomato. Mum shook some salad cream onto her plate. I was parched. I poured a tumbler of orange squash and downed it in one.

"So, what have you been up to all day?" asked mum.

"Nothing much," I replied, rolling up a slice of ham and stuffing it into my mouth.

"At least use a fork," said mum.

"And wash your hands," added Libby.

Mum leaned toward me and sniffed.

"What that smell? Is that perfume? You been out with that Debbie Marshal?"

"Deb," I corrected. "She likes to be called Deb."

Libby sniffed as well. "Doesn't smell like any perfume I've heard of."

"It's from an incense stick," I said. "Danno found one under his cousin's bed and we tried it out."

"Hippy-trippy shite," said mum and Libby together.

We all laughed.

It felt like a long, long time since we'd sat together like that. It kind of reminded me of the last clear memory I had of my dad. I must have been around six. We had spent a wet summer week in a caravan at Whitley Bay, rain rattling down on the roof and lashing against the window. The caravan rocking as it was buffeted by huge gusts of wind blowing in from the coast.

We played this seemingly endless game of Monopoly that lasted, on and off, for around three days. Dad and me versus mum and Libby - dad and I won, piles of money, dozens of green houses and red hotels all over the board. Libby had thrown a strop and knocked the board over. We'd all ended up laughing in a pile on the floor.

Six months later he was gone, packed up, walked out the door, never to return. We didn't have the slightest clue as to where he was. He never wrote. He never sent birthday cards or Christmas cards. For all Libby and me knew he could have been dead or on the moon. Libby was sure mum knew where he was. But I wasn't convinced.

Mum had bought a strawberry trifle for our afters. She portioned it out into bowls. It was only about the second time in my life I'd tasted trifle. I loved the contrast between the fruit and the sponge and the jelly and then the custard and whipped cream on top. The crunch of the multi-coloured hundreds and thousands under my teeth was immensely satisfying.

I decided it was a good time to broach the question of money for the Youth Club disco. Mum pinched my cheek again and fished a pound coin and fifty out of her purse. I was in luck. She was flush and in a good mood. She usually only managed a pound at best.

I wolfed down the rest of my trifle and went to get ready. There was a bottle of real bubble bath in the bathroom. I soaked myself in foamy water, sweating gloriously from the combination of the sultry evening heat and the hot water, hoping that I was also sweating out all the bad stuff that might have seeped into me from Maggie's house.

I dressed.

The uniform requirements for the Youth Club disco were entirely different to day-to-day wear. Jeans, Ben Sherman shirts and scruffy baseball boots were out. You had to look sharp for the disco. In came my red college jumper, with its twin yellow lines tracing the V of the neckline and its twin yellow hoops on the arms. I wore it without any shirt underneath, the sleeves rolled up to the elbows.

Next came my sky blue *Sta Pressed* casuals, turned up at the hems. Finally, my oxblood leather Monkey Boots, with yellow stitching and yellow laces. They'd been my Christmas present. The boots from mum, the yellow laces from Libby. They were my pride and joy. When I walked down the street with them on, I felt like one of the characters on the front of one of those skinhead novels.

I arrived at the Youth Club just before half past seven.

There was a big queue snaking along the front, waiting to go in. The sun was low in the sky and the air was close and muggy. I saw Deb and Shona and went and said hi. Deb had her blond hair braided into pigtails. Her pale cheeks were liberally dusted in rouge and her eyelashes were thick with black mascara. She smelled of Aqua Manda.

Both she and Shona were dressed in billowy smock top dresses, with short, puffy sleeves. They had leather Dr Scholl sandals on their feet. It seemed that most of the girls waiting in line were dressed similarly. For that matter, most of the boys were dressed pretty much like me.

No sooner had I started chatting to her than Danno and HC called to me. They were at the back

111

of the queue with Dan McCutcheon and his crowd. I told Deb I'd see her inside and went to join them. Dan was fifteen and big for his age. His nickname was Clutch. His hair was a red as HC's but it was so curly it looked like an Afro. He always put me in mind of Hair Bear from the Hair Bear Bunch cartoon. I'd never said this out loud, not even to HC and Danno, in case it got back to him.

He had broad, bullish shoulders and was already sprouting bristly ginger hairs on his chin. He'd even managed a couple of times recently to pass himself off as eighteen to buy some tins of beer from the off license.

The stalwarts of his gang were the Robertson twins, Henry and Ron, who may not have been identical in appearance, but were pretty much identical in their sadistic outlook on life, Jimmy Scott, an actual skinhead, whose face was pock marked and cratered from constant outbreaks of acne, and Clutch's faithful lieutenant, Lanky Branning, who was as tall and skinny as his nickname suggested.

The three of us often hung around with Clutch and his mates. It kind of felt like that the fact they were all a year older than us gave as some sort of status in the pecking order of the housing scheme. If we'd had enough of a structure to call ourselves a gang, Clutch would have been our leader and Danno would probably have outflanked Lanky Branning his second in command. The two Dans. A delinquent version of the two Ronnies.

"So where have you three been this past week?" Clutch was asking when I sauntered up.

"Just hanging around, here and there," answered Danno. "Surprised we haven't bumped into you."

"Actually, it's a bit of a secret," interjected HC. "We're not supposed to talk about it, but my uncle has got us keeping an eye out for this fugitive IRA gunman that's supposed to be hiding out in the area."

"Shut the fuck up," said Clutch and slapped HC on the side of his head.

The smack echoed so loudly that everyone the queue turned to look. Clutch's group of mates started laughing. I saw Danno's fists clenching a little. HC rubbed his ear. "You shouldn't go round slapping people on the head like that," he whined. "There was this kid who got slapped like that once and it brought on this huge brain tumour."

"You'd need a brain in the first place to get a tumour," said Clutch. He raised his hand. "How would you like another slap?"

"Just leave him be," said Danno.

"You mind your own business," one of the Robertson twins butted in.

HC pushed him.

"You want to have a go?" challenged the twin, arms wide, chest puffed.

His brother came up alongside Danno.

Clutch and Danno started staring each other out. Lanky Branning loomed over me, face tense with anticipation. Jimmy Scott had somehow managed to work his way round behind HC. I could see that at any minute it was all going to descend into some sort of chaotic ruck. If that happened the lot of us would probably get banned before the doors even opened.

I stepped into to defuse the situation. Wrapping my arms around HC's shoulders I did my impersonation of Ian Cuthbertson, playing Charlie Endell from the Budgie TV series. *"You might think it was just bad luck that you got slapped in the head, Budgie,"* I said. *"But let me tell you, it was Kismet. That's what it was, Budgie, my old son, Kismet."*

"Haw, haw," went Clutch. "Time you went on Opportunity Knocks."

The doors opened.

Thankfully queue started moving.

The hall felt as steamy as the jungle depicted a Tarzan film. The curtains were closed but they'd opened the fire doors to dissipate the heat. Other than letting a long wedge of light into the dimness of the hall it wasn't having much of an effect. As the sun set lower a couple of brown moths were flitting from outside to inside and back out again.

The usual unspoken ritual began to play out. Boys assembled on one side of the hall, girls on the other. In the little kiosk situated at the back of the hall a couple of the volunteers were frying onions for the hamburgers and hotdogs. The tangy, acrid smell quickly filled the hall.

Up on the stage, Gordon Aitken, who was the grandson of the Aitkens who owned the newsagents, had just finished setting up his equipment. He'd been in the same year at secondary school as Libby. She said he was a spoilt brat. He certainly had plenty of expensive toys to play with -

decks and tall stereo speakers, a bank of coloured bulbs that flashed blue-green-red and then red–green–blue. He also had a strobe light and a projector with a set of oil filled slides that would cast swirling psychedelic patterns against the wall.

Gordon flipped his long black hair back over his shoulders as he dropped the first record to the turntable. He was wearing a Led Zeplin T shirt. Libby said he was a big fan. But he was smart enough to understand an audience of thirteen, fourteen, and fifteen-year-olds weren't going to have any real appreciation of that kind of music.

The first record he put on was an oldie. Knock Three Times by Tony Orlando and Dawn. It got the crowd going, stamping our feet to the *knock three times* line, and clapping our hands to the one that went *twice on the pipes.* Gordon followed swiftly with another by Tony Orlando and Dawn – Tie a Yellow Ribbon Round the Old Oak Tree. A huge hit that summer. We all sang along with the chorus, chanting as if we were on a football terrace.

Gordon had us in the palm of his hand and his next back-to-back double whammy sealed the deal. Slade's Skweeze Me Pleeze Me, swiftly followed by Cum on Feel the Noize. Everyone was up stomping. I made a beeline for Deb, sweat already glistening on my brow.

When I tapped her on the shoulder, and she turned around her smock dress billowed around her pale legs as her braided pigtails swayed about her slender neck. She smiled when she saw me. The smile made me shiver. I couldn't quite believe I was going out with her. I don't think I've ever met anyone as beautiful as Deb was at fourteen.

Shona started dancing with one Clutch's crew. I saw Danno leaning sullenly against the wall, looking over at her. He'd been trying for months to pluck up the courage to ask her out and he'd told me that this was going to be the night he finally did it.

HC was in the corner with Karen Hogg, a thirteen-year -old he'd been going out with since the end of term. She was one of his little sister's mates and she was probably exactly right person for him. She was so gullible that she ate up every ridiculous thing that came out of his mouth. She was sitting to his left, wide eyed, nodding her head enthusiastically as HC yammered on, no doubt spinning a fantastical yarn about some fictional aunt or uncle.

Suzie Quatro's Can the Can came on. I asked Deb if she wanted to share a hotdog. We weaved our way between the dancing couples to the back of the hall, where half a dozen tables and chairs had been set out. I bought a hotdog and asked for two paper plates. Deb bought a cola and asked for two straws. We sat down. The hotdog bun was stuffed with greasy onions. I broke it in half and slid Deb's portion across the table to her on one of the paper plates. Deb dropped the straws into the fizzling cup of cola.

"Do you think Shona would ever go out with Danno," I asked, struggling to be heard over Mott the Hoople's Honaloochie Boogie.

Deb sucked her straw and then shook her head. "I told you. Shona wants to get with my cousin. He's coming down from Aberdeen next week."

I bit into the hotdog. Deb nibbled daintily at hers. The Groover by T Rex came on. Libby and couple of her pals mooched in through the open fire doors. They stood against the wall, passing a can of cider back and forth, doing their best to look moody as the psychedelic projections from the oil slides snaked and oozed all over them. One of the volunteers came and told them to leave. They put up a bit of an argument and then slouched off.

The Sweet's Hell Raiser came on. I finished my half of hotdog and took a long suck of cola from my straw. Deb finished her half of hotdog and dabbed her lips with a paper napkin. We went back to the dance floor and slow danced to Lou Reed's Walk on the Wild Side. Deb ran her fingers through my hair and stroked my ear. We snogged a bit. I saw that Danno was slow dancing with Shona. He asked her something. She shook her head and turned away.

When the song was finished Danno went hurrying through the double doors that led from the hall to the corridor. I told Deb I was going to the toilet. Danno was by the sinks, washing his face in cold water. "How come I can't get anyone to go out with me?" he asked when he saw me in the mirror.

"Maybe you haven't asked the right person yet," I replied.

The water from the tap looked cool. I scooped some up in my hand and washed the greasy onion residue away from my lips.

117

"Do you think girls like me?" asked Danno.

"I think maybe they're scared of you," I said.

Danno's reflection stared back at me. His mouth was half open. "They think I'm like my old man?"

I nodded. "Maybe."

"Fuck," said Danno, and splashed more water onto his face.

We both went back to the hall.

Gordon had put Nazareth's Broken Down Angel on. The floor was vibrating from the sounds coming from the speakers. I found Deb on one of the seats at the side of the hall, close to where HC and Karen Hogg were sitting. I slouched down beside her. HC was still rambling on, arms gesticulation widely. Karen was still nodding her head at almost everything he said. He must have been over the moon to have someone who was ready to go along so willingly with his tall tales.

I watched Danno swaggering rapidly across the dance floor till he reached the little bunched up group where Clutch and his mates were hanging out. Danno walked straight up to Clutch and said something to him. Clutch reacted instantaneously by throwing a wild punch. Danno dodged the punch and took three steps back onto the dance floor. Clutch followed him, roaring out something that was drowned out by the music. There was going to be a fight, and it seemed that Danno had set out to deliberately provoke it.

That was often the way with Danno. If he got upset or frustrated with something he'd look for someone to beat on. If a teacher ever pulled him up about anything in class, it would inevitably lead to him having a fight in the playground. Clutch swung another punch. It made contact with Danno's head. His neck jerked and he staggered to one side. HC and I jumped to our feet as everyone else hurriedly vacated the dance floor. Danno ran at Clutch, head down and knocked the wind out of him.

One of Clutch's mates launched a kick at Danno. Clutch used the advantage to deliver a punch straight between Danno's eyes. The lights went up. The music went off. I saw Danno stumbling in a kind of daze. He reached into the pocket of his *Sta Pressed* and I knew without the shadow of a doubt that he was about to pull out the Swiss Army knife. I managed to grab his wrist and forcefully hold it in place before he could do something stupid.

Gary, the Club's youth leader, came rushing into the hall and stepped into the gap between Danno and Clutch. He was dressed in a purple shirt, green bellbottoms, and white platform shoes. He sported a thick black moustache like Burt Reynolds. He'd apparently been trained to defuse conflict situations, or so he'd told us.

"What's the problem here, gentlemen?" he asked.

"None of your fucking business," said Clutch and slammed him hard on the nose with the flat of his hand. Blood spurted from Gary's nose. Several of the girls in the hall screamed. Gary's knees seemed to buckle. I thought he was going to faint. Then he stood upright, hand cupped over his nose.

"You're banned, Mr McCutcheon," he said. "Get out now, before I call the police and have you arrested for assault."

Clutch shook his head and turned to his gang. "Come on guys. Let's get out of here. It's shite anyway. Full of teeny boppers."

He headed for the door. His gang followed like a herd of sheep. Before he left, he turned and pointed at Danno. "This isn't over. You hear? It's not over by a long shot."

The lights went out again. Gordon dropped Barry Blue's Dancing on a Saturday Night to the turntable. The dance floor started filling up once more. I asked Danno if he was OK. He still had his hand in his pocket, fist closed around the shape of the Swiss Army knife. "Clutch better not be hanging around when we go outside," he warned.

"I don't think it's a good idea to get on the wrong side of him," I said.

"It's even less of a good idea for him to get on the wrong side of me," said Danno. "I'm going for a cola, you coming?"

Deb was sitting on the chairs by the wall. She was staring expectantly at me, eyes big and blue behind the spidery mascara of her lashes. "I'll catch you later," I said and went to sit beside Deb.

"I hate it when there's a fight," she told me.

Barry Blue faded out.

"Wasn't much of a fight," I pointed out. "Over before it started really."

"I still hate it," said Deb.

See My Baby Jive by Wizzard came on.

We both got up to dance. Up on the stage Gordon switched on his strobe lamp. Before me I saw Deb frozen like stolen snapshots in various poses as she danced. I wished that I could capture them and fill up an entire photo album. As the strobe flickered, I looked around the hall at how everyone was caught by each flash in a different position, expressions on their faces held for that split second between light and dark.

Then I saw him, looking hopelessly out of place, a scruffily dressed old man, bending down to pick something off the floor. The strobe light flashed. He was captured examining a cigarette end held between a finger and thumb. The strobe light flashed again. He dropped the crushed butt into an empty crisp packet. The strobe light flashed once more. He picked up another butt, raised it to his lips and searched his pockets for a match.

The chorus of See My Baby Jive boomed from the speakers. I could hear some of the kids singing along. The strobe light flashed. The old man turned to face me. It was Catweazle's fuzzily bearded face that I saw. There were flies humming around his head. Hundreds of them. A new smell seemed to pervade the aroma of fried onions, a horrible, cloying smell, like the smell that had filled the little bedroom in Maggie's house. The strobe light flashed. Catweazle's ghostly form bent down to pick up another cigarette end. The clammy air in the hall became thick with stench of rotting meat.

The strobe light flashed. Deb danced toward me. I smelled her Aqua Manda perfume. Somehow it reminded me of the smell of burning incense

121

stick. Behind it the rotten stink of overripe cadaver intensified. It was so overwhelming that I felt bile rise in my throat. I gagged. Before I could do anything I spewed up the contents of my stomach in one, huge, gushing flood of brown vomit.

Deb let out shocked yelp and stumbled away from me. Someone else danced into the splattered mess of the vomit, skidded across it, and landed flat on their back. Everyone gave me a wide berth, some of them cursing, some of them gagging.

The lights went on and the music came to a halt. Gordon turned off his strobe. Everyone stared down at the pool of vomit on the floor. A couple of the volunteers rushed into the hall thinking there had been another fight. When they saw the wet, lumpy they held their hands to their mouths.

Gary came in seconds later. He had wads of toilet paper stuffed into his nostrils. There was dried blood caking the wiry hairs of his moustache. His platforms slipped on a stray splat of vomit, and he did a comical Fred Flintstone style run on the spot till he caught his balance.

Gary slapped his forehead. "Could this night get any bloody worse?"

He turned to one of the volunteers. "Get the mop and bucket."

One of the women who had been working in the kiosk came and gave me a glass of water. "I saw you earlier," she said, mothering me a little. "Wolfing down that hotdog and then going straight back to jumping around. No wonder you made yourself sick."

122

HC and his girlfriend seemed to find my whole situation hilarious. Shona took Deb to the toilets to wash the vomit from her sandals and ankles. Everyone else was just staring at me. I felt my face flush from embarrassment.

I looked around for the old tramp I'd seen under the strobe lights. It didn't surprise me that he was nowhere to be seen. I doubted he'd ever been there in the first place. The volunteer came back with a mop and bucket. The smell of disinfectant started to make the hall feel like a hospital ward.

They washed the floor twice more before Gary said the lights could go off again. Gordon put on Rubber Bullets by 10cc, but nobody seemed to be in the mood for dancing any more. I sat down at the side of the hall. Deb came and joined me.

"I think I'm just going to go," she said.

"I'll walk you home," I offered.

"There's no need," she replied. "I mean, if you're not feeling well."

"I'm better now," I said, standing up. "I had this strawberry trifle for my tea and then with the hotdog and onion on top. I think a walk and some fresh air would be good for me."

Deb only lived two streets away from the Youth Club. When we arrived at her front gate, I leaned in to kiss her. "Better not," she said, turning her head. "You still smell of sick. And my dad's bound to look out of the window any minute now."

I stepped back from her, feeling embarrassed all over again.

"See you at one tomorrow, outside the Pavilion?"

She nodded and pushed the gate open.

I walked back through the housing scheme. It must have been around half past ten, but it was still oppressively warm. My throat felt raw and sore. There was a hollow humming in my ear from the aftermath of the music pumping out of the speakers. I turned a corner. Further along the street I saw a man standing beneath one of the lampposts. At first, I thought it was someone who had just popped out for a smoke. But then I realised that the twin streams of smoke coming out of his nose were hissing out at a constant flow.

The man pointed upward with his index finger. When I looked up, I saw a woman's corpse dangling from the lamp with a length of electrical flex around her neck. Not sure whether I was seeing this or imagining it I turned on my heels. I knew the housing scheme like the back of my hand. There was more than one way to the flats. As I crossed the road, I saw something moving in the gutter. A bloated, warty toad was waddling fatly through the dust.

Chapter Twelve

Deb and me both arrived at the steps to Pavilion Cinema at almost the same time. She had her blond hair swept back in a ponytail. She was wearing a pink blouse, with button down pockets on the breasts. It was tucked into a pair of high waist-banded brushed denims. She'd swapped her Doctor Scholl sandals for a pair of red plastic ones. I felt a bit of a scruff, dressed once more in my increasingly crumpled Ben Sherman, faded jeans and battered baseball boots.

It was another intensely hot day. A dog padded lethargically past us on the parched pavement, mouth foaming a little, and tongue hanging heavily to one side as it panted rhythmically. I could feel the uncomfortable prickle of sweat on my back. I couldn't wait to get inside to the darkened shade of the cinema hall.

"Are you feeling better now?" asked Deb.

"I'm fine," I said. "I just ate too much."

It was a complete lie. I'd never felt so lousy in my life. I'd lain awake all night. Disturbed by the ghostly visions I'd seen at the Youth Club and on my way back from Deb's. I'd been afraid to let myself fall asleep in case I dreamt of my soul rising from my body on its *Silver Chord* and setting off on a nocturnal wander along the railway track, back to Maggie's house.

That morning I'd stumbled through my paper round, strap of my canvas bag eating into my shoulder, head bowed low, not wanting to look ahead of me in case I saw something manifesting itself in the street. When Mr Aitken handed me my wages of £2.00, I fumbled with it and dropped all four 50p coins. They scattered in opposite directions across the shop floor. I had to crawl around for ages, trying to gather them all back up.

Back at the flat, mum and Libby were both still in bed. I slumped down on the sofa, tried to read a bit of the T. Lobsang Rampa book, and then dozed off watching an episode of H.R. Pufnstuf. My head fell against my shoulder. I woke up with a stiff neck. Now I had a thumping headache that wasn't being made any better by the heat.

We went into the cinema foyer. I offer to buy Deb a raspberry Mivie from the freezer cabinet in the little shop. "OK," she said. "But I'm paying for my own ticket." We sat down in the back row. There couldn't have been more than eight people in the place, most of them school age couples like us.

The cinema wasn't half as cool as I'd expected it to be. The place stank of stale cigarette smoke and the floor was sticky from where someone had spilled a soft drink. I unwrapped my Mivie and bit through the fruit flavoured ice to the vanilla ice cream beneath. It felt good sliding down my throat, but it didn't ease my headache.

There was a solitary fly flitting about in the darkness. I heard its buzz grow steadily louder as it approached us and then slowly fade to nothing as it disappeared into the gloom. The same thing happened again. In it came, like a plane circling a runway, then off into the void. I wondered, with more than a touch of morbidity, if it had been feasting on a corpse recently.

126

The big screen flickered to life and the Pearl and Dean theme tune filled the cinema. There was an advert for Player's No6. Deb said she wished I'd stop smoking. After the ads, they showed a couple of Warner Brothers' cartoons – Daffy Duck and Porky Pig. I amused Deb with some of my impersonations.

I did Bugs Bunny. *"Eh, what's up doc?"*

Then Sylvester. *"Thufferin' thuckotash!"*

Followed swiftly by Tweety Pie. *"I tought I taw a puddy tat,"*

Deb finished her Mivvie and folded the wrapper around the wooden stick. She took my stick and wrapper from me and pushed them down into the little metal ashtray on the back of the seat in front.

The main feature came on.

Stay Away Joe turned out to be mainly a comedy, with some Elvis numbers thrown in almost as an afterthought. Elvis played this ex-rodeo star called Joe Lightcloud, who was half Navaho Indian. The plot centred on him returning to the reservation and trying to make a heap of money by establishing a herd of cattle.

Only his wayward family kept getting in his way.

His father ate his prize bull for dinner and his sister sold his cows. Burgess Meredith - who also played the Penguin in the Batman TV series, played Elvis's father. It was the first time I'd seen him in any other role. He was hoot, hamming it up and stealing the show every time he appeared in a scene with Elvis.

Elvis looked weird. They tried to make his complexion look darker by smothering him in some kind of fake tan. His face was all orange and shiny. Inevitably there was a love interest. Joe Lightcloud and this white girl kept trying to make out. But every time they almost got down to it the girl's mother would chase Elvis with a shotgun.

I was studying Elvis's mannerism and listening hard to every turn of phrase. I had no real desire to attempt an Elvis song, but I felt confident I could somehow work his drawling talking voice into my repertoire. The only thing was that my eyelids felt heavy, and my head kept nodding forward and then jerking back as I almost dropped off.

At one point Deb nuzzled her head against my shoulder. I think she was expecting me to put my arm around her. But I was so focused on trying to keep awake that I didn't manage to translate the thought into action.

A moment later I felt her stiffen a little and sit up straight. I had this thought that I'd offended her with my lack of response. I knew I should do something to make amends. But my eyelids were so heavy. And the cinema was so warm. And the fly kept buzzing back and forth. And I was so unbelievably tired.

Here I go again, I thought, as my soul came levitating forth, snaking its *Silver Chord* behind it. I tried to exert my will over it and shake myself awake. But it seemed there was no way to control the dream once it set its course. I rose above the rows of seats. I saw the aisle of stairs that cut down through middle of the chairs. I saw myself and Deb and the rest of the audience members illuminated by the cinemascope glow washing back from the screen.

I rose again and found myself looking down on sun-drenched streets full of the hustle and bustle of Saturday shoppers. I floated over the town. I thought I saw HC and Karen on one of the benches in the town gardens, HC talking twenty to the dozen, Karen nodding her head enthusiastically. I knew exactly where I was being taken. It felt as though I was groaning and moaning in consternation as I slept. I had no idea if the noises were coming out loud. I floated down and came to land on the old railway track. When I looked back, I could see the *Silver Chord*, like some huge, writhing serpent, stretching all the way back to the town.

I saw the copy of the Daily Record sitting face up on the path. The front cover was torn and shredded. There was a black footprint with the sole marks of a baseball boot on the picture of the kid with his melting ice cream cone. Along the old track I went, and down the weed lined embankment, and over the collapsed fence, and through the overgrown garden, and in through the back door to Maggie's house. As I passed into the kitchen, I saw that a gas cooker now filled the gap in the worktop. Maurice was there, down on his knees, his head resting on the lower shelf of the oven.

Along the hall I went, and up the stairs. I saw the graffiti on the wall in the big bedroom. *Eric Clapton Is Dog*. I passed the bathroom to the little bedroom. In through the door, I went. Catweazle was there, bloated in the old armchair, covered in *Shake 'n' Vac* and decked with flypapers. Maggie was standing behind him, with the rubber flex around her neck. Her bugged-out eyes were staring greedily at something. I turned to look. Danno was sitting on the floor, with his back to the blown plaster of the wall, in the same position that he had been the previous afternoon.

He had the Swiss Army knife in one hand and a wooden stick in the other. He was whittling the end of the stick to a fine point. The shavings were falling amongst HC's abandoned Bazooka Joe wrappers. He was staring vacantly at Catweazle, looking like Van Helsing, preparing to stake a vampire.

Maggie came stuttering toward him in a series of bone chilling staccato movements. She prowled before him, hem of her sodden hospital gown swishing back and forth. Then leaned down and whispered in his ear. Danno turned his head to one side, as if he had heard her. He folded the away the blade of the knife and slipped it into his pocket. Slowly he rose to his feet and walked up to Catweazle's chair. He held up his stick and touched the point to one of Catweazle maggoty eyes.

"Yes," went Maggie. *"Yes. Yes. Yes."*

For a horrible moment I truly thought that Danno was going to plunge the stick right into Catweazle's eye socket. Then he gasped and stepped back. He took one look at the sharpened stick and tossed it straight out of the window. Then he turned and fled, slamming the door shut behind him.

130

Maggie looked straight at me, wet rattails of her hair falling about her shoulders.

"Soon," she said. *"Soon. Soon. Soon."*

I was so shocked at the notion she could see me there that my soul rose rapidly. I immediately found myself floating high over Maggie's house. I could see the pigeons roosting in the rafters of the collapsed roof. I saw Danno scrambling up the embankment and running hell for leather along the old railway track.

Something jabbed me in the ribs.

The *Silver Chord* went taut.

"Ranks," said a voice. "Wake up, Ranks. The film is over."

Another jab poked me in the ribs.

My eyes snapped open.

"I can't believe you feel asleep," said Deb. "Like I didn't even exist."

She stood up and went storming toward the exit. I had to run to keep up with her. When we got outside her pale complexion was almost purple with fury. "I can't believe you fell asleep," she yelled at me again. "You were whimpering like you were a little puppy dog, or something."

"Sorry," I tried. "I was tired. I had a bad dream."

"Sorry isn't good enough, Ranks."

She started crying. "I've had enough of being ignored by you."

I tried to put my arm around her.

"I wasn't ignoring you."

She pushed me away and unbuttoned one of the breast pockets on her pink blouse. From it she produced a neatly folded sheet of lined paper that looked as if it had come from an old exercise book from school. She forced it into my hand. "I wrote this because I thought this was what might happen," she said, tears washing streams of mascara down her flushed cheeks.

"What's happing?" I asked, genuinely perplexed.

"We're breaking up," she said and walked away.

I unfolded the paper. A forlorn love torn poem of sorts was neatly written onto it.

<u>I gave you my love</u>
<u>But it wasn't enough</u>
<u>I gave you my heart</u>
<u>But you tore it apart</u>
<u>We could have had kisses</u>
<u>Instead of near misses</u>
<u>We could have had cuddles</u>
<u>But it's all in a muddle</u>
<u>Now I've stopped believing</u>
<u>And so, I am leaving</u>
<u>I know I will cry</u>
<u>But it's really goodbye</u>

"Deb," I called after her.
She started to run.

I should have run after her. But I was somehow stuck to the spot, the sun scorching down on my back and the eerie residue of the dream still crashing around in my head like a revenant echo. Deb disappeared around the corner. I knew that my

132

hopes of somehow salvaging my situation had disappeared with her.

Sometimes a lie serves you better than the truth. If I'd have gone after her, I'm sure I'd have told her everything. She'd have found out that Danno, HC and I had found a dead body in Maggie's house. That we'd kept it a secret. That we'd played with it and abused it. Allowed some dead entity to come creeping and corrupting. She'd have found out what a sick and depraved person I'd become. She'd have hated me instead of just thinking of me as a neglectful fool.

My headache came back, throbbing against my skull with an almost blinding force. I walked along the street in a daze. In think I may have blacked out for a while and fallen into some sort of walking trance. I found myself at the checkouts in Fine Fayre. I had a new set of flypapers and a pack of Juicy Fruit chewing gum in my hand. I couldn't even remember picking them up.

Chapter Thirteen

Libby and mum were in the kitchen when I arrived back at the flat. Libby was dressed in her Woolworth's uniform, having just finished her Saturday shift. I hovered momentarily by the door and gave them a cursory nod before smuggling the flypapers and chewing gum up to my room. By the time I went back down they'd finished eating and had drifted to living room to watch TV. Mum had made sandwiches with the left-over ham and tomatoes and there were tinned sliced peaches, with Carnation milk, for afters.

My head was thumping, and from where I was sitting, the sun glaring in through the kitchen window was hitting me right in the eyes. I struggled to swallow down my sandwich. The half-chewed bread and ham felt like lead weights forcing themselves in stodgy masses down my throat. I couldn't face the bowl of peaches, so I stuck it in the fridge.

I went upstairs, stripped down to my Y fronts, and lay on top of my bed. I picked up the T. Lobsang Rampa book from where I'd left it on top of the bedside cabinet. I went to *Supplement A: Breathing.* There was an exercise there which involved holding you thumb against one nostril and then breathing in through the other, holding it in for what was called eight *Oms (apparently pronounced Ohm)* and then swapping your thumb to the other nostril and breathing out through the one you'd just held.

I tried it, breathing in through one nostril, holding it, breathing out through the other, then swapping it around and repeating it the other way. I imaged I was the young Kwai Chang Caine, practicing a lesson from Blind Master Po. After a while I felt the tension start to fall from my shoulders as my headache eased a little.

My eyelids fell shut.

I don't know if I had the dream about my soul rising on its *Silver Chord* from my physical body on that occasion. All I know is that when I awoke and looked at the clock it was past eight in the evening. I had no memory of having had another dream and I felt completely refreshed. The headache was gone.

I got dressed, went to the bathroom, and washed myself in cold water. Libby and mum had both gone out. I sat in the kitchen and poured some Carnation milk over the bowl peaches I'd seen in the fridge. My appetite seemed to have returned. I watched TV for about ten minutes. I kept thinking about Deb and the consequences of her splitting up from me. I read her poem several times before I decided that I really didn't want to be in the house by myself. I was worried that I might look out of the window and see Maggie dangling by her neck from one of the lampposts.

I headed for the park.

There was a huge and chaotic football match going on. It seemed to be boys versus girls. Lots of playful and flirtatious shoving and tickling going on - interspersed with high-pitched yelps and choruses of giggling. The ball, seemingly a coincidental element in the process, was being booted and punted and headed in all sorts of wildly erratic trajectories. The grass, burned to spiky yellow straw by the heat wave, was now being trodden into a fallow patchwork of dusty, light brown patches.

Danno and HC were there, as were Clutch and his mates. The altercation at the Youth Club seemed to have been set aside in favour of this boisterous melee. Deb and Shona were on the girl's team. But when they saw me joining in, they slunk off moodily to sit on the swings, rocking back and forth and scowling at me, every now and then leaning in to whisper animatedly to each other.

I ignored them and got in amongst the fun.

"How was the film?" asked Danno, jogging up beside me.

"Me and Deb split up," I said.

"I heard," said Danno. "Tough break."

"She said she dumped you," said HC, suddenly behind me.

Ignoring him I took a flying kick at the ball as it sailed towards me. It went off at an angle, arced over the fence, and bounced into the middle of the road. One of the younger kids ran to fetch it. Just then Danno's old man came strutting cockily along the road, heading for the bus stop.

He was dressed in a brown suit, cream shirt and a kipper tie that was striped in thick brown and yellow bands. His hair was swept back and fleshly greased with Brylcreme. His sideburns had been trimmed a little, but they still came right down to the line of his jaw. He'd adopted that arrogant swagger of his, head down, eyes focused straight ahead, puffing intermittently on a Woodbine. He looked like a mean little dog on the prowl, ready to tear the throat out of any other dog that unfortunately crossed his path.

He seemed so consumed in his own self-importance that he didn't turn his head or bother to look over to the park as he strutted past. But Danno watched him go, eyes full of a mismatched mixture of fear and hatred, fists firmly clenched at his sides. It reminded me so much of the look he'd had in my dream as he stared at Catweazle while sharpening that stick. I found myself again questioning whether it had been a dream or an actual experience.

"He was boasting at teatime about how tanked up he's going to get," said Danno, and tentatively touched the dry scab on his lip.

"You want to sleep at mine tonight?"

I felt genuinely worried for him.

Danno turned to me. "Do you think your mum would mind?"

"I think she's out with old Dougie Four Eyes," I said. "We'll be asleep before she gets home."

The kid came back with the ball and booted it into play. Everyone made a mad dash for it. Danno's dad stood at the bus stop and stubbed out his cigarette under his heel. A bit of a scrum ensued, everyone barging and shoving and hacking at the ball. The bus arrived. The doors hissed open. I saw Danno step to one side and watch his old man snap the collar on his suit and climb inside. Danno had that same hate filled look on his face.

Someone ran straight into me and knocked me from my feet. I went sprawling to the ground and tasted dirt in my mouth. I saw one of the Robertson twins stood over me smugly nodding to his brother as if it had been planned. Clutch ran his fingers through his ginger curls and grinned.

Danno squared up to Henry, the twin who'd knocked me over "That was deliberate!"

Clutch stepped between them. "You want to make something of it?"

Someone kicked the ball. It hit Danno hard on the side of the head. He stumbled a bit. Someone else ran in and kicked the ball back in the direction it had come from. It hit Clutch right between the legs. He doubled over. The playful and boisterous mood began to deteriorate rapidly.

Most of the girls departed the makeshift pitch, heading for the benches, some of them joining Deb and Shona on the swings. The younger kids suddenly got really interested in climbing the steps on the slide or clambering onto the roundabout to spin it around. Two gangs began to form. Clutch and his mates at one side of the park. Me, Danno, HC and three other fourteen year olds from our year at school at the other side. This was a grudge match in the making. We were like the young stags in a herd of deer, testing the limits, seeing how far we could push things, ready to lock horns.

Scores were about to be settled.

At first it played out like an actual football match, the ball being passed back and forth, kicked up and down the park, a couple of kids from each side taking on the role of goalkeepers, dancing crablike between makeshift goalposts made from tee-shirts whose owner were playing bare chested. Then the dirty tackles gave way to barging and pushing and shoving. Soon altercations were breaking out all over the park. Soon these altercations gave way to potential fist fights. I saw HC get hit hard on the side of his face by Jimmy Scott. I ran to help him.

The twin who'd knocked me over earlier kicked the legs from under me as I ran. I landed heavily on my shoulder and felt the skin on my left elbow tear against the hard ground. I looked up and saw that Clutch had Danno in a headlock. Lanky Branning kicked Danno hard in the stomach. His knees folded under him.

I tried to stand up. But, in a rapidly moving blur, the other Robertson twin knocked me back to the ground again and straddled my chest. I dodged my head left and right as he swung wild punches at me.

There were several scraps taking place now. The younger kids evacuated the slide and the roundabout and began to gather in little clusters around the skirmishes, chanting in that tribalistic manner, that even then, was as old as the hills. "Fight! Fight! Fight!" Some of the girls joined the chant. Most of them, however, hurriedly departed the park.

I bucked and somehow managed to throw off my assailant. As he fell back, I managed a kick in the chest for good measure. His head thumped against the sun-baked ground. I got to my feet and examined my elbow. Blood was trickling in jagged red streams down my forearm to my wrist. Something caught my eye, something furtively moving just beyond the bushes to the rear of the park.

The sun was on the wane. I squinted through the gathering gloom. That was when they stepped into view. Maggie and Maurice, Maggie with her rubber flex necklace and Maurice hissing gaseous vapour through his nostrils. They were laughing. As if the near riot playing out in the park was the most hilarious thing they'd ever seen.

A hand grabbed the collar of my Ben Sherman shirt. I was yanked so forcefully backwards that I was almost pulled from my feet. I managed to twist myself around to see that it was Henry Robinson who had hold of me.

"You nearly knocked my brother out," he snarled.

The other twin was sitting cross legged on the ground, groggily rubbing the back of his head. I struggled to free myself from Henry's grip. He twisted his hand tighter into the material of my shirt collar. I heard the material rip and when I looked, he had half the collar in his hand. He stepped back, eyes wide, apparently shocked at what he'd done. Anger erupted inside me. Henry dropped the piece of chequered collar.

"That's my favourite fucking shirt!" I roared and launched a punch that hit him right between the teeth.

He staggered away, spitting blood.

His brother swung a punch so wild that it missed me by a mile.

"Clear the park!" A man's baritone voice rang out above the shouts and grunts and curses.

"Clear the park - or I swear to God I'll arrest the bloody lot of you."

Everyone fell silent. Kids wrestling on the ground disentangled themselves from each other. Clutch released his headlock on Danno. I noticed that Danno's lip was spit open again.

A police officer dressed in a white short-sleeved uniform shirt and a peaked cap stepped into the middle of the park. Outside the gate another police officer, similarly dressed, was standing by a patrol car. He was speaking into his walkie-talkie. One of the people living in the houses opposite the park must have called them.

No one had noticed them arrive.

"I won't ask you again," said the police officer. "I want you all out of this park by the time I count to ten. It's Saturday night and me and my mate are going to have to deal with the mayhem that's going to ensue when your drunken relatives fall out of the pubs. We don't need the hassle of dealing with a bunch of bloody morons that have got nothing better to do than knock fifty pieces of shit out of each other."

The younger kids immediately began to drift toward the gate.

Clutch stepped up in front of him, looking somewhat smug, clearly aiming to play to the audience. He scratched his curly red hair and looked the officer up and down. I had to bite my lip. He was like Hair Bear confronting the zookeeper. "This is a public area," said Clutch, chest puffing. "You've got no right to chuck us out."

The police officer sighed. "You've got two choices, son. You can leave peacefully, or you can try out the upholstery in the back of the Panda car."

"You're going to arrest me?" said Clutch, sounding genuinely offended. "What for?"

The officer sighed again. "Public affray."

Clutch grinned at him. "You can't arrest all of us."

"I'm not planning on arresting everyone," replied the officer, tapping the metal handcuffs looped through his belt. "Just you, if you keep mouthing off."

Clutch's top lip quivered a little. Then he turned to his mates, and it was like a replay of his confrontation with Gary in the Youth Club, backing down in contradiction to his aggression and bravado. "Come on," he said. "We're wasting our time hanging about round here. It's a kid's playground."

With that he headed for the gate. Henry and Ron Robinson followed. As did Jimmy Scott and Lanky Branning. Then so did everyone else, HC and Danno included.

I turned and stole a quick glance back at the bushes. The apparitions of Maggie and Maurice were gone. I looked back round at the police officer. There were wet patches of sweat beneath his armpits. He took of his cap and wiped his brow. Out by the gate his colleague was busy shooing everyone along the pavement. In the houses across the road curtains were twitching.

This is another opportunity, I thought. *I can bring it all to an end right now.*

142

"Got something you want to say, son?" the police officer asked, noticing my reluctance to leave. "Something you want to get off your mind?"

Words started forming themselves inside my head in a tumbling, rambling stream. *It's like this, officer. You know that run down house by the old railway line? The one all the kids on the scheme call Maggie's House? Well, the other day, my mates and me went in there and we found this dead body upstairs in one of the bedrooms. It's the old tramp that's always hanging round in the bus station. And we were going to report it. But then we decided to keep him so we could watch him fester. And since then, I keep thinking that I can see ghosts and I keep having these weird nightmares. And the body is still there now. I could show you. I could get in the Panda car, and you could drive down there. And then it would all be over and...*

"Stop gawping and start walking," said the officer, clearly reaching the end of his patience.

The sentences were still bouncing around in my head, fully formed and ready to articulate. My lips moved. But the words were somehow trapped deep inside me, and they simply wouldn't take shape in my mouth.

The officer reached for his handcuffs. "I won't tell you again." He called over to his companion. "If this idiot isn't out of the park by the time I count to five, cuff and him and haul him into the back seat."

I walked to the gate with my head bowed in defeat.

HC and Danno were waiting for me on the other side of the road. HC was holding the side of

143

his face. Danno was dabbing his lip with the back of his hand. The remains of the collar of my Ben Sherman flapped limply around my neck. I could still feel blood trickling down from the gash on my elbow.

We could see Clutch and his gang farther along the road. We turned and headed off in the opposite direction. When we came to the next corner a crowd of the girls, including Deb and Shona, were congregated around the red phone box that was located there.

"Idiots," said Shona, as we walked past. Then she turned to Deb. "I don't know what you ever saw in him."

Deb blushed and hung her head, not even looking at me.

"Danno is staying at mine tonight," I said to HC, in a quiet, whispering voice. "You want come back to the flat and see if there's a good film on TV?"

HC shook his head. "I'm going home to stick some frozen peas on my face."

"We'll meet you at the usual place at nine thirty tomorrow," said Danno.

There it was then. We were going back to Maggie's house and the whole sorry saga was going to continue.

Chapter Fourteen

I lay in bed, silently crying in the darkness. I was crying for all sorts of confused reasons. Some, in the grand scheme of things, were trivial. Like the untimely end of my Ben Sherman shirt, which was beyond repair, and had been unceremoniously dumped in the bin.

Others were far more serious.

Like the fact that we had found a dead body and had pretty much set our course to continue abusing that fact, rather than reporting it. Yet others were so full of the inexplicable they terrified me. Such as apparently having ghostly apparitions regularly materialise before my eyes, or being afraid to fall asleep for fear of what new terrors my dreams might reveal.

I think mainly though I was crying for my friend. Someone I'd known since we were hardly out of nappies. Danno was on the floor of my bedroom, zipped up in Libby's old Girl Guide sleeping bag, which we had retrieved from the under stairs cupboard. I'd given him a cushion from the sofa as a pillow.

Before I'd turned the light off Danno had hurriedly stripped down to his underpants. His chest and back were covered in bruises. At first, I thought they might have been from the fight in the park. But then I saw that many of them had turned to that awful yellowy-brown hue that old bruises take on when they lose their purple. Clearly this was his old man's handywork. I didn't say anything. The way he stared me out when he noticed me looking kind

145

of confirmed that it was better not to mention this at all. More lies constructing themselves around things unsaid.

When the lights were out and all these jumbled thoughts started running around in my head, I imagined the cruel delivery of the blows that caused those wounds. A lump came to my throat. I turned my face to my pillow and wiped my tears on the pillowcase. The window was open. It was still hot and sticky. I could hear a motorbike engine revving somewhere on the housing scheme. I could hear a moth that had flown in when the light was on tic-tic-ticking inside the light shade. I'd washed the gash on my elbow, but I could still feel it throbbing beneath the Elastoplast that Danno had helped me apply.

I jumped when Danno spoke "You ever think about dying?" he asked.

The question sent a shiver running through me. I turned over and wiped away the remainder of my tears with my hands. I squinted down at Danno. He had one arm resting on his forehead. He seemed to be looking up to the ceiling.

"I think about it," he said, without waiting for my response. "Sometimes, when my old man comes home pissed out of his head. And my mum has locked her bedroom door. And he's banging on it and roaring to get let in like some big beast. That's when I think I'd be better off dead. It would be better when he kicks my door open ready to take it out on me that he just finds me there, dead in bed."

146

The lump came to my throat again. I tried to make light of it with a bit of Kenneth Williams. *"Stop messing about."*

"I'm not messing, Ranks," said Danno. "I used to wish that Roy would kill him. When he came home drunk, and Roy stood up to him, and they both ended up lugging it out in the back garden, I'd wish that Roy could just land a punch that would send the mean old bastard straight to his grave."

I found that I was crying again.

I didn't want to talk in case Danno could hear the sobs in my voice.

Danno didn't seem to notice my silence. "Maybe it'll come down to me or him in the end," he went on. "Now I've got a knife, maybe it'll come down to me slashing my wrists or stabbing him in the guts."

"It won't come to that," I said.

"It might," he replied.

I heard a key being turned in the door to the flat. The door opened and closed. I heard Libby come clomping upstairs in her platform shoes, and then sound of her bedroom door shutting. I heard the click of the compartment of her cassette player being pushed shut. She had the volume down low, but I recognised Brian Ferry's vocals singing The Strand and figured it was For Your Pleasure by Roxy Music that she'd put on.

Danno fell silent. I didn't want to reopen the conversation again. It was far too uncomfortable to hear. I turned and wiped my tears onto my pillowcase again. After a while I heard the door open again, followed by the sound of whispered voices.

Mum had brought Dougie home.

When they came creeping up stairs, giggling drunkenly, Libby turned off her music. Danno began to snore. Somewhere far away an owl hooted. I turned and lay on my back, listening to the pathetic struggles of the moth inside the lampshade. I breathed in through my left nostril and then out through my right. I hoped if I did some of the breathing exercises from the T. Lobsang Rampa book it would stop me from dreaming.

It didn't.

But this dream was something entirely different.

I felt my soul separate from my body and rise. The *Silver Chord* snaked behind it. I looked down and saw myself asleep on the bed. I saw Danno curled up in the sleeping bag. My soul rose and passed through the ceiling. And that was when the dream changed from what I'd previously experienced. The block of flats seemed to dissolve into nothingness. I found myself staring down at open fields, interspersed with little outcropping of trees, and a couple of narrow lanes, no more than dirt tracks, lined with untended hedgerows.

I remembered what the book had said about those who engage in *Astral Travel* being able to pass back and forth through time. I wondered if I was imagining what the area the housing scheme had been built on had looked like before the first phase of construction began in the early 60's.

I passed over the fields and treetops and found myself once more on the old railway line. This time some of the tracks and sleepers were still in place. There was a long truck parked at the bottom of a makeshift slope. It was loaded with sleepers and bits of track that must have been lifted the previous day.

My dream had taken me to the time immediately after the decommissioning of the line. I could see tools at the side of the track, alongside piles of iron couplings. I drifted along the partially disassembled line and came to the embankment that looked down onto Maggie's house. The house was restored to its former glory. Not long built. Glass in all the windows. No collapsed roof for pigeons to roost in. Guttering neat and tidy, drainpipe still attached to the perfectly pointed brickwork. The back door on its hinges, freshly painted and firmly closed.

A light was on in the kitchen. There was coarse grass on the slope leading down to the upright garden fence, a few shrubs growing here and there, no weeds of any consequence. I passed through the fence. The garden was well stocked with roses and azaleas, held up on bamboo canes and bordering a well-tended lawn. I passed through the door and into the kitchen. There were cupboards on the walls. The worktops beneath them looked spotless and new. In the gap between the worktops sat a gleaming white cooker.

Maurice was seated at the kitchen table. Spread out before him were papers that looked like bundles of bills and invoices held together with bull-clips. To his left there was a wad of banknotes and beside that a heap of pre-decimal brass and silver coins. Maurice had a pencil in his hand. He was scribbling a sum down into a little notebook. He stared at the sum, as if he was working back through the figures, then he tossed his head back and rubbed his temples with his knuckles. He stared at the sum again. Then crossed it all out, tore out the page, crushed it, and then started all over again.

This was the story being played out before my eyes, the one that you were supposed to recite to someone else just before they made the *run*. Here was Maurice fretting over his mounting debts. They were set out in the bills he had spread across the kitchen table. There was the cooker, just waiting for him to become so overwhelmed by it all that he switched on the gas and stuck his head in the oven.

A movement in the dark shadows of the corridor caught my eye. Someone was there, creeping up behind Maurice, laying their heels cautiously onto the carpeted floor and easing the soles of their feet slowly down. The figure stepped stealthily into the kitchen. Maurice was far too focused on his calculations to notice. He was sweating profusely as he poured over the sum. The creeping figure was right behind him now, mere inches away, but still he remained oblivious.

The intruder was a teenage boy of around seventeen. He had on a leather pilot's jacket, a white tee shirt and blue denims held up with a leather belt that had a big, cowboy style buckle. His hair was greased back. He had thick, black sideburns that came down level to his earlobes. He looked up and straight across at me. His eyes went wide. His mouth dropped open. It was as if he could see me standing there. Although it was pock marked with acne, I recognised his face. It was Danno's old man, or what my subconscious clearly believed his old man had looked like when he was a teenager.

He shook his head, forcefully denying my presence, and turned his attention to the wad of notes and pile of coins. A greedy grin spread across his face, a grin full of malevolence and malice. He stepped closer to Maurice and passed his hands around either side of his head. Maurice jumped, noticing now that he wasn't alone. Danno's old man clamped his hands over Maurice's mouth, fingers and knuckles interlocked, and pulled back. Maurice struggled to breathe, jerking violently in his chair.

Danno's old man pressed his thumbs hard against either side of Maurice's nostrils. Maurice tried to shake himself free. The chair shot sideways from under him. But Danno's old man pulled back tighter, holding his weight, hands and thumbs preventing him from drawing breath. Maurice began to turn purple. His eyes started to bulge. He started to look how Catweazle's corpse had looked when it began to bloat. I watched in horror. I was hoping for the tug of the *Silver Chord*, drawing me back to my physical body. It didn't happen. It seemed that whatever grotesque events my dream wanted to throw at me I was expected to witness them to the bitter end.

Maurice went limp. Danno's old man eased him down onto the floor. He took a steel comb from the back pocket of his jeans and flicked back his greasy hair, admiring his reflection against the outside darkness shown in the kitchen window. I watched him split the wad of notes into two and then stuff them into the pockets of his leather jacket. Then he filled the pockets of his jeans with the coins. He was about to leave when he seemed to notice the cooker.

He opened the oven door and dragged Maurice's limp body across the kitchen floor. I heard Maurice groan a little. Danno's old man rested Maurice's head on the shelf and turned the gas to full without igniting it. He took a step back and then, seeming to notice something else, he crouched low and lifted Maurice's limp left arm. There was a gold signet ring on his little finger that had been designed to look a little like a wheat sheaf. The design seemed vaguely familiar to me. But at that point I didn't realise its significance.

With the gas hissing all around him Danno's old man diligently manoeuvred the ring back and forth until he'd managed to twist it over the knuckle. He held it up to examine it and grinned greedily. He slipped the ring on his own outstretched pinkie. Then, with a last sweep of his steel comb through his quiff, he was gone, swiftly inserting himself back into the darkness of the corridor.

Maurice coughed and tried to raise himself up. But a combination of concussion and seeping gas overwhelmed him. He slumped back down onto the shelf. What I was witnessing in my dream was a murder. But not the murder that Libby claimed had happened. When Maggie came home and saw the bills scattered there and Maurice's desperate calculations it would seem to her and, for that matter, anyone else who could put two and two together, that it was a suicide.

*

It was about half past eight in the morning when Danno and I started getting dressed. No paper round on a Sunday. The only day I could sleep that late. Danno didn't mention the conversation we'd had before he went to sleep, and I didn't mention the dream that I'd had. More lies grew from our mutual silence.

We found mum, Dougie, and Libby in the kitchen, eating toast with rhubarb and ginger jam. There was a big pot of tea in the centre of the table and mum had brought out the little souvenir milk jug she kept for special occasions.

"Daniel," she quipped when she saw Danno. "If I'd have known you were coming, I'd have baked a cake."

The joke went over Danno's head. He'd never quite gotten the hang of mum's sense of humour. I don't suppose that there was ever that much to laugh about in his house.

We sat down.

Mum stuck some more bread under the grill of the cooker.

"It's going to be another hot day," she said. "We're planning to take a run down to Berwick if you boys want to come."

"You said I could bring one of my mates," complained Libby.

"There's room for four of you in the back," said mum.

Libby put down the piece of toast she was holding. "Four of us? In Dougie's Cortina?"

Mum turned the toast over and looked to Dougie for confirmation that we'd all fit. Dougie looked across the table at us through the milk bottle lenses of his glasses. The morning sun was glinting from the smooth crown of his bald head. "It'd be a squeeze," he said.

"No way," said Libby. "I'm not being squashed up amongst two stinky fourteen-year-olds. Especially in this heat."

Mum set out a plate with four slices of toast onto the table. Danno picked up a slice and started spreading it with jam. "We can't really come, anyway, Mrs Rankin," he said. "We've got something planned."

A big part of me wanted to contradict him. A trip to Berwick would be another way of breaking the cycle. Maybe if we went for a walk along the cliffs, we could somehow force each other to talk about what we'd gotten ourselves into.

"Nothing stupid I hope," said mum, pinching my cheek. "I don't want my little soldier getting into any trouble."

This time Danno laughed at the joke.

I blushed.

"The river is really low," said Danno. "We're going to go down and see if we can net some minnows."

I bit off a mouthful of toast and gave him a sideways glance. The lie had tumbled out his mouth as easily as if it had been HC sitting there and not

154

Danno. Danno folded his slice of toast in half and bit into it.

"Well, I don't want you coming back here and trying to cook them like you did the last time," warned mum.

I groaned. "We were nine years old."

Libby rolled her eyes. "You're both still just as stupid as you were back then."

"Ruined my best frying pan, so they did," mum told Dougie.

Dougie chuckled, teacup held halfway to his lips.

Chapter Fifteen

The inevitability of the heat was becoming monotonous. In the sky above us there was nothing but vast miles of blandly uninterrupted blue, pierced by a fat, burning sun. As Danno and me walked lethargically through the housing scheme the dust gathering on the pavement made it feel like one of those desert towns from an old western. I half expected to see a ball of tumbleweed come bouncing along the road.

I wondered how people in hot countries coped with the predictability of it all. What must it be like to experience day after day of the sun beating relentlessly down, draining you of your energy and your ability to think straight? I wondered if it might be any cooler at Berwick. Maybe there would be a breeze blowing in from the North Sea.

I was just plucking up the courage to tell Danno about how his old man had appeared in my dream when he came to a sudden halt. "I need to go home to pick something up."

"You sure that's a good idea?" I asked, fanning myself with the pack of flypapers that I'd only just remembered to bring with me.

"It's not a problem," he replied. "The old bastard won't get out of bed till gone two. Then he'll demand that my mum makes him some bacon sandwiches with the off cuts he brought home on Friday. Then he'll have another sleep. Then he'll bugger off down the Legion. It's the same routine every Sunday. You go and meet HC. I'll be in and out in a couple of minutes."

"If you're sure," I said, thinking that maybe his real intention was to check up on his mum.

I found HC sitting on the pavement. There was a huge bruise on his left cheek, black and badly inflamed. "That from last night?" I asked, sitting down beside him.

HC nodded. "I think I might have fractured my cheek bone," he said.

For once I didn't think he was exaggerating. I started tapping my knee with the pack of flypapers, beating a kind of nervous rhythm.

"Sometimes I reckon this is all we've got," he said, and started counting off on his fingers. "Beating up each other. Beating up other people. Getting beat up."

He had a point. In the case of Danno it even applied to his home life. I thought about the slap that mum had given Libby when I'd burned the fish fingers, and how many times that sort of thing happen, and all those times that Libby and I ended up in a screaming match. Maybe my own home life was only a tad better than Danno's.

"If we were posh kids, this wouldn't be happening," said HC, rubbing his cheek. "We'd be going to piano lessons or doing a thousand-piece jigsaw."

I laughed. "A thousand-piece jigsaw. Who'd have the patience for that?"

"Kids who have some sort of calmness in their lives," said HC. "Kids who can do things like read a book."

That set me thinking. Other than the T. Lopsang Rampa book, which I was dipping in and out of, rather than reading straight through, the only books I had really read since I was twelve were the skinhead novels by Richard Allen. I estimated that I'd probably read five of them - Skinhead, Skinhead Escapes, Trouble for Skinhead, Suedehead and Boot Boys. The lives of the characters in those books seemed to mirror our own. Every second or third page brought with it another random act of violence.

I had a theory that there was only one copy of each novel, perpetually circulating amongst the kids on the housing scheme. Reading them was a much a rite of passage as making the *run* at Maggie's house. No sooner had you started at secondary school than someone pressed one of those novels into your innocent hands and seduced you into the bizarre notion that violence was somehow a cool thing to be involved in.

I tried to remember the last *proper* book I'd read.

I guessed it must have been Stig of the Dump by Clive King. It had been the last birthday present I'd received from my grandma before she passed away. I seemed to remember that I'd gotten about halfway through the book when Bernard Cribbins, or someone like him, had started reading it on Jackanory, and that had made me question the whole point of seeing the book through to the end. Why bother reading it if someone else was doing the job for you?

"Sometimes I think we go too far," said HC. He was clearly skirting around the edges, trying to broach the question of Catweazle's body.

"Do you think we're getting in too deep?" I prompted.

"I think we're going to go to hell for what we're doing."

I told him about the dream and how, in it, Danno's old man had murdered Maurice.

"That might be exactly what happened." HC turned to me squinting against the sun. "You said yourself no-one really know what happened in that house."

"I was my mum who said that," I pointed out. "This was a dream. I didn't go back in time and witness an actual event. That's not even possible."

HC yawned loudly. "Holy fuckeroni, Ranks," he said. "I can't even sleep at night without the light on. I keep thinking Maggie's ghost is creeping around in the darkness."

I was about to tell him about the ghosts I'd been imagining seeing all over the place when Danno showed up. He had a Fine Fayre bag tucked under his arm. Whatever it was that was wrapped in there it looked bulky and heavy and it certainly wasn't another pack of incense sticks.

"Ready?" he asked.

Neither of us offered any form of protest. We just rose to our feet and followed him. He was like some aberrant shepherd; we were his sheep, happily traipsing behind him as he led us to the abattoir. The mood was subdued. None of us were talking. For once HC wasn't prattling on about some uncle or aunt, engaged in some exaggerated enterprise, and I wasn't even remotely inclined to try out any of my impersonations.

The sun just went on beating down on us. By the time we reached the old railway track the red tee shirt that I'd worn to replace my Ben Sherman was showing wide patches of sweat. We walked past the copy of the Daily Record, still sitting face up on the path. The front cover was torn and wrinkled. There was a black footprint on the picture of the kid with the melting ice cream, exactly as it had appeared in the dream I'd had when I'd fallen asleep in the cinema. My heart started to thump. How could something that had appeared in a dream be there in physical reality?

"Did either of you go to Maggie's house yesterday?" I asked.

"By myself?" said HC. "No fear."

"Not me," said Danno.

I looked back at the paper. Maybe it was just coincidence. We climbed down the weed-infested embankment and picked our way through the jungle of thistles and goldenrods in the overgrown garden. I kept remembering the well-tended lawn and flowerbeds I'd also seen in my dream.

The interior of the house was already fiercely hot, dust motes dancing in the shaft of light that had wedged in through the back door, spiders prowling the tight webs that hung in the corners of the corridor ceiling. Danno climbed the stairs. We followed. A couple of black-shelled beetles scuttled away on our approach. A little patch of crumbling plaster fell from the wall.

The warning was still there in wax crayon on the little bedroom door.

Maggie waits...

Still with the Fine Fayre bag held tightly under his arm Danno pushed it open. The smell in the room didn't seem as bad as it had previously. It was kind of sickening to contemplate, but I thought that maybe I was getting used to it.

"Holy fuckeroni!" cried HC as soon as we entered.

He was pointing at the flypapers that we'd stuck to Catweazle two days earlier. They were scattered on the floor. They looked like little, overcrowded fly cemeteries viewed from a bird's eye point of view.

"Somebody's been here," said HC.

"It's just the heat," said Danno. "It dried up the gum and the papers fell off."

"Heat doesn't dry gum," said HC. "Cold does. If someone didn't take them off, then it was Maggie. Maggie's ghost." He looked cautiously over his shoulder.

"Fuck off," said Danno. "It was the wind then. It blew in through the window last night."

"You fuck off," replied HC. "There was no wind last night. We're in the middle of a heatwave!"

I was only vaguely listening to the argument. My attention was fixed on what was else on the floor. In amongst the discarded Bazooka Joe wrappers lay a little heap of curly wood shavings, some still bearing the brown bark of the stick they been shaved from. Again, my heart began to thump. Danno had been whittling a stick in my dream. This had to be more than coincidence.

161

I looked at the Fine Fayre bag tucked under Danno's arm. In my dream he'd thrown the sharpened stick out of the window. Maybe he'd retrieved it. Maybe that's what was in the bag. I felt a twist tighten in my belly. Was he planning to do what Maggie had been urging him to do in my dream? Stab a sharpened stick into Catweazle's dead eye? Had it been a dream? Or had I somehow witnessed an actual event? If I had, what did that mean for the other dream? The one in which Danno's old man committed a murder and covered it up as a suicide?

"What's in the bag, Danno?" I asked.

He grinned back at me. "All will be revealed shortly."

HC was still staring down at the flypapers.

"I'm going to light a couple of incense sticks," said Danno. "You and HC put some of them new flypapers on our friend." He laid the Fine Fayre bag down in the corner and picked up the pack of incense sticks he'd left there.

"I still think someone's been in here," said HC.

"Probably your uncle, looking for IRA fugitives," said Danno. He lit one of the incense sticks and poked it into the upholstery of the tattered armchair.

"Fuck you," said HC.

I brought out the pack of Juicy Fruit from my jeans' pocket and handed a couple of slices to HC. "I wish you'd brought Bazooka Joes again," he said. "I could do with reading a couple of them comics to cheer me up, because right now I'm shitting my

162

pants about how those flypapers ended up on the floor."

I felt the same way about the wood shavings. But I didn't say anything. Danno lit another incense stick. HC and me chewed on the Juicy Fruits and then pressed wads of gum to the new set of flypapers. Since we'd last seen him Catweazle had deflated a little. He was no longer so bloated. The heat seemed to be quickening his descent into decay.

The flesh above his trimmed beard was marbled. The skin had split in several of the places where there had previously been blisters, exposing dark, and meaty lesions. His nose had turned a greenish black, fluid was leaking from it like streams of glutinous snot. His eyes seemed to be sinking backwards into their sockets. His fingernails were disappearing into the flesh of his swollen grey fingers.

A new generation of flies was buzzing about his head and a new generation of maggots was squirming inside the open sores, wallowing in the putrid discharge. There was a horrible, discoloured wet patch between his legs. I could see a procession of tiny ants climbing up one of his scuffed old boots and into his trouser leg.

We began sticking the flypapers onto him. Pretty soon the flies began sticking to the papers. I affected a Charlton Heston, biblical epic, kind of voice. *"And low it came to pass that fly begat maggot and maggot became fly."*

Neither Danno nor HC seemed to find it funny.

163

HC picked up the old flypapers and set them down beside the shattered remains of the Fyffes banana box. Danno fetched the Fine Fayre bag and dipped his hand into it. My heart began to thump again. I'd expected to see the sharpened stick. I didn't expect to see a gun. It was a black pistol, with a metal handgrip and a long barrel. Danno pointed it at HC and managed to do a Clint Eastwood that was just as good as anything I could have come up with. *"Go ahead, punk. Make my day."*

HC ducked down. "Holy fuckeroni, Danno, you don't want to go pointing that thing at people."

Danno laughed, holding the gun steady. "Don't shit a brick, it's not loaded."

"Where the hell did you get that?" I asked.

Danno lowered the gun. "I found it under Roy's bed when I was looking for more incense sticks."

"Roy had a gun?" My mouth went slack.

"It's not a gun that fires bullets," HC pointed. "It's an air gun. Looks like a .22. Probably a Webley and Scott."

"Listen old mastermind," said Danno, nonchalantly tossing the pistol from left hand to right.

"I'm not shitting you," said HC. "Read what it says on the side of the barrel."

Danno turned the gun over and squinted. *"The Webley MK 1,"* he read out.

"Told you," said HC. "My uncle had one of them."

I could see that he wasn't lying this time. It didn't seem that far-fetched, given HC's uncle had been in the army. And if the rumour was true about him being involved in an armed robbery, then maybe it was an airgun he'd used, pretending it was real.

"It fires lead pellets," said HC.

The airgun seemed to be drawing his attention away from the conundrum of how the flypapers had ended up on the floor. The fact that Danno had produced the gun from the bag and not a sharpened stick had kind set my mind at ease about the dream being real. But it still didn't explain the wood shavings. Unless HC was right and someone else had been in the room.

Danno reached down into the Fine Fayre bag and brought out a little cardboard box. "Like these?" he said to HC, opening the lid and holding out his hand. The box was filled with little grey pellets. They had round tops and they fanned out like skirts at the bottom.

"Exactly like them," said HC. "You load them in the magazine that's in the handle. But you need an air canister too. It'll only fire if there's enough compressed air to launch the pellet."

Danno handed the box of pellets to HC and reached back into the bag. Again, he was like Danno the magician. This time he produced four silver cylinders, each about the length of an index finger, all of them bound together with a brown elastic band.

"Let me see the gun and I'll load it for you," said HC.

Danno handed him the airgun. I felt as if I'd ended up on the periphery of this mutual interest in weaponry that was being shared between the two of them. I looked at the new set of flypapers we'd hung on Catweazle. They were quickly filling up with tiny twitching bodies. The spicy scent of the incense sticks had started wafting smoky serpents about the room.

HC flipped something on the underside of the handgrip and pulled down the magazine. "There's already a cylinder here," he said, and started pressing pellets into the little round housings in the magazine clip.

HC was in his element. I could imagine his uncle, dressed in his tartan trimmed K.O.S.B. uniform, showing him how to do this, explaining how it all worked. I could imagine HC at ten or eleven years old, listening in wide-eyed awe. I could imagine too how all sorts of stories about his uncle might have started forming in HC's impressionable head.

Now he and Danno had something in common, a shared experience. Danno looked up to his cousin as much as HC looked up to his uncle. They were linked by the fact that both relatives had seemingly possessed an airgun. The very fact that HC knew how the gun worked appeared to have pushed him up several notches in Danno's estimation.

HC clicked the magazine back into the handle grip. He held his arm out straight and took aim at the wall. His finger pulled back on the trigger. There came a click, followed by the hiss of the pellet slicing through the air, then a dull thunk as it embedded itself in the plaster.

HC and Danno rushed to examine the little hole it left.

I hung back – not part of this new intimacy.

"Still compressed air in the cylinder," said HC.

"Let me have a go," said Danno, holding out his hand.

They were like a couple of kids with a new toy at Christmas.

HC handed him the airgun.

"You still got that wax crayon?" asked HC. "I could draw a target on the wall."

Danno turned and aimed the gun at Catweazle's corpse.

"No need to draw a target when we've got one ready-made," he said.

"No," yelled HC and pushed his hand away. "We agreed to show him some respect. You already punched him in the head. I'm not going to let you shoot him as well."

Their tentative alliance was breaking down already. I shuffled a little to the side in case the air gun went off by mistake. Danno barged past HC. "*You* said we should show him some respect. I never agreed. The smelly old fucker is dead."

HC grabbed his shoulder. "That's even more reason to respect him. You have to show respect for the dead. That's what people do."

Danno shrugged off his hand and pressed the barrel of the airgun to Catweazle's left eye. "Do you think if you did this in real life you could kill a person?" he asked. "You think if you crept up on a person when then were asleep and tipped the gun at the right angle the lead pellet would go right through their eye and into their brain?"

This was his old man he was talking about. He had that same look on his face, the one that I'd seen in my dream, when he was sharpening the stick to a point. The same one I'd seen in the park as he watched his old man swaggering toward the bus stop.

"Don't do it, Danno," pleaded HC. "We're damned as it is. Don't go making it worse."

"One pull of the trigger," said Danno, pressing harder against Catweazle's eye. "That's all it would take."

The smoke from the incense sticks seemed to gravitate in his direction. It settled around him. It looked as if someone was standing behind him, guiding his hand. There seemed little doubt to me that Maggie herself was present within the swirl of the smoke, full of malicious intent.

"We could do the Golden Shot," I blurted.

I've no idea where it came from. The words just formed in my head and then flew out of my mouth a fast as the pellet had shot out of the airgun when HC pulled the trigger. The smoke dissipated. Danno turned to look at me. His finger eased back from the trigger.

"We could use the apple cores that are in the duffel bag," said HC, taking my lead. "I could be Bernie the Bolt."

Danno lowered the gun and let it hang by his side. "We have to put the apple cores on Catweazle though," he said. "Just to keep it interesting."

"OK," I said. "But we aim at the apple cores and not at Catweazle."

Danno nodded.

"What if we hit Catweazle by mistake?" asked HC.

Danno glared at him.

I knew it was down to me to be the diplomat.

"Then it wouldn't be disrespectful," I said. "Because it would be a mistake."

Danno and HC stared each other down.

"Fair enough," said HC.

Danno stuffed the barrel of the gun down the front of his jeans and went to rummage in the duffel bag for the apple cores. They'd become dried and spotted with mould. He used the Swiss Army knife to cut each of them in half and then placed the four halves on Catweazle. One on the blackened hand that was resting on the armrest, one on each of his shoulders, and the last nestling amongst the grey hair on the top of his head.

He turned to me.

"You be Bob Monkhouse then."

"Monkhouse was ages ago," I said. "I was thinking of doing it as Charlie Williams."

Danno shook his head. "You're the wrong colour for Charlie Williams."

"You don't have to be black to do Charlie Williams," I told him. *"Y'just 'ave t' talk wi' a Yorkshire accent."*

"It has to be Monkhouse," insisted Danno. "You can't have the Golden Shot without Bob Monkhouse."

"How about Norman Vaughan?" I asked.

I put both thumbs up and did his catch phrase from the Cadbury advert. *"Ooh, Roses grow on you."*

"Na," said Danno. "Norman Vaughan was crap on the Golden Shot. It has to be Bob Monkhouse. He was the original."

"Danno's right," agreed HC. "Monkhouse is the man."

At least I was providing them with some common ground to build on.

"I'm not very good at Bob Monkhouse," I admitted.

"Jesus Christ, Ranks," said Danno, "you're not on Opportunity Knocks yet. Just do Bob Monkhouse and let's get on with it."

Danno pulled the gun out of his jeans. HC and me pushed Catweazle in his armchair across to the wall. The remaining flies followed, jittering in the air like a squadron of WW1 biplanes. The smoke from the incense sticks made my eyes water. The apple cores fell off. We rebalanced them. I crossed the room and dragged my heel across the floorboards, making a line in the dust.

Danno stood behind it and raised the airgun.

"Not yet," I told him. "We have to do it right."

I cleared my throat and recited the opening announcements from memory. *"Live from Birmingham, it's the Golden Shot. And here's the man who keeps it bang on target. He-e-e-res Bobby."*

I made as if I was walking on set. Then I adopted what I hoped looked like a smarmy Bob Monkhouse type stance and did my best to remember his voice. We played out the part when someone phones in to the show.

"Who do we have on the line today?"

"This is Gladys Saggyboobs from Manchester," replied HC, hand cupped over his mouth, so it sounded like a phone call.

I had to bite my lip to stop myself from laughing. *"Saggyboobs?"* I said. *"Now that's an unusual name."*

"Oh, I come from a long line of Saggyboobs," said HC.

Danno and me cracked up.

"You understand how the game is played, Gladys?" I managed to ask.

"Oh yes, Bob," said HC. "I'm a big fan of the Golden Shit."

"That's Shot, Gladys," I corrected. *"Golden Shot."*

"Sorry, Bob," said HC. "That was a slip of the tongue."

"But talking of shits," I went on. *"Today's target is based on the theme of that smelly old tramp, Catweazle Shitypants. Can you see the target, Gladys?"*

"Oh yes, Bob," said HC. "He's a right ugly old bastard."

"And can you see the targets that have been placed about his person?"

"Yes, Bob. There's a couple on his shoulder. One on his hand and one on his head."

"So, are you ready to play the Golden Shot?"

"My saggy boobs are trembling at the thought," said HC.

171

Danno and me cracked up again.

I motioned to Danno to raise the gun.

"Bernie the bolt, if you please," I said.

HC stepped forward and pretended to load a bolt on top of the barrel of the gun.

"You have fifty seconds starting now," I said.

"Left a bit," said HC in his Gladys voice. "Left a bit and left a bit more."

Danno followed the instructions, moving the gun slowly leftwards.

"Stop," said HC. "Now down a bit."

Danno moved the gun down.

I could see that it was HC's plan to direct him to the apple core on Catweazle's hand. He wasn't taking any chances.

"Down," said HC. "Down some more. Stop."

Danno stopped.

"Right a little," said HC.

Danno moved the gun to then right.

"Fire!" yelled HC.

Danno pulled the trigger. A click followed by a hiss and a little puff of dust as the lead pellet penetrated the front of the armrest.

"Oh, bad luck, Gladys," I commiserated.

Danno lowered the gun.

"You be Anne Aston and tell us the scores," said Danno, looking at HC.

"I can't be Anne Aston," said HC. "She's a woman."

"If Ranks can be Charlie Williams, you can be Anne Aston," said Danno.

"Ranks isn't being Charlie Williams," said HC. "He's being Bob Monkhouse."

"You just pretended to be Gladys Saggyboobs," I pointed out.

HC shook his head. "OK, you win."

"And here to tell us the scores is the lovely Ann Aston."

HC went flouncing up to the armchair. He bent down and looked at the hole left by the pellet, wiggling his bum in the process. Then he stood up, put his hand on his hip and fluttered his eyelids. "I'm afraid Gladys missed the target completely, Bob."

He held out his hand to Danno. "My turn now."

Danno hesitated and then handed him the air gun.

HC went and stood behind the line in the dust.

I pretended to pick up the phone.

"Who do we have on the line now," I asked, in my attempt at Bob Monkhouse's voice.

Danno's response was predictable and lacking in imagination. "Malkie the alcie from Mary Hill," he slurred.

It seemed that imitating drunks was the best he could stretch to.

"Well, Malkie," I said. *"Are you ready to play the Golden Shot?"*

"Sure am," replied Danno, slurring the words again.

On my signal HC raised his arm and aimed the airgun at Catweazle.

"Bernie the bolt – if you please."

Danno assumed the role of Bernie the Bolt and pretended to load the bolt into the barrel of the gun. Then he stepped back and swayed deliberately,

173

getting into the character of Malkie the alcie. His head turned to the side a little and yet again I had the impression that he was listening to something being whispered into his ear. A spiteful little grin formed on his lips.

"Up a bit," he said.

HC raised his arm a little.

"Up some more," said Danno.

I could see where this was going. He was going to make HC take a shot at the apple core on Catweazle's head. I hoped that HC would have the sense to shoot wide.

"Left," said Danno.

HC moved his hand left.

"Down a bit," said Danno. "A little to the right."

HC followed the directions.

"Fire!" yelled Danno.

I saw HC narrow his eye to the sight at the end of the barrel. He lifted his hand a fraction, the pulled the trigger. A click, followed by a hiss through the air. The pellet hit the apple core, splitting it in two and sending the two parts spinning through the air.

"Holy fuckeroni!" cried HC.

Danno shimmied up to Catweazle.

"Malkie the alcie scored a bullseye, Bob," he said.

I looked at HC. He was grinning like the cat that got the cream.

"How the fuck did you manage that?" I asked.

"My uncle taught me," he replied. "We used to shoot empty beer cans in the back garden."

HC tried to push the airgun into my hand. "Your turn now, Ranks."

I declined. "I can't I'm doing Bob."

"You can do Bob and fire the gun," said Danno.

I really didn't want to have anything to do with the gun.

"I'm OK," I said. "You have another go, Danno."

Danno walked across the room toward me. "We're in this together," he insisted. "If HC and me had a turn, you've got to take your turn as well."

I gesticulated with my arms. "I wouldn't even know how to fire the thing."

HC grinned, corners of his lips turning up to his freckle filled cheeks. "It's easy," he said. "Just hold the handle and pull the trigger. Nothing to it."

He offered me the gun again. With a sigh, I took it from him. It felt heavier than I expected. The handle was hard and awkward in my palm. When I curled my index finger around the trigger my hand began to tremble a little.

"Who's on the line now?" I asked.

"Never mind who's on the line," said Danno. He looked tense. I saw his fist clench. "Let's just get on with it."

"Bernie the bolt – if you please," interjected HC.

I raised the gun.

HC made as if he was loading the bolt.

"Up," said Danno.

I moved my hand slowly up.

The smoke from the incense sticks was curling around Catweazle's corpse. By then all the flies had either gotten trapped on the flypapers or had been chased away by the smoke. There was a little piece of apple core stuck to the tainted flesh on Catweazle's forehead. The discharge from his nostril was melding with the blue toilet flush stain on his beard.

"Up some more," said Danno.

I moved my hand up again.

The heat was making me sweat. The sweat dripped from my eyebrows into my eyes, blurring my vision. In thought I caught the fleeting glimpse of a shadowy figure moving across the room. I thought I caught the sensation of something creeping up behind me, and then the flutter of cold breath in my ear.

My wrist started to strain a little from the weight of the airgun. I really didn't like how it felt in my hand. My palm was sweating, and I could feel a pulse in my index finger throbbing against the trigger.

"Left," said Danno. "Left, left, left."

At first it felt as if he was guiding me to one of the apple core halves on Catweazle's shoulders. But the more leftward he urged more the more suspicious I became that he was lining me up with Catweazle's head. Just as he had done with HC. Only there was no apple on Catweazle's head now. I glanced at Danno. His eyes looked cold. His face was so taut that there were veins standing out on his temples.

"Left," he said. "Left some more."

I tried to do what I'd seen HC doing and line my eye to the sight. I narrowed my eye and found myself looking straight at Catweazle's rotting face. I had the distinct sensation of someone pressing intimately close to my back, of fingers wrapping around my wrist, of my arm being held forcefully steady.

"Fire!" cried Danno.

I jerked my hand to the right and pulled the trigger. I heard the click, followed by the hiss of the pellet as it sliced through the air. Then there came the little thump of the pellet embedding itself in the plaster.

"Oh, dear, Bob," said HC, in his Anne Aston voice. "Looks like another one missed the target completely."

Danno shook his head, as if he was thoroughly disgusted by my actions. "Deliberately more like."

I realised that my arm was still outstretched. I lowered the airgun to my side. "Told you I didn't know how to shoot," I said.

Danno snatched the airgun from my hand. "Never had you down for a coward, Ranks."

"If he missed, he missed," said HC. "You can't just go around calling people cowards."

"Speak as you find," said Danno.

"Still doesn't give you the right," insisted HC.

Danno's fist tightened around the handle grip of the airgun. "Fuck you, Anderson. You want to make something of it?"

"Come on, Danno," I said. "It was only supposed to be a bit of fun. If it makes you happy,

I'll admit I missed deliberately. I didn't want to risk hitting Catweazle."

"Makes you a coward, Ranks," he said.

"Out of order!" yelled HC, squaring up to him.

"Out of order?" Danno yelled back. "Out of order? Who are you to tell me I'm out of order?"

He jabbed the barrel of the gun forcefully into HC's belly. HC doubled over in pain. The hinges on the door creaked. A shadow passed swiftly across the floor. Still doubled over HC made a swipe for Danno. Danno dodged it and made a grab for his hair.

"Just stop it," I said, getting in between them. "Can't you see this is what *she* wants?"

The two of them looked at me and I could tell from the stunned expressions on their faces that they both knew exactly what it was I was alluding to. But before either of them could say anything in response we heard a loud jumble of boisterous voices drifting down from the railway track.

Chapter Sixteen

The three of us froze, listening intently. The voices drew nearer. We recognised Clutch's voice. "Let's knock the rest of the glass out of the windows." Crouching low we shuffled across the floor and wedged ourselves beneath the sill of the back window so we couldn't be seen from up on the old railway line. A second or so passed before HC scrambled back, snatched the incense sticks one by one, and crushed them out under his baseball boots.

"In case they see the smoke," he whispered, joining us again.

We heard something clatter against the outside wall. We knew one of Clutch's gang had thrown a stone, aiming at one of the windows. The three of us had been engaged in this activity on a couple of occasions, lobbing stones down the embankment to see who could smash out the ever-diminishing shards of jagged glass left in the rotting window frames.

There came another couple of noisy clatters against the wall, then the sound of something crashing down in the kitchen, followed by a triumphant whoop. Then more stones came raining down, clatter, clatter, clatter against the brick walls.

"Do you think they'll come in here?" whispered HC.

"They've all made the *run*," I whispered back. "No reason why they should."

Danno held up the airgun. "If they do come in, they're in for a big surprise."

A stone came sailing through the window and landed by Catweazle's feet.

Another hit the window ledge and toppled down into my lap.

We heard glass smashing along the corridor in the big bedroom.

There came another loud whoop from the railway track.

I started to feel as if I was in the cantina scene at the end of Butch Cassiday and the Sundance Kid, Butch and Sundance under siege from the Bolivian army, bleeding from various gunshot wounds. As if to emphasise the notion a stone hit the window. We were showered in little slithers of glass. HC picked a jagged piece out of his hair and a little bit of blood trickled down to his brow.

Out in the corridor there came a loud, clearly audible creak of a floorboard, followed by the sound of the door to the big bedroom slamming violently shut. HC clamped his hand over his mouth as if to stop himself from screaming. Danno and me looked at each other. Danno's eyes went wide.

Clatter, clatter, clatter went the stones against the wall.

"I'm bored now," came the sound of Clutch's voice. "Let's go and see who's hanging around in the park."

"What if Danno and the other two are there?" asked one of his mates.

"Even better," said Clutch.

They all started laughing. The laughter started to fade as they walked away along the track. The three of us remained kind of frozen to the spot. HC dabbed his index finger against the little cut on his scalp and wiped the spot of blood that came away with it onto the floor.

I felt pretty sure we were all thinking about the big bedroom door slamming shut and how it had done that without there being so much as a breeze. I tried to lighten the mood by mimicking Paul Newman's lines from the end of Butch and Sundance.

"You didn't see Lefors out there, did you?"

Danno came back as Robert Redford. "Lefors? No."

"Oh, good," I said. *"For a moment there I thought we were in trouble."*

None of us so much as smiled at the quip. Danno rose to his feet, crunching glass beneath the soles of his baseball boots. He snuck a look out the window. "They're gone," he said. HC went to the door. I followed him. Along the corridor the door to the big bedroom was firmly shut. "Holy shit," said HC. "Holy, holy shit."

"We should go," I said.

"If that door handle turns," said HC. "I swear I'll jump right out the window."

I turned to Danno. "We should go," I repeated.

Now that the incense sticks were doused, flies were starting to drift back around Catweazle's mouldering cadaver. More of them were getting stuck in the glue of the flypapers. Some of them were exploring the disgusting sewer of seepage oozing from his nostrils.

Danno went and fetched the Fine Fayre bag. "I'm going to hide this first," he said, dropping the

181

airgun into the bag and scooping up the box of pellets and the air canisters from where they'd been left on the floor. He knelt down and used the Swiss Army knife to wedge up one of the floorboards. Then he dropped the Fine Fayre bag down into the gap and stamped the floorboard back into place.

The three of us left the room.

Danno pulled the door shut.

'Maggie's Ghost Waits Behind This Door,' read the wax crayon warning.

Maybe not this time, I thought. *Maybe she waits in the other room.*

We crept slowly down the stairs. It was as if we each felt that if we made too much noise the door to the big bedroom might crash open and Maggie would be there, rubber flex, bugged out eyes, and all. When we reached the foot of the stairs I couldn't stand to so much as glance in the direction of the kitchen. I was convinced I would witness a vision of Maurice on the floor with his head resting on the oven shelf. I didn't dare draw breath for fear that there might be the hint of the smell of gas in the air.

Danno led us along the litter strewn corridor and out through the front door. The glare from the sun stung at my eyes. I saw HC reach up and touch the scratch on his head again. We passed through the gateway and along the road till we reached the path that led down to the river and found ourselves once more on the white stone bank.

The river chuckled downstream in a ponderous current that tossed up silvery glints of reflected sunlight. Within its shallows the minnows and sticklebacks darted here and there, some of them occasionally rising to harvest the cloud of midges that hovered just above the surface. Danno produced a twenty pack of Woodbines from his jeans pocket. He flipped open the lid. There must have been at least thirteen or fourteen cigarettes inside.

"Holy fuckeroni," said HC, scooping up some water to wash the tiny wound on his head. "Where did you get them?"

"Nicked them from my old man's suit pocket when I went back to get the airgun," said Danno.

"Fucking hell, Danno," I said. "What if he finds out?"

Danno smiled at me. The scab on his lip was almost healed over now. "Sunday is the best day to rob the old bastard," he said. "He never remembers what was in his pockets on Saturday night."

HC and me took a Woodbine each. Danno clamped one between his teeth and slipped the pack back into his jeans. We lit up. I coughed when I inhaled. I wasn't keen on cigarettes with no filter tip. A bit of tobacco got stuck to my tongue. The taste was bitter. I spat it into the river.

We all sat down. The argument we'd been having before Clutch and his gang started bombarding the house with stones was already forgotten. The implications of the door slamming became silently unacknowledged. What I'd said in the moment before we heard the voices drifting down from the railway track went unspoken.

"We should go up to the quarry," said Danno.

HC blew out a gush of smoke. "We haven't been there in ages."

"What do you reckon, Ranks?" asked Danno, turning to me.

The limestone quarry was cut into the side of a hill, about a mile away, on the other side of the river. Kids from the housing scheme often drifted over there on a Sunday when there were no workmen.

The quarry was like a film set. It could be anything your imagination wanted it to be. It could be a bleak, distant world, like the Forbidden Planet or Robinson Crusoe on Mars. It could be an episode of Doctor Who. It could be the Arizona desert of a spaghetti western like The Good, The Bad and The Ugly. It could be the vast, undulating dunes of the Sahara where marauding Bedouins lay in wait to charge you on camelback.

Once around thirty of us had acted out a huge battle between the French Foreign Legion and Bedouin tribesmen. Another time a whole gang of us had gone there on Boxing Day and had a massive, chaotic snowball fight. Going to the quarry seemed like a great idea to me. The perfect antidote to all the poison we seemed to be sucking up between us. "Why not," I said, and flicked the horrible tasting Woodbine into the river.

HC started unlacing his baseball boots. "Let's wade across," he said. "It's shallow enough and it's too hot to walk down to the bridge."

We all took off our socks and baseball boots and rolled up our jeans. Despite the heat the water was refreshingly cool. It felt good gathering up in churning ripples around my ankles. We splashed our way across the opposite embankment, bare feet skidding on slimy stones, minnow and sticklebacks scattering before us.

The crow that seemed to have a favoured branch in one of the trees over there alighted on our approach and went gliding away, black wings outstretched, in the direction of Maggie's house. I didn't look back. I didn't want to look back.

To get to the quarry you had to climb a steep incline. There wasn't any shade. It was hard going in the heat. My tee shirt started to stick to my back. My socks had been made uncomfortably damp by putting my wet feet back in them. Now they became sopping in sweat.

To keep our spirits up HC led us in a comical recital of theme songs from TV shows. We quickly made our way through the Flintstones, the Jetsons, Top Cat, Scooby Doo and the Wombles. HC wanted us to sing White Horses. Danno objected, saying it was a girl's song from a girl's programme.

We sang the Flashing Blade instead, swiftly followed by I Wish I Was a Spaceman from Fireball XL5. Then we sang Come Away with William Tell, in celebration of HC and the apple core. That led to Robin Hood, Riding through the Glen, which in turn led to Champion the Wonder Horse, followed by Flipper and Skippy the Bush Kangaroo.

We sang the songs boisterously and somewhat tunelessly, as if we were chanting in a football stadium. For a while we were like three fourteen-year-old kids again, enjoying the freedom of the summer holidays, not a burden in the world. It was

185

the type of summer day we should have had by rights. It was the type of summer day we might have had if Danno and I hadn't been so insistent on HC making his *run*. If HC hadn't stumbled on Catweazle's corpse.

It proved one thing to me. We were different people inside that house than we were outside. Outside we were just three teenage kids who aspired to look cool and act tough to conform to the misguided mores of our peer group. Inside Maggie's house we became monsters. Sadistic, mean-spirited monsters. Every nasty thing we did somehow engineered and imposed upon us by Maggie's malevolent influence.

We reached the crest of the hill that led down into to where the quarry sat on the other side and stopped to catch our breaths. From the vantage point of the hill, you could see the stone bridge that spanned the meandering stretch of river. Beyond that you could see whole the town, laid out like something constructed from Lego. In the foreground of the town the housing scheme was nestled on the lower slopes of another hill. I recalled the green fields and meadowlands I'd seen in my dream and again found myself nagged by the possibility that what I had witnessed had been real.

The houses and blocks of flats were all laid out in neat uniform rows, shades of beige and dirty off-white. Our lives were constrained by those narrow and wholly artificial boundaries. The buildings themselves put me in mind of song my dad used to sing when he was driving us in the car. The one that was about these little boxes on the hillside that were

186

made out of something called ticky-tacky. It had always seemed to me that the song had been specifically written about the place I was growing up in.

I could see some tiny little figures kicking a ball around in the park. I presumed it was Clutch and his gang. I wondered if Deb would be there with Shona. I wondered if one of Clutch's mates might try and chat Deb up now that she'd dumped me. A little flutter in my belly told me I still had feelings for her.

My eyes wandered from the housing scheme to the old railway track and then fell on the ruin of Maggie's house. I wasn't sure if it was the hazy beating down of the sun playing tricks on me, but there seemed to be someone standing in by the front window of the little bedroom, gazing up the hill at us. The flutter in my belly twisted to a knot.

HC came and stood beside me. He looked down at the lazily winding course of the river. "Remember when we snuck into the Pavilion to watch Deliverance? It looks just like that river."

He did a snatch from Duelling Banjos. *"Da-da dum-dum-dum."*

Behind us Danno came back with the response. *"Da-da dum-dum-dum."*

I mimicked one of the notorious lines from the film. *"You sure got a purdy mouth."*

HC grimaced. "Aw, shit, Ranks. Why did you have to go and say that? Now that scene is going to get stuck in my head all over again. The one where the ugly hillbilly is bumming the fat guy in the forest."

I shuddered, recalling.

"Come on," said Danno. "We can't hang around here all day."

We started to make our way down the dusty, winding track that descended through the limestone terraces carved into the lower slopes of the hill. Usually, you couldn't go to the quarry without bumping into someone else from the housing scheme. Today it was deserted, and we soon understood why.

Days of endless sun had baked the limestone almost as white as the stones on the riverbank. The intensity of the heat reflecting from it was like the raw fury of a furnace. By the time we reached the belly of the quarry every inch of me was drenched in sweat. I could see big beads dripping from Danno's nose. HC was a red as tomato.

"It's like the desert that Kwai Chang Caine is walking through at the beginning of Kung Fu," said HC, panting a little.

We all adopted exaggerated marshal art poses. Then we started play fighting, launching slow motion kicks at each other. After a while the heat made it feel like too much of an effort and the novelty wore off. HC lobbed a couple of stones at the gouged terraces, pretending they were grenades, making the sound of explosions as they hit. I did my impression of Peter O'Toole in Lawrence of Arabia. *"The desert is an ocean in which no oar is dipped – and on this ocean the Bedu go where they please and strike where they please."*

Then I did Phil Silvers in Carry on Follow That Camel. *"Stop making promises I can't keep."*

188

I followed through with John Mills in Ice Cold in Alex. *"The next drink I have is going to be a lager – ice cold."*

That last one kind of ruined the mood. I realised how dry my throat was and how parched my mouth was. I recalled the coolness of the water around my ankles half an hour or so earlier and tried, with some effort, to muster enough saliva in my mouth to swallow down the dryness.

We stumbled our way across the creviced and powdery crater of the quarry's floor, kicking up puffs of dust, till we came to the little hut where the workmen and lorry drivers took their sandwich breaks. The door was locked. So were the windows. The padlock on the door was so hot it stung when I touched it. We stumbled again toward the barn-like construction where they stored the tools and some of the tipper trucks.

That was locked too.

"We could try to break in," suggested Danno.

"It would be even hotter inside," I pointed out.

We gave up on the quarry and climbed the side of the hill till we reached a little shaded cluster of trees. Wearily we sat down amongst the latticed shadows cast by their branches. There was dust in my hair and gritty flecks in my eyes. I could feel it in my nose when I breathed in.

I had one stick of Juicy Fruit left. I divided it into three and passed round the pieces. When I chewed it some much need saliva mercifully materialised in my mouth. But it didn't do anything to quench my thirst. When Danno offered me another Woodbine I declined.

On the sloping field to the right of the quarry a scattered herd of black-faced sheep were bleating as they grazed. I saw the glint from the windscreen of a car as it wound its way along narrow the road that cut through the hills. I watched an orange hued millipede as it doggedly negotiated the tangle of grass stems that clung to the parched earth. Wasps were buzzing back and forth all about us. Danno reckoned there might be a nest in one of the trees farther up the slope.

It was HC who finally put what we were all thinking into words. "She's there, isn't she? Maggie? She's there in the house?"

Danno nodded. "I feel her every time we're in that room."

"Maurice is there too," I said, and told them about the smell of the gas.

Danno nodded again. "I think I smelt that too."

"Maybe ghosts are like are like flies," said HC. "Maybe they're attracted to dead things. Maybe it's Catweazle's body that brought them out."

"I think it's the opposite," I said, swallowing down the sugary taste of the chewing gum. "I think ghosts are attracted to living things. It's us that attracted them."

"Holy shit," said HC.

"Maybe ghosts feed on the all the bad stuff that comes out of us," I said. "The way flies feed on the bad stuff that oozes out of corpses."

"This is what she wants," said HC. "That what you said just before Clutch and his lot turned up."

Despite the chewing gum my mouth felt immediately dry and parched again. I swallowed

190

and turned to HC. "I hear her whispering in my ear," I said. HC's mouth dropped open a little. "Me too," he said. "At first, I thought it was one of the flies buzzing around my head. Then I realised it was a woman's voice."

We both looked at Danno to see what his response was. Danno took a long draw on his Woodbine, sucked it in, blew smoke down his nostrils, then nodded his head and looked away.

"You were there yesterday," I said. "You went to Maggie's house by yourself, didn't you?" Danno said nothing. He took another long draw on the Woodbine and dodged his head as a wasp flew in his direction.

"What are you talking about?" asked HC. "Danno wouldn't go there by himself. None of us would."

"But he did," I insisted. "He went there yesterday afternoon. He sat on the floor sharpening a stick to a point. And he was going to plunge it into Catweazle's eye."

HC laughed and tried to turn the tables on me. *"Hans Christian Andersen, Andersen that's you."*

Danno scowled at me. "Did you follow me? Were you spying on me?"

"It's true?" cried HC. "I thought you went to the pictures with Deb?"

"I was kind of in two places at one time," I said.

I told them about T. Lobsang Rampa and *The Wisdom of the Ancients* and how astral travel was supposed to work. I didn't tell them about the scene I'd witnessed in the kitchen with Maurice and

Danno's old man. I was determined not to give up on the notion that part had to be simply a dream.

"You're saying you were in the room when I was there yesterday afternoon?" said Danno.

"How else would I know what you were doing?"

"You could have followed me."

"I was in the cinema with Deb, watching Stay Away Joe," I reminded him. "Deb broke up with me on the pavement outside the Pavilion. She told you both about it in the park."

"Holy fuckeroni," said HC. "It's true. She did."

"Still sounds far-fetched," said Danno. "You rose out of your body on this *Silver Chord* thing?"

"Don't ask me to explain it." I said. "All I know is I saw you. And I saw Maggie. She was creeping around you. I saw her whispering in your ear."

Danno blew more smoke out of his nostrils.

"It was like she was in my head," he admitted. "Egging me on."

"But you managed to resist," I said. "You threw the stick out of the window."

Danno nodded. "Today when I was going to fire the airgun at Catweazle it was the same thing."

"I've seen her you know," I said. "Maggie and Maurice. Catweazle too. I've seen their ghosts. They never speak. But I've seen them."

Danno swatted at a wasp that was buzzing at his head. "You said. You've seen them when you do this *astral travel* thing."

I shook my head. "I mean I've seen them. Outside of my dreams. On the housing scheme. At the Youth Club. In the cinema."

I told them about the apparitions I'd been witness to.

"You're psychic," said HC. "You can commune with the dead."

"Well, I won't be making a career out of it any time soon," I told him.

"I've seen stuff too," confessed Danno. "Not full-blown ghosts like what you've just described. Just kind of shapes moving out of the corner of my eye."

HC stood up and started pacing around under the trees. "We're in deep shit, guys," he said. "We're really in deep shit. You don't want to go round messing with the supernatural."

"We can't go back there," I agreed. "We just have to keep well clear of Maggie's house."

"I need to get the airgun," said Danno. "I need to put it back under Roy's bed. In case he comes back for more of his stuff."

HC sat down again. "It's not just the gun," he said. "We have to tidy up all the mess we made. Otherwise, when someone finds Catweazle's body they're going to know what we did."

"They won't know it's us," said Danno.

"Our fingerprints are all over the place," said HC. "And our footprints."

"Wouldn't they have to have our fingerprints on record in the first place for them to tell it was us?" I asked.

"They'd know it was kids from the housing scheme," said HC. "They'd pull us all in and take our fingerprint us to find the culprits. My uncle told me it's what they do in some areas of Belfast when they're trying to track down IRA suspects."

"Don't start on that crap," warned Danno. "I'm not in the mood."

"OK," said HC. "But I'm just saying, there would be some sort of investigation. Mr Renton saw us. That first day when we came along the track when he was out walking Captain."

The realisation hit me like a hammer blow. "Fuck," I said. "So he did."

"When the police start asking questions, he'd say he saw us," said HC. "We'd become the prime suspects. Then they'd definitely take our fingerprints. We might even get accused of murdering Catweazle."

Danno heaved a sigh. "That's it then, we've got no choice. We have to go back to get the airgun and cover up anything that links us to the house. We have to wipe all the surfaces."

"And after we're done we never go back," I said. "We never even go within a mile of the railway track again."

"But let's not go back today, guys," pleaded HC. "I can't face going back today."

"In the morning, then," said Danno, and flicked the stub of his Woodbine down the hill.

"You shouldn't go round throwing away lit cigarette ends in this heat," said HC. "You could set the whole hillside on fire." He stood up and went to search for the cigarette end.

194

Chapter Seventeen

The flat was empty when I arrived back home. My legs were aching from the climb up to the quarry and my feet were blistered from sliding about in my sweat-drenched socks. I had the beginnings of a headache coming on. I ran three glasses of water straight from the tap and drank them all down. Then I splashed my face in cold water to wash off the dust.

I went up to my room and hunted out the T. Lobsang Rampa book, opened all the windows in the living room, and sat down on the sofa to read. The smell of Libby's Aqua Manda perfume still clung to the cushions. I was again unsettled by the way it reminded me of the incense sticks.

I found an entry for *Ghosts*. It wasn't that much help. I was hoping that maybe the ancients had some wisdom to offer about how to rid yourself of malevolent spirits that somehow attached themselves to you. But the entry simply suggested that a ghost was an *etheric* force that was left to drift aimlessly about once the *Silver Chord* was cut by the act of death. It said that a ghost was just a mindless, homeless waif and nothing to be too concerned about.

Nothing to be too concerned about? That didn't seem right. Maggie definitely had a home and all the evidence suggested she had a mind too. I tossed the book across the room. What did this T. Lobsang Rampa character know anyway? *Enough to know that you can go wandering out of your physical body and witness what your friend is doing in a different part of town,* I reminded myself.

I heard a heard a key turning in the lock of the front door and then someone thumping upstairs. A moment later Buick McCaine from the T Rex Slider album came on at full volume from Libbie's cassette player. Mum blustered into the room. She was wearing a sleeveless dress with big, yellow sunflowers on it. Her shoulders had gotten too much sun. They looked red and angry. She raised her thinly plucked eyebrows to the ceiling.

"Madam is in a foul mood again."

"What happened?" I asked.

"We took Big Moira with us to Berwick," said mum.

Libby and Big Moira had been friends since primary school. She had these long, lanky legs that meant she'd always been at least a head shoulder taller than most of her schoolmates. At sixteen she was almost six foot in her socks.

"On the way back, Big Moira was telling us how she's starting work in that new electrical component factory that's just opened where the old woollen mill used to be," mum went on. "All I did was suggest that Libby might want to apply for a job as well and she threw a hairy bloody fit."

Mum yelled up the stairs. "You turn that down right now, young lady!"

The volume went down a tad.

"Catch any minnows, soldier?" asked mum, returning her attention to me.

"Not really."

196

It felt like I was blushing from being caught up in Danno's lie.

I hoped she didn't notice.

"You eaten?" she asked.

"Not yet," I replied.

She held up a plastic bag.

"I brought you some chips."

"They'll be cold," I said.

"I'll refry them," she said.

Ten minutes later we were sat together on the sofa, watching an episode of the Fenn Street Gang, dipping refried chips into a saucer of tomato ketchup. I couldn't help wondering how she'd react if I told her what Danno, HC and me had really been up to.

Mum had a potent temper when she really got worked up. She usually reserved it for Libby. But I could imagine her slapping me in the face just as hard as she'd slapped Libby the other day. It was exactly as HC described it. Our lives were full of beating each other up and getting beat up. They were as full of violence and the imminent potential for violence are they were full of lies and little deceits.

Besides, it had gone too far now. I no longer knew how I might begin broaching the subject. This was more than simply - *we found this dead man and didn't bother reporting it*. Over the past few days, it had become - *we found this dead man and set about abusing him. We covered him in Silverkrin and Shake 'n' Vac. We stuffed blue toilet flush into his mouth and covered him in flypapers. We took pot shots at him with an air pistol.*

197

How would you go about confessing stuff like that to your mum? What would she think of you? It could destroy your relationship with her beyond any chance of repair. HC was right we could never mention any of this to anyone.

When the Fenn Street Gang came to an end mum stood up and picked up the empty plate and saucer. "I'm going to put some washing on," she said. "Be a doll and bring down those jeans. They're starting to look a bit manky."

When I went upstairs the door to Libby's room was ajar. She was lying on her bed reading a copy of Jackie. David Bowie's Hunky Dory was playing in the background. I shouted *hi* to her. She didn't reply.

I wondered what posh kids did on a Sunday. I was pretty sure they sat down to a proper Sunday roast and not just refried chips and ketchup. But did they argue? Did they fall out with each other? Did they keep secrets and tell lies to each other? It couldn't all be piano lessons and thousand-piece jigsaws, could it?

I took off my jeans and pulled on my PE shorts. When I checked the pockets of my jeans, I found the little brown pebble that I'd picked up from the gutter when I'd been waiting for Danno and HC. I turned it over in the palm of my hand. If only it truly had the power to give me the courage to face the challenges that were before me.

Hippy-trippy shite, I told myself. *The only one who's going to going to give you courage is yourself.*

Mum put on the washing machine.

198

The BBC was showing a series of Peter Sellers' films on Sunday nights. This week it was What's New Pussycat, which also starred Peter O'Toole. Sellers played this long-haired character with a German accent.

I thought that if I memorised some of the dialogue, I might be able to do him. I wondered if Danno and HC were watching the film and if they'd get it if I tried out the impression out on them. But I couldn't concentrate. I kept thinking about returning to Maggie's house. I suspected I'd be going there twice. Once with Danno and HC in the morning. Once on my own, when I went to sleep.

Mum loved Peter Sellers. When she was a teenager, she said she'd listened to the Goon Show on the radio with my granddad. She was laughing away. Every time she turned her head to look at me, I had to pretend I was sharing her amusement so she wouldn't notice how deeply I was becoming engrossed in my morbid thoughts.

I was contemplating the possibility that my nocturnal sojourn might involve returning to the scene in the kitchen of Maggie's house when Danno's old man crept up on Maurice and faked his suicide. I started wrestling with the notion that what I had witnessed was an actual event. Didn't T. Lobsang Rampa claim that you could cross time and space through *Astral Travel*?

Hippy-trippy shite, sneered Libby's voice inside my head.

"Mum?" I asked. "Didn't you go to school with Danno's old man?"

199

Mum had her eyes focused on the TV. She was only half listening.

"Pardon?"

"Danno's old man?" I said. "Were you at school with him?"

"Johnny?" She nodded her head. "Worst luck."

"What was he like?"

"He's couple of years older than me. But he was as much of a spiteful little bastard as he is now," replied mum. "Always getting in fights. He was a petty crook. He got sent to a young offender's institute for breaking into houses when he was sixteen."

My heart did a little flip in my chest. Housebreaking? That fit perfectly with what I'd seen in my dream. I had to stuff my hands into the pockets of my PE shorts to hide the way they'd started to tremble.

"Why did you want to know?" asked mum, eyes still fixed on Peter Sellers' antics.

A pulse started pounding in my chest. "It's just that he's always on Danno's case," I replied.

Mum shook her head. "More than just getting on his case, I'd say. I'm surprised no one has contacted social services about what goes on inside that house on Saturday nights."

We watched the rest of the film in silence, mum chuckling every now and then at something Peter Sellers said. Me engrossed in my brooding thoughts. When it was finished, mum hung the washing onto the clotheshorse and went to bed, reminding me not to forget to shut the windows.

For a while I did my best to avoid going upstairs. I knelt in front of the TV pressing the white buttons to change from one channel to the next. BBC1 – BBC2 – ITV – BBC2 – BBC1 and then back again. I tried to watch the news, but my attention soon wandered.

I picked up the T. Lobsang Rampa book and flicked absently through the pages. Then I tossed it to the side again in case I was tempted to start reading one of the entries. In case whatever might be written in that entry put a suggestion into my head that might lead to a new variety of nightmare. In the end I shut all the windows and climbed up the stairs. Libby's door was ajar. Her light was out. She was listening to Rod Stewart's Never a Dull Moment, with the volume down so low it was little more than a vague whisper.

I stripped down to my underpants and lay on my bed without putting on the light. My hair still felt gritty from the quarry. I wished I'd taken a bath and washed it. I set my alarm and fumbled around for the little brown pebble I'd left on the bedside table. I hoped it would fortify me with the courage to see me through the night. My one positive thought was that in the morning after my paper round it was all going to come to an end at last. We were going to clear away any hint of our presence in that horrible little room and we were going to finally leave poor Catweazle to rest in peace.

My soul rose from my slumbering body almost the moment my eyes closed. Once more the housing scheme was gone and in its place were fields, hedgerows, and narrow tracks. I passed along the railway line, where more of the sleepers seemed to have been lifted, and then down the embankment into Maggie's back garden.

It was only then that I noticed how badly it was raining. Great grey sheets of it lashing against the walls and the windows, battering down the roses and Azaleas, waterlogging the lawn. I held out my etheric hand and watched the fats drops pass straight through the palm. I entered through the kitchen door, *Silver Chord* meandering behind me, glistening in the rain. The house was in darkness, its silence only broken by the machine gun rat-tat-tat of the rain against the windows.

I found myself in the hallway, facing the front door. In the gloom I could see what appeared to be something in a large square frame on the wall to my left. I couldn't tell if it was a painting or a mirror. To my right I could make out the shape of a coat stand.

I was waiting. It seemed that I was expected to wait there for something. I thought I knew what it was. I hoped I was wrong. I heard the key turn in the lock. There came a flash of lightening and in the illuminated hallway I saw that Maurice was waiting there with me, or at least the ghost of Maurice, gaseous vapour ponderously hissing from his nostrils.

The door came crashing open. Sheets of rain lashed diagonally into the hallway. The light went on and there stood Maggie. She was just the way we would describe her in the story we'd tell each other before the *run*. The sodden gown, issued to her on the ward of the mental hospital, clinging wetly to her pale flesh, hair hanging around her shoulders in fat, matted rattails, her eyes juddering in stuttering fits of psychosis.

I stepped backwards as she stepped in.

Far, far away, on some distant and different plane, I could hear my own voice.

No. Please. I don't want to see this. Don't make me watch this.

I was talking in my sleep.

I knew exactly what was coming.

Maggie passed straight through me and headed along the hall, leaving dark, wet footprints on the carpet in her wake. The coils of my *Silver Chord* billowed around her as she moved. Maurice's spectral image followed her, gushing gas. I followed Maurice. Maggie stopped at the kitchen door and clicked the switch on the wall. Light from the kitchen bled into the light from the hall. The kitchen table was bare, no longer piled high with Maurice's bill and invoices. The gas cooker had already been removed. The space between the worktops looked like the gap left behind by a missing tooth.

Maurice's ghost fussed around Maggie. It seemed to me he was trying desperately to gain her attention. Maggie grabbed a sopping handful of her hair and rang it out with a tight twist. Her shoulders seemed to spasm as she let out a strangulated sob. I could sense my physical body thrashing on my bed, trying to draw back my *Silver Chord*. But my astral self was obstinate. I was firmly trapped within the bounds of my dream. I believed that I was about to be forced to bear witness to the inevitable turn of events that was about to play out.

Maggie headed for the stairs. Maurice threw his head back and issued a silent scream. He was definitely trying to warn her about something. The rain lashed noisily against the kitchen window, as if it too was trying to gain her attention. Maggie climbed the stairs, dripping dirty water from her hospital gown. Maurice rose and followed her. Against the resisting will of my physical self I followed on in my astral form.

Maggie entered the small bedroom.

It was not the room I'd come to know so well, the room where Catweazle sat festering in the old armchair. It was brightly decorated, with blue wallpaper depicting swallows soaring amongst billowing clouds. There were net curtains in the windows and expensive looking drapes on brass curtain poles.

Along one wall ran a long clothes rail, from which hung dozens of designer dresses. Beneath this lay stacks of shoeboxes. By the wall that ran parallel to the door was an ornamental dresser, littered with perfumes, powders, and make up, an ivory handled hairbrush, scissors and cuticle cutters, hair curlers and a blow dryer. This had been Maggie's den. The place where she hoarded the best of all the material things she'd had Maurice buy for her.

And someone had invaded it.

He was crouched low leaning toward one of the open drawers on the dresser, fist full of necklaces and jewellery in his greedy little hand. I recognised the leather pilot's jacket straight away. Danno's old man had come back for second helpings. He clearly hadn't expected to be disturbed. When he looked over his shoulder and saw Maggie there in the doorway, he dropped his haul and ran at her.

She backed away into the corridor. But she was too slow. Danno's old man already had her by the throat. She kicked him in the shin. This just riled him more. Now he had two hands wrapped around her neck. He pushed her against the bathroom door, squeezing tighter. Maurice danced around them, trying in vain to catch the attention of Danno's murderous old man. But he was as impotent and helpless as me. All we could do was watch in horror as the life was squeezed out of Maggie. When she finally slumped to the floor Danno's old man took the stairs two at a time. I followed him down. He didn't flee from the house as I'd expected. Instead, he ran to the kitchen.

He skidded wildly on the floor tiles made wet from the rainwater that had dripped from Maggie, then caught his balance on the worktop. He brought out a carving knife from one of the drawers. Then he returned to the hallway and crouched low to the under stairs cupboard. Before he even produced it, I knew that what he would emerge with was a vacuum cleaner.

And there it was, upright, gleaming chrome, green dust bag hanging down. And wrapped around its handle, a length of black, rubber electrical flex. Frantically now he began to unravel the flex. He used the carving knife to cut the flex from the vacuum and then cut the plug from the flex. He dropped the knife to the carpet and then climbed the stair with the flex dangling from his left hand.

Maurice was on his knees, sobbing beside Maggie's body. Danno's old man wrapped the flex three time around her neck and dragged her to the door of the little room.

He slung the flex over the top of the door and then heaved on it till Maggie's feet hung limply on her slack ankles six inches or so from the carpet. Then he tied the end of the flex to the door handle and set the stool from the dresser on its side just next to her feet, so that it would look as if she'd climbed up on it and kicked it away.

Maurice fell once more to his knees, engulfed in a mist of ghostly gas. Maggie hung there, strangulated, looking for all the world as if she'd taken her own life in a fit of grief. Danno's old man coldly filled his pockets with the necklaces and jewellery, looked at himself in the mirror, ran his steel comb through his teddy-boy quiff, and twisted Maurice's wheatsheaf signet ring where it sat on his finger.

My physical body tossed and turned in my bed. I think I may have cried out. I think once more Danno's old man may have caught a fleeting glimpse of me. But it was too late for Maggie. It was entirely possible that she'd still been alive when the flex was wound so cruelly around her neck. Now her eyes were bugging out and her face had turned grotesquely purple.

Chapter Eighteen

When the alarm rang, I found that I'd been holding the little brown pebble so tightly in my sleep that it had made an indent in the sweaty palm of my hand. I dug it out and placed it on the bedside table, shaking my head to try and free myself of the stubborn residual image of Maggie dangling on the rubber flex as Danno's old man brushed coldly past her and made his escape into the night.

I was determined that this was the day that things were going to change, and I wanted it to start off as normal as possible. I went to the bathroom and washed my face. I combed my feather cut hair and teased it about a bit until it was as close to Rod and Ronnie as I could manage.

I crept downstairs to see if my jeans were still dry. When they turned out to be too damp to wear, I went back to my room and hunted out an old pair of faded denim flares. With my Ben Sherman in the bin and my Levis out of commission I didn't feel I looked much like someone from the front cover of one of the Skinhead novels any longer. It didn't matter. I'd finally decided that aspiring to be like one of the characters in those books was a dumb thing to do anyway.

I poured myself a bowl of Sugar Puffs. Mum had already left for work. She'd placed a tinned Fray Bentos pie on the table with a pack of Smash instant potatoes and a note for Libby on how they should be prepared and what setting the oven should be at. The thought of oven settings made me think about Maurice and how Danno's dad had dragged him unconscious to the cooker and left him there with his head resting on the shelf. I lose my appetite quite rapidly.

Determined not allow this to be a set-back I fetched my canvas bag from under the stairs and set off for the newsagent. Outside it felt as if there might be a change impending in the air. The sun was already up, and it was starting to get hot, but for the first time in days there were white steaks of cloud slashed across the blue sky and just the faint hint of a breeze.

Mr Aitkin was on early turn. He had the Times spread out across the counter as usual. He hardly acknowledged me when I entered the shop and started to load my bag with the papers set out on the floor. I was about to make my attempt to pocket a handful of Bazooka Joes when someone else came through the door.

When I looked up it was Danno's old man who was standing there. He looked rough. His face was unshaven. His eyes were slightly bloodshot. His hair was standing up at the back and it didn't look as it had yet seen a fresh dab of Brylcreme. His shirt was all crumpled and looked as if it had been slept in.

Mr Aitkin looked up from the article he'd been reading in the Times. "Early one this morning, Johnny?"

"We've got four sides of lamb coming in this morning that need cutting to into joints," said Danno's old man.

When he spoke, I could smell the stale reek of booze on his breath, even from my crouching position. On the other side of the counter Mr Aitkin seemed to get it face on. His nose creased a little. But he was clearly determined to maintain his professional decorum. "What can I help you with?" he said.

Danno's old man scratched the bristles on his chin and yawned loudly. "You got any Alka Seltzer behind there?" he asked. "I had a heavy session at the Legion last night. My head is thumping like there's no tomorrow."

Mr Aitkin produced a little pack of Alka Seltzer. "Will that be all, Johnny?"

Danno's old man kind of stepped from his left foot to his right, as if he was trying to keep his balance. I thought he might still be drunk. He yawned again and twisted his head as though his neck was stiff. "I'll have twenty Woodbine and packet of Polo Mints," he said.

Mr Aitkin tallied up the total on the cash register and it was when Danno's old man reached round to his back pocket to get his wallet that I saw what he wore on his little finger. A gold signet ring, fashioned into a wheatsheaf. Exactly the same design as the ring that he'd stolen from Maurice in my dream.

"Stop gawping at the customers," said Mr Aitkin, noticing me there. "You need to get out on your rounds. My customers are waiting for their morning papers."

Danno's old man looked down at me. He'd seen me with Danno thousands of times since we were little kids. But he was so full of his own meanness and self-importance that I hardly registered with him. I hefted the paper bag over my

209

shoulder. Danno's old man was right behind me when I left the shop. I didn't look back at him. I knew he'd be heading for the bus stop. I was headed in the opposite direction. My thoughts were heading all over the place. Going off once more at all sorts of tangents.

I stumbled through my paper round in a daze. In terms of which morning paper should be delivered to which house I was kind of on autopilot, my hand instinctively dipping into the bag and coming out with a Record or a Mail or a Herald commensurate with the street I was on and the number on the house door. Memory patterns formed from day after day of repeating the same thing.

If an apparition had materialised to stalk me as I moved through the housing scheme, I don't think I would have even noticed. The thought of the wheat sheaf signet ring was making my head hurt with the improbability of what it might signify. Had I truly travelled back through time in astral form just like T. Lobsang Rampa suggested a person could do? I didn't think it was possible. *Hippy trippy shite*, I kept telling myself.

Yet the evidence was there. I had seen Danno's old man removing a signet ring with a wheatsheaf motif from Maurice's finger. And that very same ring was right there on Danno's old man's finger almost twenty years later. If this was true, then it followed that he was the cause of everything. He'd murdered Maurice and made it look like a suicide. That deception had led Maggie to have a breakdown and then escape from the hospital to the house where Danno's old man did the exact same thing to her. No doubt it was that tragic sequence of events that led to Maggie and Maurice haunting that old house of theirs.

I thought about the *run* and all the kids who had been egged on to do it. And how when you did the run you could truly sense the presence of ghosts in that dilapidated old house. And how Danno and me egging HC on to make his *run* had led to the discovery of Catweazle's corpse. And how that, in turn, had led us into the situation we found ourselves in now. One thing inevitably leading to the next, and all of it starting that night years earlier when Danno's old man crept into Maggie's kitchen as a delinquent teenager.

All of it building up from one huge and dreadful lie.

I finished the paper round still mentally wrestling with the notion. It couldn't be the way I was thinking it was. It simply couldn't be. The ring must be a coincidence. Or, more likely, something my subconscious had made up. Maybe I'd seen that ring on Danno's old man's finger one time when I'd been at his house. Maybe I'd been seeing it all my life and not really registering. Maybe that was why it materialised in my dream. Dreams were mostly just jumbled fragments of things you see in real life, reassembled in a manner that didn't often make sense.

But that didn't account for the fact that I had witnessed Danno in Maggie's house by himself on Saturday afternoon when I had dozed off sitting next to Deb in the Pavilion. I felt cheated. I had started off the day genuinely feeling optimistic that

211

I was going to be able to draw a line under recent events and move on. Now there was this dreadful conundrum to contend with and it terrified me that I'd never be able to draw that line until I had the answer.

One thing I felt sure of though, was that I was going to get rid of the T. Lobsang Rampa book. Let the ancients keep their wisdom. I wasn't going to have all that *hippy-trippy* nonsense screwing with my head anymore. I was going to take the book with me to Maggie's house and it was going to get dumped with all the other junk from that room.

I was the first to arrive at our usual meeting point. It seemed to me that nine times out of ten it was always me that was the first to arrive when the three of us planned to go anywhere. Our days seemed destined to start with me on my own, waiting for the other two to show.

The sun was up. Despite the clouds, which were thickening now, it wasn't feeling that much cooler. The spiky rays were already burning the back of my head. I sat down on the pavement. The T. Lobsang Rampa book was an uncomfortable bulge in my back pocket. My thoughts were still full of the wheatsheaf cygnet ring, and what that implied, and, whether I should speak about it to Danno and HC.

I attempted to distract myself by trying to remember some of Peter Sellers' dialogue from What's New Pussycat, muttering under my breath as I attempted the slightly exaggerated German accent. Danno laughed at my old flares and red tee-shirt when he saw them. "For fuck's sake, Ranks. You look like one of the Brady Bunch."

I stood up. "My mum washed my Levis last night," I explained. "They're not dry yet."

HC seemed deathly serious. I could tell he hadn't slept all night. There were puffy red bags beneath his eyes. Somehow his preponderance of freckles made them look far worse. "We have to get in and out as quick as we can," he said. "No messing. Just grab everything we need to cover our tracks and end it once and for all."

I nodded my agreement with undisguised enthusiasm.

That same painfully awkward silence fell over us as we made our way along the railway track. The copy of the Daily Record was still there in the exact same spot, baking to a crisp and jaundiced yellow from the heat, front page crumbled from a baseball boot footprint, that I now had no doubt belonged to Danno.

The sight of it riled me. It seemed symbolic of the terrible bind we were in. The same dreadful thing, in the same predictable place, every single time you were forced to revisit it. I kicked it into the nettles. It floated downward - pages hung open over the leafy green canopy, like some huge, dead butterfly. The sun too was a like a symbol, fat, fiery and angry, not ready to let up on its oppression for even a moment. If I could have kicked it out of the sky, I would have.

The doors to both bedrooms were wide open when we reached the top of the stairs in Maggie's house. "Holy shit," said HC. "Holy, holy shit."

"You think someone's been here?" asked Danno.

"I think we know the answer to that question," I said. "I think we know who's here. We know who's been here all along."

Cautiously we entered the little bedroom. Catweazle was seated in his armchair. The new flypapers that HC and me had stuck to him were scattered on the floor. We didn't react this time. I think we all kind of expected this to be the case. The green tinge was almost gone from Catweazle flesh. It had turned dark brown, shaded here and there with streaks of black. He seemed to be drying out, no longer bloated, skin tightening back to the bone. The lesions left by the blisters were drying out too and the seepages from his nostril and eyes had caked and crystallised, giving them the appearance of caked streams of snot.

Catweazle's lips were curling back to his black gums, revealing his teeth, which were a grotesque blend of nicotine brown and toilet flush blue. The cake of blue flush itself still sat on his chest. It had shrivelled to a dark little kernel. There were a few flies buzzing around here and there. But they seemed far more interested now in the bits of apple core that were scattered across the floor.

HC produced a pair of yellow rubber Marigold gloves from his pockets. He pulled them on. "Nicked these from the kitchen," he said. He picked up one of the Fine Fayre bags, took the kernel of blue flush between his finger and thumb and dropped it into the bag.

He started apologising profusely to Maggie. "We're sorry, Mrs Henderson," he said. "We're sorry we made such a mess of your bedroom. We're sorry if we didn't show Catweazle the respect he deserved. We're sorry that those other guys threw stones at your house."

I didn't think he needed to apologise to Maggie for what we'd done to Catweazle. It seemed to me that she had her hand in all the sick and stupid things we'd gotten ourselves into. HC began rolling up the flypapers and dropping them into the bag. "We want to apologise to Catweazle too," he said. He was down on his hands and knees now, picking up stuff from the floor. "We shouldn't have done what we did. We're going to try and put it right."

He looked up at me. "We could still report it, Ranks. We could make one of them unanimous calls."

"I think you mean anonymous," I corrected.

"Whatever," said HC, rolling up another flypaper. "We could just call 999 and tell them where he is. Then they could come and fetch him and give him a proper burial."

Danno took out the Swiss Army knife and unfolded the long blade. He crouched down and wedged it between the floorboards where he'd hidden the airgun.

"Just so you're both clear," he said. "The gun isn't getting dumped with the rest of the stuff. It's going back under Roy's bed, with the pellets and the air canisters."

Before either of us had time to say anything the sound of a girl, giggling loudly, drifted up from the

215

road outside the front of the house. I immediately crouched down beside Danno and HC. We heard the chatter of voices. It sounded as if they were coming through the gateway into the yard.

One voice was louder that the other two. "You just have to run into every room and check behind every door."

I recognised it straight away. It was Shona.

"Why don't you do it first to show me?" asked a boy's voice.

"Girls don't do the run," replied Shona.

"We're not that stupid," said another girl's voice.

That one belonged to Deb. It was Deb and Shona, and they'd brought Deb's cousin, *who wasn't really her cousin*, to Maggie's house to make the *run*. Girls did do the *run*. I knew loads of girls who'd done it. Libby had done it. Except, according to her, she'd done it as a leisurely walk. They were lying to him to egg him on.

"Maybe you're just cowards," said the cousin.

"Maybe you're the coward," said Shona. She giggled in an exaggerated manner. There was clearly a whole lot of flirting going on between the two of them.

"You calling me a coward?" teased the cousin.

Shona let out a shriek. "I told you not to tickle me like that!"

"Would you two just get a room," sighed Deb, sounding a little weary of it all.

"Are you going to do it, or what?" asked Shona.

"Aren't we supposed to tell him the story first?" asked Deb.

"What story?" asked the cousin.

"The one about how Maggie hung herself because her husband committed suicide," said Shona. "And how she might be still hanging from a rubber flex behind one of those doors right now."

"I heard that Maurice killed himself because Maggie had an affair," said Deb. "Then she killed herself because she found out she was pregnant by her lover."

"Have you got a lover?" teased Shona.

"That's for me to know, and you to find out," the cousin teased back.

"Maybe you shouldn't do this," Deb interjected. "My dad says it's not safe in that house. He says one of these days someone is going to fall right through the floorboards."

"If he runs fast enough, he'll be fine," said Shona.

"Bring on the story, then," said the cousin, clearly putting on a bit of bravado. "I'm all ears."

I looked at Danno and HC. What were we going to do? Any minute now Deb's so-called *cousin* was going come helter-skelter up the stairs and we were all going to be caught in the act.

"I've got this," whispered Danno.

Before HC and me could do anything, he'd scrambled into the hall and risen to his feet. He turned and winked back at us, then disappeared into the stairwell. We heard the stairs creak and crack as he crept slowly down. Outside Deb was telling the story of how Maurice married Maggie and how he'd built the house for her and brought her everything she wanted.

The sounds of Danno's footfall thumping noisily along the downstairs corridor came echoing up to us. "Gaah!" went Danno. It sounded as if he'd kind of skidded through the front doorway.

Shona and Deb both screamed.

"Oh shit!" exclaimed the cousin.

"Jesus Christ, Danno," yelled Shona. "I nearly wet my knickers."

"That was out of order," said Deb.

Danno laughed. "Got you good. The lot of you."

"Were you in there by yourself?" asked Shona, sounding impressed.

"I was out the back looking for Ranks and HC when I heard your voices," replied Danno. "I just came straight through from the kitchen. You haven't seen Ranks have you, Deb?"

"If Deb ever sees Ranks again in her life it'll be too soon," said Shona.

I felt a little flutter of disappointment in my chest.

"You remember my cousin, Terry?" said Deb. "He's down for the week from Aberdeen."

"I'm not really her cousin," Terry pointed out.

"What are you lot up to?" asked Danno.

"Terry was about to make the *run*," said Shona.

"I'd leave it a couple of days," said Danno. "It stinks in there. I think there might be a dead cat or something."

Nice touch, I thought.

218

"Yuk," said Shona. I could imagine her wrinkling her tanned nose.

"It's so hot," said Deb. "We were planning to go for a swim down by the bridge."

"I could come with you," suggested Danno.

"You haven't got a towel or swimming trunks with you," Deb pointed out.

"I'll go in my underpants," said Danno. "And dry myself on my shirt."

"Hope you've got no skid marks on your underpants then," taunted Shona.

A second later she let out another shriek.

"What is it with boys and wanting to tickle me?" she complained.

"I wonder," said Deb. I felt there was more than a hint of sarcasm in her voice.

The sound of their chatter began to drift away as they passed back through the gateway and along the road. HC and me rose slowly to our feet.

"What now?" I asked.

"I can't believe Danno just pissed off and left us," said HC.

"He was making sure they didn't come inside the house," I said.

"He didn't have to offer to go swimming with them though," said HC.

He had a point.

"So, what now?" I asked again.

"We finish the job," said HC, glancing at the door as if he might have just seen some movement behind it. "I want to get out of here as soon as possible. It's starting to feel even worse with just the two of us here."

I knew what he meant. With Danno gone it was like we were going to be more susceptible to Maggie's influence. I didn't know how Danno had plucked up the courage to come to the house by himself. But I could remember from what I'd witnessed how easily Maggie appeared to be manipulating him.

HC removed the rubber glove from his left hand and passed it to me. "If you put it on backwards on your right hand the thumb'll be the right way," he told me.

I did as he asked. He started picking up Bazooka Joe wrappers and stray cuts of Catweazle's hair and dropping them into the Fine Fayre bag. I started dropping the splinters of the shattered Fyffes box out the back window.

"What are you doing that for?" asked HC.

"It's just bits of wood," I said. "There's so much junk out there already. No one is going to think anything of a smashed-up box."

"Do you think we should try and gouge them pellets out of the wall," said HC, looking at the little holes in the plaster.

"Doubt anyone's going to notice them either," I said.

I plucked the burnt out ends of the incense sticks from the upholstery while HC gathered up the apple cores, swatting the flies away with his yellow glove. He handed me the bag and then went and got the other one, which still had his comb and scissors in it. While I picked up some incense stick that had dropped to the floor, he gathered up the Shake 'n' Vac and the aerosol can of Silvekrin.

When HC wasn't looking, I slipped the T. Lobsang Rampa book from my back pocket and dropped it into the bag with the rest of the rubbish. "What about Catweazle's duffel bag?" I asked.

"Reckon we'll have to dump that as well," said HC. "Everything in there has got Danno's fingerprints on it."

"The gun," I said. "We need to get the gun as well. If we don't, Danno's going to insist we come back here."

"Holy fuckeroni," said HC. "Danno took the pen knife with him. What are we going to use to wedge the floorboard back up again?"

"We'll think of something," I said. I saw a flicker of shadow draw close to me and felt a shiver run through me as a cold hush of breath whispered in my ear. I couldn't make out the words. But a wicked little thought seemed to plant itself inside my head. *Wonder what it would be like to shoot a lead pellet into Catweazle's eye?* I didn't have to see her to know that Maggie was prowling somewhere close to me. Who knew what she might have me do if we didn't get out of there soon.

But it seemed that fate had other plans for us.

From the road outside there came the staccato put-put-put of a motor scooter engine. It didn't pass by as I'd hoped. Instead, it came through the gateway, tyres crunching on the dry dirt of the driveway as it slowed to a halt.

"What now?" HC mouthed at me.

I snuck to the front window in time to see a couple of teenagers dismounting what looked to be a shiny new moped. They were both wearing white

221

crash helmets and black tee shirts. One of them kicked down the footrest and leaned the scooter against it. When they removed their helmets, I saw that it was Gordon Aitkin and his girlfriend Eleanor. They both had shoulder length black hair, combed to a middle parting. Gordon had a Led Zeppelin motif on his tee shirt. Eleanor had a Deep Purple one. They looked like a pair of creepy, incestuous heavy metal twins.

Gordon hung both crash helmets by their straps over the handlebars of the moped. I figured this was the latest toy he'd pestered his parents into indulging him with. He was wearing a pair of expensive looking Ray Bans. He removed them, folded the arms, and then hung one arm down through the neck of his tee shirt, so they were dangling down the front.

He took Eleanor's hand and led her toward the doorway to the house.

"Isn't this place supposed to be haunted or something?" she asked.

Gordon laughed. "Old wife's tale."

I turned to HC. "They're coming in."

Without a word the two of us removed our rubber gloves, dropped them to the floor, and then hurried out of the room into the corridor. HC pulled the door quietly shut. We could hear the two of them thumping around downstairs in the living room. It went quiet for a moment - then Eleanor said, "Not here. Someone might walk in on us. If we're upstairs at least we'll hear them coming."

I found myself frozen to the spot. Next to me HC was turning red from holding his breath.

Another terrible thought popped unbidden into my head. *Wonder what it would be like to shoot someone in the eye when they're still alive?* Half way up the stairs Gordon looked up and saw us standing there on the landing. He was still holding hands with Eleanor. "What are you two looking so guilty about?" he asked. "Been tossing each other off?"

Eleanor let out a little giggle.

"What are you up to then?" I shot back. "Come here to finger your skanky girlfriend?"

Eleanor's mouth popped wide. The heat had brought out her acne. She looked like she was suffering from a severe bout of chicken pox. She was a couple of steps behind Gordon on the stairs. She looked up at him. "Are you going to let him talk to me like that?"

HC stuck his tongue out at her.

I did my Humphrey Bogart. *"Out of all the old houses in all the world, you have to walk into mine."*

"Gordon," whined Eleanor. "They're taking the piss."

Gordon looked at me. Then he looked at HC. He seemed to be sizing us up, working out what his chances might be if we got into a scrap. His cheeks flushed red. I could tell he was conflicted. He didn't want to lose face in front of his girlfriend. But he was no fighter. When he was at our High School he was more likely to be the one taking the beatings than handing them out. Gordon didn't really understand the concept of fighting. He'd never had to fight for anything in his life. It was all there for him on a plate. That gave him a different kind of advantage.

I could see it slowly dawning on him. He shook his hand free of Eleanor's and climbed another step. "Rankin, isn't it?" he said, attempting to stare me down. "You've got a paper round with my granddad. Would you like to keep it?"

He had me and he knew it. I didn't quite know what to say.

Luckily HC stepped in. "Why don't you both fuck off and finish your thousand-piece jigsaw."

The two of us cracked up.

Gordon's brow creased. "What's that supposed to mean?"

"I think they're on drugs," said Eleanor. She was stationary on the stairs. She didn't look as if she had any intention of moving.

"Want to see something?" asked HC. "Come up here and I'll show you something."

Gordon seemed a little more confident now. He climbed the last couple of stairs to the landing. Eleanor hung back. She pushed her hair behind her ears and nervously scratched at her angry spots.

"Read what's written on that door," said HC.

Gordon mouthed the words.

Maggie's Ghost Waits Behind This Door.

He laughed and called down to Eleanor. "You should see what they've written on the door. And they've written it in wax crayon. Like some primary school kids." He turned back to us. "Only a pair of idiots would think this place is haunted."

"Oh yeah?" said HC. "You'd shit your pants if you knew what was really behind that door."

224

Gordon sneered and shook his head.

"Maggie's rotting corpse," said HC. "Swinging on a length of rubber flex from her hoover. She all blistered and festering and crawling with fat maggots."

I let out the breath I'd been holding in. I'd thought he was going to tell them about Catweazle.

"Crap," said Gordon. "Utter crap."

HC stepped to one side. "Have a look for yourself if you don't believe me."

Gordon looked at the door. His cheeks blushed red again.

"Me and Ranks were just waiting for someone a lot older and braver to come along and double check that we weren't imagining things," said HC.

There came a moment of thick and ominous silence. Up in the rafters the pigeons cooed in the morning's heat. *Droo-droo droo droo-droo.* I thought I heard a little creak along the corridor behind the door to the big bedroom. I imagined Maggie spying on us through the crack beneath the hinges. I breathed in. It seemed to me there was a hint of the smell gas in the air.

Another thought ugly seeped into my head.

Get them both into the room and see what fun you can have.

Suddenly Gordon broke the silence. "Fuck you, Anderson," he spat. "You're full of shit. Everybody knows it. That's why your little mates call you HC. Hans Christian Andersen, that's you."

He turned to Eleanor. "These two idiots are getting on my nerves. Let's take a run into town and

225

I'll treat you to a Knickerbocker Glory at the café in the High Street."

"A whole Knickerbocker Glory?" asked Eleanor. "Not one to share between the two of us like last time?"

Gordon sighed, as if this was something which was getting old between them.

"Yes, a whole one," he said. "We'll have one each this time."

They began to descend the stairs.

"Enjoy your piano lessons," I called after them.

HC laughed.

"Idiots!" Gordon back, from down in the hallway.

A minute or so later there came the sound of the scooter starting and the put-put-put of its engine as it passed back through the gateway and along the road.

"What did you do that for?" I challenged HC.

"It worked, didn't it?" he said. "Sometimes it's a bit of an advantage to have a reputation as a liar."

I couldn't believe he was being so dumb. "So now there are two witnesses who can swear we were in here. Who'll say we both seemed pretty damned keen that no one should go in that room."

The realisation seemed to hit HC like a ton of bricks. He slapped his forehead so hard that the sound of the smack echoed along the hallway. A little clump of plaster dropped down from the ceiling and landed on the floor between us. "Holy fuckeroni, Ranks," said HC. "What have I done?"

Chapter Nineteen

The two of us panicked. We just grabbed the Fine Fayre bags and the rubber gloves and the fled. Danno's airgun and Catweazle's duffle bag were forgotten and left behind. I'd kind of expected that we'd head over to the little woods near the quarry and that's where we'd bury all the evidence. But when we reached the bottom of the stairs HC ran for the kitchen door and I followed him.

As we scrambled over the collapsed fence and up through the weeds on the embankment it seemed to me that HC had made the right decision. If Danno and the others were swimming down by the bridge then they'd have been sure to see us when we climbed the hill. HC was just like he had been on the day Danno and me had goaded him into making his *run*, all tightly wound and twitchy. As we made our way along the railway track, he started tossing the contents of the Fine Fayre bag into the nettles.

"Holy fuck," he began repeating. "Holy, holy fuck."

He was walking fast, tossing items left and right. I had to run to keep up with him. Nevertheless, I thought he had the right idea. By the time winter came, and the nettles died, whatever was dumped there would just be considered random bits of junk. No one would ever join up the dots. I followed his lead, arm jerking as I slung the burnt-out remains of the incense stick as far as I could. When I came to the T. Lobsang Rampa book something held me back. I slipped it into the back pocket of my jeans and began disposing of the rest of the bag's contents.

When both bags were emptied out HC turned to me. His face was creased in consternation. "I'm sorry, Ranks," he said. "I've screwed up. I've dropped us all completely in it. Danno's going to kick my head in when he finds out."

"He won't," I tried to assure him. "I'll talk to Danno. I swear, mate, I'll make him understand."

HC's eyes met mine. "I bet you feel like kicking my head in yourself."

I didn't. "I don't see what choice you had. If you hadn't said that stuff about Maggie they'd have probably gone into that room. And then we'd have been in even more trouble."

"You think?"

"I know."

Even though HC could wind me up beyond endurance with his exaggerated tales there had never actually been a time when I'd even considered getting into a fight with him. There was the slapstick rough stuff that the three of us always got into, but I didn't count that.

Danno was a different story. When we were all younger, I must have gotten into a good three of four punching, gouging, biting fights with Danno before I realised that I was never going get the better of him. It was the same with HC and Danno. But HC and me had never gone one to one. I didn't have any intention of changing that. I grabbed him round the shoulder and rapped his ginger head playfully with my knuckles. "Let's go into town and get some chips," I said. "You're the smart one. You'll come up with something."

HC turned his head and looked up at me. "You think?"

I wasn't all that convinced, but he didn't need to know that.

"I know," I said again and let go of him.

We screwed up the Fine Fayre bags and tossed them to the nettles with the rubber gloves and then set off the town centre. The sun beat down on our backs. Coal dust, kicked up by our feet, danced in eddies before us, midges hummed in huge, annoying clouds around our heads. Neither of us once looked back in the direction of Maggie's house.

You could follow the railway track all the way into town. They'd built a car park where station and goods yard had once stood. We were about halfway there when we saw Mr Renton approaching from the other direction. He had his dog with him again. The Alsatian had its head down. It didn't look happy at being dragged out for a walk in the type of heat we were enduring.

"Act normal," whispered HC.

When captain approached him, HC crouched low and ruffled the dog's head again. It looked at him with doleful eyes, panting rhythmically as its tongue hung from the side of its mouth. Just seeing it like that made me feel thirsty.

"Where's the third musketeer today?" asked Mr Renton.

"Gone swimming down by the bridge," replied HC, still stroking the dog, in what I suspected was an attempt to avoid eye contact.

"You two didn't fancy it then?" asked Mr Renton.

I delivered a response in the style of Top Cat. *"It's like this, officer Dibble. Choo-choo here has got an aversion to water, on account of him never having had a bath in his life."*

Mr Renton chuckled. "Not half bad," he said. "Sergeant Bilko, right?"

"Not quite," I said. "But same thing really."

He picked up a stick and threw it along the track. Captain looked disdainfully at him and padded away, completely ignoring the stick. Mr Renton shrugged his shoulders and followed. When he was far enough away that he couldn't hear us, HC turned to me.

"Now we're doubly fucked. He's seen us twice. In fact, if you take into account Gordon and his spotty girlfriend, we're doubly fucked with a cherry on the top."

"Well," I said. "If you take Deb and Shona and what his name into account, and the fact they saw Danno coming out of Maggie's house, we're probably knickerbocker glory triple fucked – with a cherry on the top."

Despite the seriousness of the situation, we both managed to laugh.

We pooled what money we had and found we had enough between us to pay for a sausage in batter and a can of Coke instead of a portion of chips. We sat on the same bench in the gardens that we had sat on with Danno a couple of days earlier, nibbling at halves of the battered sausages and passing the can of Coke back and forth.

Gordon's scooter was leaning on its footrest outside the High Street Café. We could hear music thumping out from the jukebox. It sounded like Deep Purple's Strange Kind of Woman. I had this horrible notion that he and Eleanor would come out at any minute, and when they saw us, they'd jump on the scooter and head off for Maggie's House to get down to whatever it was they'd been planning to get down to.

Instead, it was Danno's old man who came out of the café. He must have been on his lunch break. He was dressed in his butcher's overalls. He lit up a Woodbine and leaned for a moment against the outside wall of the cafe. Then he ran his fingers through his hair, swaggered along the pavement, took a few more puffs, stubbed out the cigarette and went into the bookies.

I turned to HC. "You ever notice that ring that Danno's old man wears?" I asked.

HC nodded. "The one that looks like a wheatsheaf?"

I nodded back. "How long do you think he's had it?"

HC licked grease from his fingers. "As long as I can remember."

That was it then I'd probably just stored the image in my head and the somehow it had gotten muddled in with my dream.

"Remember when Action Man first came out?" asked HC. "And me, you, and Danno all got one for

231

Christmas and we went round to his house after Boxing Day?"

"What were we? Eight or nine?" I asked.

"Something like that?" said HC.

He took a swig from the can of coke.

I swallowed down the last bite of my half of the sausage.

"I think that was the first time I noticed the ring," said HC. "Danno's old man came home while we were there. And he was happy drunk for once, instead of fighting drunk."

"He'd had a big win on the horses," I said.

HC took the coke can from me when I offered it to him. "And he started putting all these old rock'n'roll records onto Danno's mum's Dansette."

"*Chuck Berry and Jerry Lee, them were the boys, lads,*" I mimicked.

"Exactly," said HC. "And he was tapping his fingers on the armrest of the chair in time to the music. And that's when I noticed the ring."

He finished the coke, crushed the can, and tossed it into the rubbish bin.

"I had a dream about that ring."

I told him what I'd seen in my dream.

"Holy fuckeroni, Ranks," he said, when I'd finished. "Maybe it wasn't a dream. Maybe you witnessed an actual murder! Maybe you witness two actual murders."

I shook my head. "It couldn't have been real."

I could feel the outline T. Lobsang Rampa book in my back pocket. I could almost remember word for word what it said about people who travelled in the astral plane being able to go back in time. I didn't want it to be true. With everything else that was going on the notion that the root cause went back to something cold and evil that Danno's old man had done when he was a teenager like us was just too much to cope with.

The clouds were thickening in the sky now, but it was still impossibly hot. Bees were humming around the flowers in the ornamental beds. The sun suddenly broke through a gap in the billowing white blanket above.

HC squinted as he looked at me. "You saw Danno in Maggie's house when you fell asleep in at the pictures," he said, "And it turned out he really was there. So, it is possible you saw something that really happened. You've got to do something, Ranks. You can't just go around ignoring a murder. Even if it did happen years ago. My uncle would know what to do. Do you want me to ask him?"

"You know you can't do that," I said.

HC looked hurt. "What's that supposed to mean?"

Across the road Danno's old man came out of the bookies. He had a face like thunder. He screwed up his betting slip, tossed it into the air and then kicked it into the road as it fell. Scowling he spat on the pavement. Then he stuffed his hands into his pockets and marched head down for the butcher's shop. Poor Danno, his old man was going to be in a foul mood when he got home.

"Are you trying to say something about my uncle?" challenged HC. The tone of his voice had gone from hurt to confrontational.

"I think you know what I'm saying," I replied.

233

I burped and the meaty taste of the battered sausage repeated in my mouth.

Gordon and Eleanor came out of the café. They kissed on the pavement before putting on their crash helmets and climbing onto the scooter. I wondered if they were planning to set off for Maggie's house. Part of me hoped they were. I just wanted it all to finally end, for better or worse.

"My uncle's in Barlinnie jail," admitted HC in a quiet voice.

"I know," I said. "Everyone kind of knows. He got done for an armed robbery on a post office."

HC nodded. "It's not his fault. He really is a hero. When he was in Ireland his patrol got blown up by a roadside bomb. He got medal for dragging three of his mates to safety. But it was too late for one of them. I heard that bits of the guy were splattered all over my uncle's face."

There it was, the same old story, acts of violence with every page that turned in our lives. "Shit," I said.

"I know," said HC. "My mum says that's what changed him. After he got his medical discharge, he just couldn't cope."

He looked at me. "The army never gave a fuck about him once he got out, Ranks."

"Maybe nobody gives a fuck about any of us," I said.

The air was getting thicker. I was finding it a bit of a task to breathe.

"That's why if Danno's old man committed a murder, we can't just let it stand," said HC. "*We* have to give a fuck, even if nobody else does."

234

I could see sweat running down the side of his face. My tee shirt was sticking to my back. I wondered if this was the kind of damp and muggy heat you would experience in a jungle. I took the T. Lobsang Rampa book from my back pocket, flicked through the pages till I found the entry about astral travel, and then handed it to HC.

HC's lips moved with every word as he read the entry. He'd been doing this since we'd sat next to each other in primary school. I could hear each sentence whispered under his breath. When he'd finished, he looked straight ahead, freckled brow creased, tiny stream of sweat still running down the side of his face.

"It says you can travel through space as well as time," he said, turning to me again.

"It says a lot of things," I replied. "But that doesn't make them true."

"It's kind of like a Doctor Who Tardis," he said. "Except it's inside your head."

A little groan rose in my throat. I had hoped HC would laugh at me for buying into T. Lobsang Rampa's hippy-trippy shite. Instead, he seemed to be giving it some credence, forcing me to speak out loud what I been secretly going over inside my head.

"I don't think you actually travel back in time," I told him. "I think it kind of gets mixed in with your dreams. I mean the first time went to Maggie's house the actor that plays Catweazle on TV was with Maggie and Maurice."

"Maybe he died?" suggested HC.

Not this again. "It would have been in the papers, and I'd have seen it when I was delivering them."

HC shook his head. "Not if it was on the inside instead of the front page."

"He isn't dead," I said. "I didn't really see him. He was in a dream. But somehow the dream got all mixed up with reality. Maybe I did see Danno's old man though. Maybe things that happen in the past are kind of recorded like scenes from a film, especially bad things. Maybe they leave a big mark. If you can somehow tune in, you can watch them play out. But you can't change them. Maybe that's how astral travel really works."

"You're like Nosferatu in reverse," said HC. "He could see into the future. You can see into the past."

"I think you mean Nostradamus," I said.

HC grinned. "See? I told you I wasn't the smart one."

"Smart enough," I said.

He handed the book back to me. "I think we should go to the library," he said.

Chapter Twenty

"They're not going to have any more T. Lobsang Rampa books in the library," I called after HC as he walked swiftly through the ornamental gardens.

HC turned. "We're not going to look for a book," he said.

"We're not?"

HC shook his head. "We're going to look at old newspapers." Above us the clouds were rapidly darkening from white to dirty grey. There seemed to be a charge in the air that was making the little hairs on my forearms stand up. "They've got big folders of all the back issues of the local papers," said HC. "There might be some picture from when Maurice had his toyshop. We could see if he's wearing the ring. It's what they do on the detective shows on TV. They go and look at old newspapers for clues."

That made sense to me. At least we might find out one way or the other.

"I bet there's a picture of the wedding, when he got married to Maggie."

HC nodded his head. "And if we can see what's on his finger."

"Maybe Maggie gave it to him," I said.

"You mean like a wedding ring?"

"It's possible."

"If that's what it was then what Danno's old man did is even worse."

"If Danno's old man did actually do anything," I pointed out. "And it isn't all just some weird dream that got mixed up in my head."

We arrived at the stone steps to the library.

"Only one way to find out," said HC.

When we reached the desk, the librarian was full of questions and thinly disguised suspicions. She was dressed in a tweed suit that looked far too warm and stuffy for the weather we were having. Her salt and pepper hair was moulded into a huge perm that looked as if it had so many layers of hairspray you would need to chisel through it to reach her scalp.

She fired off challenges and allegations in quick succession.

"You're from that housing scheme, aren't you?"

"We don't want any of your shenanigans in here."

"You do realise this is a library and that means you can't make a lot of noise?"

"Can I trust you to behave yourselves if I give you access to the reference area?"

In my head I was coming up with dozens of quips and comebacks that I could deliver in the voice of this or that actor. Somehow though I managed to hold my tongue. HC went on a charm offensive, spinning her a line about a summer project set by our history teacher to find out what had happened in the town in the year we were born.

Eventually she relented and led us somewhat grudgingly upstairs to the reference section, insisting we both went into the gents and washed our hands on the way. When we came out, she asked us to hold out our hands so she could check them. Then she asked us to turn out our pockets.

"I want to make sure you've got no felt pens or biros," she said. "I don't want to go back and find moustaches and spectacles drawn on some of the photos in the papers."

We did as she asked. There wasn't much in our pockets other than a few remaining coppers. She showed us to these huge shelves where copies of the local paper were kept in tall binders, each with a year printed on its spine. "The 1950s are in this section," she said, still eyeing us with a great deal of suspicion. "You take care when you turn over the pages, you hear? And just so you know, I'll be popping my head around the door every five minutes or so to make sure you're behaving yourselves."

The first binder that HC pulled out was marked 1954. He laid it out on the table. We pulled up a couple of chairs. We flicked slowly through the pages of each issue. There seemed to be an advertisement for Henderson's Toy shop in the small ad column of every issue. But we could find no pictures of Maurice, or any stories that mentioned him by name. In the December issue the advertisement was adorned with bells and holly and invited children to come and see Santa in his grotto.

I closed the binder and slipped it back in place while HC pulled out the one for 1955. In one of the March editions there was a picture of members of the local Chamber of Commerce standing outside the Town Hall where they were due to attend their Annual General Meeting. That old nauseating knot twisted in my belly when I looked at the picture.

"What's wrong?" asked HC.

239

"It's him," I said, pointing to the small, wiry looking man who stood third from the left. "That's Maurice. That's how he looked in my dream. I've never seen a picture of him before. I have no idea what he looked like. But that's who I saw in my dream."

Beneath the picture was a list of the Chamber of Commerce members in attendance. And there, third along, was the name, Maurice Henderson.

"Holy fuckeroni," said HC. "It's true then. You did go back in time. You did see something that really happened."

"Keep the noise down," hissed a voice. "Any more language like that and you'll both be out on your ears."

We both looked up. The librarian, in her tweed suit and sculpted hair, was scowling at us from the doorway. When she'd said she was going to check up on us she sure as hell meant it.

"We'll keep the noise down," I assured her.

"And no more swearing," added HC.

"Let's hope so," she said. "Don't think I won't be back to check you again though."

"Holy F," whispered HC when she'd gone. "That's really how he looked in your dream?"

I felt sick to the stomach. All I could manage to do was nod my head. HC flicked through to December. There was the same advert for Santa's Christmas grotto at Maurice's toyshop. HC replaced the folder for 1955 with the one for 1956. There was nothing of much interest until we came to one of the April editions. It had a full page spread of Easter weddings.

There was Maurice in his morning coat. Beside him his young bride in her long white dress. Beneath the picture ran the line – Maurice Stanley Henderson and Margaret Ruth Dixon. I hardly recognised Maggie. In my dream she'd been rain lashed and overcome with grief. Whenever I'd seen what I believed to be her ghost she'd had the rubber flex around her neck, flesh blackened and eyes popping out of her head.

The picture showed a young woman, radiant in her white wedding dress, hair hanging in ringlets down the side of her face, cheeks dusted in rouge, smiling enthusiastically for the camera. HC looked at me. He didn't need to say a word. I nodded in answer to the earnest look in his eyes. My stomach started to hurt so much it felt as if it was being put through a mangle.

HC was about to turn the page when something else caught my eye. On the opposite page there was a collection of pictures from the Borough Sports Championships. One picture showed a young man who looked like a slightly older version of me. He was dressed in a white tee shirt with a card bearing the number 62 on it. In his left hand he held a little silver cup. He was giving a thumbs up with the right.

HC read out the line beneath the picture. "Andrew Kenneth Rankin (19) Celebrates Coming First in the Cross Country Final."

He looked at me again. "Holy F, Ranks. It's your dad."

The paper was faded and exuded a fusty smell, but there he was, my dad, frozen in that moment, just like the kid with the ice cream cone on the front page of that sun-baked issue of the Daily Record. I never even knew he'd had any athletic prowess when he was younger. I wondered where he was and what he was doing as I sat there looking at that faded, monochrome image of him.

I wondered if Libby was right, and mum knew exactly where he was and was selfishly keeping it to herself. Was he such a bad person that she wouldn't allow him to have any contact with us? Was it really the case that she didn't know where he was, and he didn't care enough to keep in touch with his kids? Those were the type of question that had endlessly gnawed away at me for years and I was determined not to get into that again.

I nudged HC. "Just turn the page."

"You sure?" he asked.

I nodded, deliberately resisting the temptation to take another glance at the photo. Part of me wanted to kind of recharge my memory so that in my head I'd have a clearer image of what he looked like. Another part of me just wanted that fuzzy image I had of him to fade even more than it already had. It was better that way.

"I'm sure," I said.

"It's your dad, Ranks," he insisted. "Don't you want to tear out the picture and keep it?"

"Just turn the page," I said.

HC began flicking through the pages again. There were a couple more adverts for the toyshop. One from early July depicted a bucket and spade and the strap line 'Get ready for the summer at Henderson's Toys.'

Further on in September there was another picture of Maurice. He was shaking hands with an elderly man with a receding hairline. They were both wearing suits and ties and grinning widely for the camera. The headline explained that Maurice had been unanimously elected as president of the Chamber of Commerce to replace Mr Reginald Barkley, who had decided to retire after fifteen years in the position.

"Look," whispered HC, pointing to the ring on Maurice's finger.

We both leaned in to take a closer look.

The wheat sheaf motif was clearly visible.

"Holy F," said HC. "That's it. That's the one that Danno's dad wears."

"It's the one I saw him take from Maurice in my dream," I said.

From outside there came a rumble. It sounded as if somewhere in the distance a thunderstorm was brewing.

"That's it," said HC. "That's the proof."

HC closed the binder.

"We've got to go to the police."

"We've been over that." I said. "If we do that it'll all come out. What we did with Catweazle. Everything. Anyway, who's going to believe us?"

"We can't just leave it," said HC. "We can't just let someone get away with murder."

I shrugged my shoulders and blew air out of my mouth. "He's gotten away with it all this time." I took the binder and slid it back into place on the shelf. As I was doing so the librarian came bustling down the hall and stopped in the doorway.

243

"We're done," said HC.

"Almost," I interjected. "Just one more to look at."

She eyed us with more than a hint of suspicion. "I thought the project was about the year of your birth?"

"It is," I said. "But I wanted to back a bit further. In case there was a picture of my parents' wedding."

"Fine," she conceded grudgingly, and bustled away again.

I brought down the binder for 1957.

"We don't need to look at that," said HC. "We found everything we need."

"We haven't found the end of the story yet," I told him.

I had kind of hoped that the end of the story would be different to the one that had been handed down through various generations of kids since the late 50's. But as it turned the story was exactly how it had been relayed.

We found the piece on Maurice's suicide on the inside pages of one of the June editions. "Tragedy of Local Business Man" read the headline. The article beneath told how Maurice's had been found in the kitchen by his young wife and how she was inconsolable. It speculated that Maurice may have been in considerable financial difficulties.

"He had money," said HC. "But Danno's old man stole it. Just like he stole that ring."

Maggie's suicide made the front page in the first week of August.

244

There was a picture of her in a smart party frock at a social event, smiling and looking carefree. "Second Tragedy at Suicide House", blared the headline. The fact that she had discharged herself from hospital rather than having escaped from some psychiatric ward was the only variation on the story we knew. The rest was the same. Found behind the door of one of the bedrooms, hanging by the neck from the electrical flex of her vacuum cleaner.

In the October issue we came across a small column that featured Danno's old man. "Local Youth Sent to Borstal on Eight Counts of Breaking and Entering".

"Bet he didn't confess to breaking into Maggie's house," said HC. "He did time for burglary, but not for murder."

Chapter Twenty-One

On the way out of the library the fussy librarian had challenged me about the book that was sticking out of my back pocket. "I do hope you're not trying to get away with pilfering that paperback," she said, stepping in front of us and effectively blocking our way.

I pulled the book from my pocket and held it up in front of her. "The Wisdom of the Ancients," I told her. "By T. Lobsang Rampa. It's mine."

She looked at the book with its dirty, half-torn and mould speckled cover and screwed up her nose as if I was holding up a piece of dog dirt I'd picked up from the pavement. With a flabbergasted shake of her head, she stepped to the side to let us past.

"Old witch," I muttered under my breath when we were back on the pavement.

"You need to get rid of that book," said HC. "It could be used as evidence against us. The same way as Danno needs to get rid of the Swiss army knife."

"Good luck with that," I told him. "In any case Gordon and his spotty faced girlfriend might have already blown everything out of the water."

"Holy fuckeroni," said HC. "I'd forgotten about them."

We walked along the High Street. The whole sky was smothered in dark clouds now. It hadn't quite dissipated the heat, but far away, beyond the heather covered hills that surrounded the town, thunder was rumbling and streaks of lightening were renting the sky.

"It'll be with us pretty soon," I said. "We're going to get drenched."

HC stopped and turned. "We should go to the police station right now and just tell them what we know."

"We've been through that," I said. "They'd never believe us. It's all too far-fetched."

"We can't just let him get away with it," said HC. "Murder is murder. Even if it happened a long time ago."

I noticed that he was looking worriedly over my shoulder. When I looked behind me, I discovered that we'd come to a halt outside the butcher's shop. Danno's old man was laying out lamb chops onto white tray in the chilled window display. When he saw us looking at him his lip curled to a scowl as he gave us the middle finger. The ring with the wheat sheaf motif was there on his ring finger, brazen and for all the world to see.

We hurried on, not looking back.

"We have to do something," said HC. "He so full of himself. He committed two murders, and he doesn't have a care in the world. Doesn't even think he has to hide the evidence."

"Maybe we're getting it wrong," I said. "Maybe there weren't any murders. Maybe I'm just having weird dreams. Maybe Maggie sold the ring after Maurice died and Danno's old man bought from a second-hand shop or something."

"He'd have a receipt then," said HC.

"After all these years?"

"That would be for the police to investigate," said HC. We were opposite the police station now. I

247

grabbed HC by the arm in case he got it into his head to cross the road. "We could send a unanimous letter," he suggested.

"I told you before the word is anonymous. Anyway, neither of us have exactly got the type of handwriting that would make the police take any letter from us seriously."

"I could get my little sister to write it," said HC. "Or you could ask Libby."

I let go of his arm. "And let someone else in on all of this? Have you gone soft in the head?"

"I'm trying to do the right thing here." He began to pace back and forth, muttering under his breath. "Holy fuck. Holy fuck. Holy, holy fuck."

A couple of uniformed constables came out to the carpark and looked over at us before getting into their Panda car. "Come on," I said. "You're drawing attention."

We found ourselves on the old railway track once more, heading back in the direction of the housing scheme. The clouds were still thickening. It had become quite gloomy. But still there was not a single drop of rain. We must have walked a good five or ten minutes before HC came up with a new idea. "We should bury Catweazle," he said. "Give him a proper send off. We could say the Lord's Prayer like we used to do in Primary School. I think I still remember the words. Or you could read something out of his book."

"Bury him where?" I asked.

"At the back of Maggie's house," said HC. "Next to the old shed. It's the perfect time. It's going to rain. The ground's going to be soft."

"How would we get him down the stairs?" I asked.

I couldn't quite believe that I was entertaining the idea.

"We'd carry him. One would take his legs and one would take his shoulders."

A shudder ran through me. "I couldn't face carrying a dead body."

"We'd have rubber gloves."

"We threw them away," I pointed out.

"I bet they're still where we left them," said HC. "Even if they're gone, I can get some more. My mum has a whole pile of them under the sink."

"How would we dig the grave?" I asked.

"We'd use my dad's shovel," said HC. "He keeps it in the shed."

"And he'd just let you take it?"

"We'd have to sneak it out."

"We?"

"My dad is out at work and my little sister went round to Karen's house. It's only my mum at home this afternoon. If you went to the front door, pretending you were looking for me, I could sneak into the shed and leave the shovel by the side of the house."

"Then what?"

"Then you could come and get it tomorrow morning when you're on your paper round and leave it somewhere for us to pick up on the way to Maggie's house."

I laughed.

It sounded just like the kind of crazy, convoluted scam we'd have gotten up to a couple of years earlier. Before everything started getting serious. Before we became so focused on looking cool and acting hard. I still wasn't convinced by the notion of burying Catweazle. But the idea of stealing the spade had me hankering for the old days, when the mischief we got up to was both innocent and foolish.

"Where does Danno fit in to all of this?" I asked.

"He doesn't," replied HC. "The two of us bury Catweazle. That puts us all in the clear. Then we can break the news to Danno about what we think his old man did. And the three of us can decide what we should do next."

I didn't want to analyse HC's plan too closely in case some obvious flaws caused it to unravel completely. It was like the whole situation - murders, suicides, ghosts, corpses, secrets, lies, was overwhelming me and making my mind shut down compartment by compartment. I could only manage to focus on one thing at a time.

All that mattered for that moment was the shovel and whether I could distract HC's mum long enough for him to get it round to the side of the house. The idea of it was bringing smile to my face. If we pulled it off, it might be something we'd laugh about when we went back to school - if we ever managed to laugh about anything again.

We headed for HC's.

The three of us had somehow managed to cover all the housing options the council had made available on the scheme. I lived in a flat. Danno lived in a maisonette. HC lived in a boxy little house at the end of a terrace. The house had a little side passage leading to the back garden. His dad, who was a keen gardener, used it mainly to store plant pots. No one ever really used the passage. They just went in and out of the garden through the kitchen door, like everyone else on the terrace.

HC snuck round the back and said he would hide behind his dad's greenhouse. I walked up to the front door and rang the bell. HC's mum appeared. She was a big, busty woman who filled the doorway so completely that I found myself taking a step back as her shadow fell on me. She had on a floral apron. Her plump, pink hands were covered with flour. The delicious smell of something cooking wafted out from the kitchen.

"Hello there," she said when she saw me. "You caught me in the middle of making a rhubarb pie."

HC's mum always put me in mind of a big old mother hen. She had a laugh that came from the back of her throat that fit the image perfectly. Everything seemed to make Mrs Anderson laugh. The fact that she had just mentioned making a rhubarb pie seemed to amuse her enormously and out came that laugh. Cluck-cluck-cluck. Cluck-cluck-cluck.

As ever it was all I could do not strut around, scratching at the ground with my foot as I descended into an exaggerated impersonation of the cartoon character Foghorn Leghorn and his southern drawl. "I was looking for HC," I said. "I haven't seen him all day. I thought he might be sick or something."

"Sick?" She looked shocked at the very notion. "He's fit as a fiddle. When he went out this morning, he said he was going to meet you and Daniel. Did you try down by the river?"

I nodded, pretending I had.

"Well, I'm sure he'll show up eventually," she said. She leaned slightly out of the door and looked up at the grey clouds. "No doubt looking like a drowned rat."

I opened my mouth. Then found I couldn't think of anything else to say. HC's mum watched me expectantly. I thought I heard a noise from the side passage. But I couldn't be sure.

"Oh well," said HC's mum, dusting off her hands and sending up a little cloud of flour. "Can't dither around all day. I've got a chicken casserole in the oven and a pie to bake." The she was off again, breasts jiggling as the laughter seized her. Cluck-cluck-cluck. Cluck-cluck-cluck.

"When he gets home, I'll tell him you came looking for him," she said as she closed the door.

As I turned to walk back down the garden path HC's head popped out around the side of the house. He gave me a thumbs-up, then quickly disappeared. Not looking back in case his mum was watching from the window I walked to the post box two streets away where we'd agreed to meet.

There was a wide smile on my face when he arrived. HC was smiling too, freckled face all wrinkled up around the eyes. We'd concocted a little plan that we'd seen through to the end of its first leg. This was what the summer holidays were supposed to be like, random acts of mischief that didn't matter and had no real consequence.

"It's by the side wall," said HC. "I covered it with plant pots. When you move them in the morning you need to be quiet. My mum's a light sleeper. You've only got to fart to wake her."

"I'm going to get up early," I told him. "Good half hour at least before I start my round."

HC nodded. "Where are you planning to hide the shovel?"

"I was going to put it at the side of the railway track and stamp some nettles down over it so we can pick it up on the way to Maggie's house."

HC nodded again. "Good plan." He looked up at the boiling grey clouds. "Let's hope it comes down in buckets, so the soil is good and soft."

My mood sank. The smile dropped from my face. This wasn't mischief without consequence. This was mischief with a purpose. A purpose that was going to lead to us burying a dead body to cover up some other terrible mischief. That wasn't innocent fun. It was sick and twisted.

"What time should we meet in the morning?" asked HC. "It should be before nine, because we want to get this done before Danno shows up. It's going to be hard enough telling him what his old man did without making it even more complicated."

"If his old man actually did anything," I tried.

"Come on, Ranks," said HC. "We both know he did it."

Did we? I still wasn't sure.

I gave a kind of non-committal shrug.

253

"Quarter past eight?" suggested HC. "We'll meet at quarter past eight?"

I shrugged again.

HC began to walk away.

"Hang on," I called after him. "Where are you going?"

"I'm going home," he called back. "I've got to spin my mum a line about how me and Danno have been looking for you all day."

There it was again. More lies piling up on top of the ones already told. I heaved a sigh and leaned on the post box as I watched him go. After a while I decided that all I could do was go home myself. I walked through the scheme in a kind of stumbling daze, oblivious to everything around me.

I've heard since of people who get so overloaded with stress and worry that their mind just wipes everything blank and kind of resets itself without the pressure of everything that's been burdening them. They completely forget who they are. They no longer recognise their friends and family. It takes them years of therapy to get back their memories.

I honestly think that something like that was about to happen to me. I think it might have happened if I hadn't walked past the little play park and bumped into Deb, Shona and Deb's *cousin*. It was the shock of seeing what had happened to Deb's cousin that snapped me right back to my horrible reality.

His nose looked mangled and swollen. His bottom lip was gashed as if he'd bitten through it with his front teeth. There was dried blood all over his face and in his hair. His tee-shirt was stained in bloody red splatters. I thought he'd been run over or something. Deb's eyes were pink and swollen. Shona had watery streaks of mascara running down her cheeks. They'd both been crying.

"What happened?" I asked.

"I tell you what happened," snapped Shona. "That psycho pal of yours, that's what happened."

That horrible knot twisted in my belly again. "Danno?"

"Yes Danno," said Shona. "Who else? We were all down at the river and me and *Derek* were just splashing around and having fun when your pal goes bananas. Punching and kicking. Howling like an animal. *Derek* nearly drowned, so he did."

Deb started to cry, burying her face in her hands, white-blond hair cascading over them.

"Then the mad bastard runs to the shore," ranted Shona. "And he pulls a knife out his jeans' pocket. A fucking knife, Ranks. Then he starts screaming that he's going to stab the lot of us."

"I don't know what I'm going to tell my dad when we get home," sobbed Deb.

"The truth," said her *cousin*, his voice thick and slightly slurred over his ragged lip. "I got into a fight, and I lost."

"It wasn't a fight," said Shona. "It was a violent assault. You should go to the police."

"Where's Danno now?" I asked.

"Who knows?" replied Shona, arm around Deb's shoulder for comfort. "Who cares? If there's any justice, they'll have carted him off to the loony bin."

I don't know what exactly I had in mind at that point. Maybe I intended to confront Danno and risk getting into a fight with him myself. Maybe I was going to console him and offer sympathy for the way the violence in his family life spilled over into the aggressive way he acted around people. Maybe I was going to blurt out everything HC and me had discovered, tell him his old man was a murderer and that if he wasn't careful he was going to end up going the same way.

All I knew for sure was that I had to find him. As I walked away, I glanced over my shoulder and saw that Deb was watching me go over her puffy pink eyes. I found myself stupidly wondering if there was still a chance for us.

If I'd been quicker off the mark back at Maggie's house that morning it might have been me who had gone swimming with them instead of Danno. Maybe Deb and me would have gotten back together. Maybe Shona would have gotten off with Deb's cousin. Maybe things would have taken a turn for the better and the four of us would have hung out together for the rest of the summer.

But that wasn't the way it was.

I headed for Danno's house.

It seemed the obvious place to start.

The maisonette was on the second floor, up a stone stairway that ran down the side of the building. The iron railings were flaked and rusty and in need of attention. There was a withered plant in a cracked pot by the door. One of the panels on the lower half of the door was split from where

Danno's old man had tried to kick it in one drunken night.

If Danno's old man had been at home instead of at work, I don't think I would have dared gone there. Danno's mum worked a couple of afternoons a week at the local chemist. I wasn't sure whether it was one of her work days. But she was so timid that even if she was at home, she'd most likely leave it to Danno to open the door.

I chapped at the knocker on the letterbox.

Chap-chap-chap.

Under the portentous gloom of the cloud filled sky the sound echoed dully across the street. No answer. I tried again. Chap-chap-chap. When there was still no answer, I knocked the door hard with my knuckles.

I waited.

Nothing.

I crouched down and shouted through the letterbox into the fusty little hall.

"Danno! Danno! Dan! It's me, Ranks. I need to talk to you."

Still nothing.

I rapped the knocker one last time. When there was still no response, I made my way back down the stairs. I wondered where Danno might be. My stomach flipped when the notion struck me that he might have gone back alone to Maggie's house. That he might at that very minute be sitting on the floor in the little room, sharpening a stick ready to plunge into Catweazle's eye, while somewhere in the shadows Maggie's ghost prowled around him, exerting its malicious influence.

I didn't think it was in me to pluck up the courage to go there and look for him. What if Maggie somehow got her claws into me? What horrible things might she have me to do to Catweazle's corpse? I couldn't risk it. I had to go back to HC's house. I had to tell him what Danno had done to Deb's cousin and how the two of us had to go straight to Maggie's house in case he was about to do something even more sick and stupid.

Behind the row of maisonettes there was a little area that consisted of a couple of dozen garages, constructed with breezeblock walls, steel doors and corrugated iron roofs. I decided to slip through there as a short cut. As I approached the garages, I began to hear shouting, followed by the sound of a loud, hollow thump, as if someone had been pushed hard against one of the garage doors. I heard a voice calling out. "Get him! Kick his head in!" It sounded like Jimmy Scott, Clutch's skinhead mate.

I broke into a trot. When I rounded the corner into the potholed little tarmac square around which the garages were built Jimmy immediately stepped in front of me. "This is none of your business, Rankin."

I looked over his shoulder.

Danno was on the ground with Clutch straddling his chest and pummelling his head with wild punches. Lanky had hold of his legs, pinning them down to stop him struggling. The Robertson twins had huge grins on their faces as they took turns at launching kicks at his side. The noise of the impact was horrible.

"Four on one," I said to Jimmy. "That's not fair."

"That's how he wanted it," said Jimmy, pressing his forehead aggressively against mine. "Came down here and said he'd fight the lot of us."

Clutch must have caught a hint of the conversation. He stopped landing punches and looked back at us. He scrambled away from Danno's chest. Lanky quickly took his place, spindly legs pressing down on Danno's arms. Jimmy stepped back as Clutch came sauntering cockily over, rubbing his fists. One of the twins launched another kick at Danno. He cried out in pain.

"Piss off, Ranks," said Clutch. "We've got no beef with you."

"I think you have," I replied. "Even if you don't. I don't think I've any choice but to make sure you have."

Clutch stared me down. "If you want it that way, I'm sure Jimmy will go one on one with you while we finish what your mate started."

"What is it he's supposed to have done?" I asked. "Is this still about what happened at the Youth Club?"

Clutch shook his head, as if he thought I was a complete idiot. "I was prepared to spit on it and let bygone be bygones. But Danno wasn't having any of it. He said he was going to have all of us. He was swinging punches all over the shop."

"Kicked Lanky in the fucking nuts," added Jimmy.

259

The second twin stepped on Danno's fingers and cruelly twisted the sole of his baseball boot. Danno cried out again.

"He's a head case," said Clutch. "It's like he's got a death wish or something."

I was instantly tempted to do a Charles Bronson impersonation.

"He needs to be taught a lesson once and for all," said Jimmy.

"What's it going to be, Ranks?" asked Clutch. "Are you going to walk away like a good little boy, or are you going to take a beating as well?"

I looked at his frizzy red hair and something just took hold of me. "Fuck off back to your cage, Hair Bear," I blurted. "Before I call the zookeeper."

Jimmy looked at me, then at Clutch, then at Clutch's frizzy hair.

His mouth began to quiver and twitch. "Hair Bear?" he repeated and creased up with laughter.

Behind him the twins started to laugh as well.

Clutch was furious. "What did you call me? What the hell did you just call me?"

I backed away. Hands held out in front of me in an apologetic gesture.

Meanwhile Danno had somehow bucked Lanky off his chest. The two of them were rolling around on the ground, each trying to better the other. The twins started launching kicks, but just as many were making contact with Lanky as they were with Danno.

Clutch wasn't distracted. He was advancing on me. Jimmy was advancing with him, but he was glancing at Clutch's hair and chuckling. I kept my hands outstretched and backed off another few paces.

"It was a joke," I said. "Just a joke, Clutch."

"See how many jokes you tell from your hospital bed when I knock your teeth down your fucking throat," said Clutch.

He raised his fist, face contorting with rage. As I waited for the impact, I saw a blue flash of lightening streaking down though the grey swell of the clouds. There came an almost sonic boom of thunder, so loud it physically rattled the roofs and doors of the garages. The heavens opened up, spewing down great sheets of pounding rain. The rain was falling so hard it was bouncing from the fissured tarmac surface of the square. Dirty puddles were rapidly forming in potholes and crevices. Torrents of gritty looking water were gushing down in tumbling cascades from the garage roofs. It was like the sky had been holding the rain in for weeks and now, finally, it had broken free.

Clutch's ginger Afro began to deflate from the assault, flopping down in wiry clumps around his shoulders. Lanky had unravelled himself from Danno's grip and staggered to his feet. He and the twins were kicking Danno around in the mud. Jimmy just stood there staring at me as the rain ricocheted from the shaven crown of his head.

"Fuck it," said Clutch. "Let's get out of here. These two are not worth getting soaked to the skin for."

He barged past me. Jimmy followed, making an attempt at a head butt, which I easily dodged. Lanky and the twins took turns at giving Danno a

261

last kick each, before sprinting away, heads down through the deluge.

Full of pent up sudden rage I roared out a pathetically petulant version of the Hair Bear theme tune. *"Help, help here come the bears. Here come the bears. Let's split!"*

The rain intensified. The ground trembled at the power of several consecutive thunderclaps. The dark clouds flashed with jagged forks of lightening. It looked to me like the way the sky suddenly erupts into rocket bursts on Guy Fawkes' night. Danno had pushed himself up onto his hands and knees. The rain was bouncing from his back. He was so weakened from the beating he'd taken that the downward force of the deluge was preventing him from rising to his feet.

I ran to him, rain stinging my eyes, water soaking through my baseball boots to my socks as I splashed through muddy puddles. I dragged him to his feet. He swayed a little and then leaned on me for support. The rainwater running down his face was mingled with red streaks of blood.

There was a vandalised garage near the end of the square, buckled door hanging half open. I dragged him in there, the two of us stumbling and weaving out of the rain. Inside the place reeked of old engine oil. The lightening flashed and illuminated its gloomy interior. A rusted wheel rim and an upturned car battery were the only items left there. The rain beat a fierce tattoo onto the corrugated roof.

"Fuck's sake, Ranks," said Danno. "What's wrong with me?" He spat blood onto the oily concrete floor. "What the hell is wrong with me?"

I tried to wipe some of the blood from his face. I didn't know how to respond. I looked at the bloodstains on my palm. *Bad blood,* that was what I wanted to say. *You've got bad blood, Danno. It comes from your old man. It comes from Maggie manipulating that fact for her own wicked ends.*

Instead, I held my tongue.

Danno looked at me. "You should have seen what I did to Deb's cousin."

"I saw," I replied.

"Is it bad?" he asked.

I nodded.

Danno started to cry. "I don't know what came over me. It was like there was this stab of white light inside my head and I just went ape shit."

I put my arm around his shoulder. Cold water dripped from his hair onto my forearm. "I knew I had to be punished for what I did that kid," he sobbed. "That's why I came looking for Clutch. I knew this was going to happen. It's what I deserve."

Outside in the square two figures had appeared, shimmering slightly behind the relentless sheets of rain. Maggie and Maurice, side-by-side, peering across at us like we were animals caged in a zoo. They seemed to be gloating, somehow smugly satisfied. As if what had happened to Danno was all part of some vindictive plan.

"Can you see them, Dan," I asked.

Still crying Danno nodded his head. "I saw them at the river too. They were watching from the bank when I laid into Deb's cousin."

Chapter Twenty-Two

I didn't sleep at all that night. Despite the downpour the air remained close and muggy. I lay on the bed sheets, sweating, afraid to close my eyes in case I went travelling through the *astral plane* to some terrible destination. I kept going over in my head what HC and me planned to do in the morning. Were really we going to pick up Catweazle's mollified body and carry the cold cadaver down those rickety stairs to bury it behind the old shed in Maggie's overgrown garden?

It didn't seem real. When I imagined how it was going to play out, I imagined it happening at midnight rather than first thing in the morning. It was like a scene from a Hammer Horror. A full moon peeping out from behind the clouds, a thin mist swirling around Maggie's house, bats flitting in the sky. Both of us creeping around like a pair of grave robbers in reverse.

And what about Maggie? Was she just going to stand by and let us carry out our plan? Or would she intervene and manipulate our actions to thwart us? Would we find ourselves going hell for leather up in that little room, beating up each other and not even knowing where the aggression came from? Or would she be waiting there at the bottom of the stairs to stop us in our tracks as we struggled down with Catweazle's cold corpse, Maurice at her side, hissing gas from his nostrils, Maggie bug eyed and black faced, with the vacuum cleaner flex tight around her ghoulish neck?

265

Around one in the morning there was another huge thunderstorm. The room lit up to violent flashes of lightening, the walls shuddered from the thunderclaps, the rain lashed against my bedroom window. I heard Libby go creeping into Mum's room. She'd never gotten over her childhood fear of thunder and lightning.

My thoughts turned to Danno. I wondered what his mum had said when he'd come home all battered, bloodied and bruised. More importantly I wondered what his old man had said when he arrived home from work to find that someone else had done a much better job on his son than he'd ever managed in his drunken furies.

A bizarre scene played out my head in which Danno's old man came home and saw the state he was in. Danno told him what he'd done to Deb's cousin. He ruffled Danno's hair and hugged him close, kissing him on the forehead. "That's my boy," he said. "Like father, like son." Danno smiled, looking proud. "Now all you got to do is kill someone," said his old man. "How about that friend of yours? That one who stares at me in the newsagents when I but my ciggies."

"Ranks?" asked Danno.

His old man nodded. "The Rankin boy. He'd be easy meat. All you'd have to do is creep up behind him. Suffocation is best. Then we could toss him in the river. Make it look like he drowned."

He demonstrated, sneaking up behind Danno. "Then you put your hand over his mouth and squeeze his nose shut with your finger and thumb, like this." I saw Danno struggling for breath while

266

his old man increased the pressure on his mouth and pressed harder with his finger and thumb. He didn't stop till Danno slumped down and lay unconscious on the floor.

"Whoops," he said. "The son is out."

Then tossed his head back and laughed at his cruel pun.

I shook my head to clear away the image.

To avoid any more of these of thoughts I began to go over my repertoire of impersonations, categorising them into three lists - good, not bad, and rubbish. Then I divided the rubbish list into two separate categories – work on and forget about completely.

From my *work on* list I selected Tony Curtis and spent the next couple of hours going over in my head scenes from films I'd seen him in and practicing dialogue in his heavy Bronx accent. I made a mental note to watch The Persuaders TV series, the next time they showed a repeat. Maybe I could work in some humorous exchanges between Tony and Roger Moore.

I was up long before the alarm went off. Mum was in the kitchen getting ready to leave for work when I went downstairs. "The thunder kept me awake," I said when she gave me a look. Mum chuckled. "Libby crept into my bed. Don't say anything though. She'll be embarrassed."

I shook some sugar puffs into a bowl and poured on some milk. "I heard her creeping into your room."

"Don't say anything though," repeated Mum.

I nodded, thinking to myself I'd probably save that one up till the threat of exposing Libby to her mates provided me with leverage for something I wanted from her. Mum put two tins on the table. Ravioli in Meat Sauce and Sliced Peaches in Syrup. "These are for your tea. Tell Libby to make some toast to go with the Ravioli."

I nodded with my mouth full of Sugar Puffs.

Mum chuckled again. "Mrs Aitken is going to fall off her bloody stool when you come in this early."

She picked up her handbag and slung it over her shoulder.

"What are you and your pals getting up to today?" she asked.

"Nothing much," I replied. And the sentence carried on silently inside my head. *Just burying the mouldering corpse of the town tramp that we've been keeping secret for the past couple of weeks.*

She came and kissed me on the forehead. "No getting into bother, you hear?"

"Sure," I said, flushing at the thought of how much bother I was actually in.

After she left, I retrieved my canvas newspaper bag from the cupboard. As the sun started to rise the dampness in the ground from the thunderstorm was evaporating, shrouding whole housing scheme in a dense, vaporous mist. I walked toward HC's house with my head down, afraid of what I might see in the white, dancing swirls.

Remembering what HC had said about how lightly his mum slept I drew in a huge lungful of breath and crept to the side of the house to retrieve the shovel from where he'd left it. I'd planned to hide it by the side of the railway embankment, but the eerie quietness that the mist was creating caused me to rethink. Instead, I hid it amongst the coarse grass behind one of the benches in the play park.

I sat there for a while, pondering on what we were about to do, wondering if it was too late to back out. Maybe we should still just do what HC had suggested and put in an anonymous call to the police. Who cared now if there were witnesses and evidence that linked us to Catweazle's body?

We hadn't killed him, had we?

It felt like from the very moment HC came screaming out of Maggie's house the three of us had been hurtling headlong down a dark road that could only lead us to some sort of tragic end. But then again, maybe we could bring about an end on our own terms. Maybe we could just bury Catweazle and all the terrible secrets that went with the discovery of his body.

I made my way to the newsagents feeling as confused and conflicted as ever. My bones ached in a way I'd never experienced before. I wanted to go back to bed. But I knew that if I did sleep would evade me once more. When I entered the shop Mr Aitken's attention was so focused on the page of The Times he was reading on the counter that he hardly even acknowledged my presence. If I'd wanted, I could have slipped a whole box of Bazooka Joes into my bag without him noticing.

Instead, I found my hand drawn to a Cadbury Raisin Bar. It seemed to symbolise everything that was lost to me. Maybe after HC and me had performed our gruesome deed I could go and find Deb and try to make up with her. Maybe I could somehow redeem what was left of the summer. But then there was Danno and what he'd done to her cousin. And there was the terrible truth that we had to reveal to Danno about what we thought his old man had done all those years ago, and where that ring he wore actually came from. Redemption it seemed was far beyond my grasp.

"Are you planning to pay for that?"

Mr Aitken's voice made me jump. For once he'd noticed my pilfering "I was thinking maybe you could deduct the cost from my wage at the end of the week," I lied.

Mr Aitken regarded me over the tops of his horn-rimmed spectacles. "Didn't you have breakfast before you left the house?"

I nodded my head. "It's just that by the time I finish my round I'm usually hungry again."

He looked at the clock on the wall behind the counter. He seemed in a good mood. "Let's call it a bonus for getting in early for once."

"Thanks," I said, and dropped the Raisin Bar into my paper bag.

I think I went into some sort of autopilot again during the paper round. By the time HC met me I had no recollection of pushing a single paper through letterbox, or even whether I'd delivered the right papers to the right addresses.

"Holy Fuckeroni," said HC when I told him where I'd hidden the shovel. "What if someone sees us when we go to get it?"

270

"You can hardly see a few feet ahead of you in this mist," I pointed out. "We can cover up the shovel with my paper bag."

"Let's hope it doesn't lift too soon," said HC. "There'll be less chance of someone seeing us from the railway embankment when we…you know…"

We made our way to the park.

"Some thunder yesterday," said HC. "You get caught in it?"

I told him the whole story about Danno, from the time I'd ran into Deb and Shona to the beating he'd been taking from Clutch and the others when I found him at the garages. HC's eyes popped wide. "Holy fuckeroni, Ranks. He's completely out of control."

"That's why we've got to end it," I said. "Maybe he's not out of control. Maybe he's *under* some sort of control. Maybe what he's doing is being influenced?"

"You mean by Maggie, don't you?"

I told him about the apparition Danno and me had seen through the sheets of rain while we were sheltering inside the garage.

"How come I've never seen her?" asked HC. "Yesterday Danno said he'd noticed things out of the corner of his eye. Now he's seen her and Maurice. Just like you."

"Believe me, it's nothing to be jealous of," I replied.

We entered the park. Instead of picking up the shovel straight away we both sat down on the bench. I took out the raisin bar and gave half to HC.

HC tried to make a joke. "This doesn't mean we're going out or anything." Neither of us laughed.

Through the mist we could make out the shapes of people waiting at the bus stop. It was entirely possible that Danno's old man was amongst them. I turned to HC. "Sooner or later, someone is going to dig up Catweazle's body. Then questions are going to be asked about who buried it."

"I know," said HC. "But it could be a long time before that happens. By then he'll be a skeleton. At the moment there's physical evidence of what we've been up to all over him. The Blu Flush, the Shake and Vac all over him, the hairspray that you used. If someone finds him now, the questions are going to go a whole lot deeper."

I swallowed down the last mouthful of Raisin Bar and wiped my hands on my jeans. "Let's get on with it then."

With the end of the shovel wrapped in the canvas newspaper bag we made our way to the old railway track. The yellowed copy of the Daily Record was still draped over the nettles where I'd kicked it. But it hung there limply. Drenched and shredded by the rain.

"Remember a couple of years ago, when they brought them Funny Face ice lollies out?" asked HC.

I nodded, slightly wrong footed by the randomness of the question.

"Remember how we spent nearly the whole summer going into shops and asking if the people behind the counter had a Funny Face?" he asked.

I laughed. It was a good memory. "And nearly every one of them said hang on a second and I'll take a look."

Now HC laughed. "That was about the best time we ever had, Ranks. We pissed ourselves laughing every time it happened."

He turned to me. There were tight lines drawn on his freckled features. "Where did it go, Ranks? When did life turn out to be so shitty?"

I gave him a shrug. "I suppose that's what happens when you start to grow up. You just lose the fun stuff like that. It slips from your grasp."

HC bowed his head. He seemed lost in his thought.

"Should we dig the hole first?" I asked, as we made our way down the embankment to the fallen fence that bounded the overgrown garden.

"I think we should get him downstairs and leave him in the kitchen while we dig the hole," replied HC. "That way we can watch the embankment and get him out and into the hole quickly when we're sure no one is walking along the track."

My heart started to quicken as we neared the kitchen door. The stairs cricked and cracked as we climbed them, HC slightly ahead, far braver now it seemed than he had been that day he'd made the *run*. The house reeked of damp and mildew now. There were streaks on the dirty wall where rainwater had leaked through the damaged roof and damp patches on some of the floorboards on the upper landing. When I looked up there was still

273

water dripping through a gap where the plaster in the ceiling had blown.

The door to the little bedroom was wide open.

"You think someone went in there?" asked HC, pausing in the hall.

I shrugged. "If someone found the body wouldn't the police have boarded up the house, or put some of that yellow tape up, or something?"

We entered the room. Catweazle was still seated in the armchair, cheeks hollowed into the crater of his open mouth, dewdrops of condensations, speckling his beard and hair and the crusted lesions that had previous blistered and burst on his face.

"How are we going to do this?" I asked.

HC reached into his pockets and brought out two sets of yellow rubber gloves. "We were stupid to throw the other ones away," he said. "But, like I said, my mum has plenty under the stairs." He handed me a pair. "One of us takes his feet. The other get his hands under his armpits."

I rested the shovel against the wall, looked at the decayed corpse and shuddered.

"I'll take the feet."

HC began pulling on his gloves.

"You think of a prayer or anything we can say?" I asked.

"Whatever we're going to say we should say it in here," replied HC. "We don't want to be paying our last respects outside where we might be seen. We need to get it over and done as fast as we can."

I took the T. Lobsang Rampa book from where it was wedged into the back pocket of my jeans. HC brushed some hair away from his face. "You can't go reading out of that. It wouldn't be right. I thought about it last night."

I opened the book. "Who says it's not right? This was in Catweazle's duffle bag. How do you know this wasn't his favourite book?"

HC face blushed a little, making his freckles stand out. "I suppose it's the best we can do," he said.

I cleared my throat. The hinges on the door creaked. There came a crack on the floorboard somewhere behind me. Over the smell of the dampness there seemed to be a hint of the noxious aroma of gas. Hand shaking, I held the book open at the page I'd selected and stood before Catweazle's addled body.

"To the lady Ke,uie," I read. *"Who taught me many Siamese cat words and always encouraged me."*

HC screwed his brow and looked at me as if I was crazy.

It was then that we heard the sudden, unexpected sounds of someone thundering up the stairs.

Chapter Twenty-Three

We stood there like a couple of yellow-gloved minstrels - caught in the spotlight, act unrehearsed as the curtain went up. It was Danno who emerged onto the landing at the top of the stairs. He'd been taking them so fast that he tripped over the lip of the top stair and went sprawling along the corridor. We'd have probably laughed if his unexpected arrival hadn't shocked us so much.

Grunting, he picked himself up and clambered to his feet. The bruising had set in on his face. He had blackened rings around both eyes and ugly purple welts on his cheeks. There was a lesion on the bridge of his nose and the healed wound on his upper lip had opened afresh. "What are you two doing here?" he demanded, when he saw HC and me.

"Could ask you the same thing," I fired back.

Danno was trembling. I noticed that he had Catweazle's penknife in his hand. The long blade was extended and covered in blood. There were dark spatters of the same blood on the back of Danno's hand. He came stumbling into the room. "I stabbed my old man."

"Holy fuckeroni!" yelled HC.

The hinges on the door to the little room groaned as it visibly moved. A floorboard creaked as though it had been stepped upon. My knees felt like they were about to buckle under me. "Where?" I asked, doing my utmost to ignore the presence that was palpably in the room with us.

"In the kitchen." Danno looked down at the knife. "Through the back of the hand. Damn near nailed him to the table before I pulled it back out."

I felt a twinge of relief. At least it hadn't been fatal.

"He started in on me at breakfast, as soon as he saw my bruises. Said I was a useless waste of space, and I should toughen up. Said no son of his would have let himself get set on that way."

The conversation hadn't gone the way I'd imagined it then.

The seeping smell of gas began to intensify.

"While he was ranting at me, I took the penknife out of my pocket and opened it on my lap under the table. When he yelled that he had a good mind to beat me up himself I kind of flipped and brought the knife down on the back of his as hard as I could."

"Holy fuckeroni," said HC again. The temperature in the room had dropped by several degrees. "There was blood when I pulled it back out, a whole lot of blood. My mum started screaming. I ran. He ran after me."

HC's eyes went wider than I'd ever seen them before. "He ran after you?"

From the top of the embankment there came a monstrous roar. "Daniel, you little bastard, I know you're in that house. Get out here now. I swear to God, I'll swing for you!"

"The gun?" asked Danno. "Ray's airgun. Did you move it?"

"We didn't get the chance," I replied.

Danno fell to his knees and started wedging the bloodied blade of the penknife between the loose floorboards where the gun was hidden. An undefined shadow seemed to coalesce at the back of him, hunching close to his arched back. I edged my way over to the rear window. Danno's old man had started down the embankment. His hair wasn't greased and slicked back the way it usually was. It hung messily over his face in a pendulous and unruly curtain. There was a tea towel wrapped around his right hand, stained darkly red.

"I swear to God, Daniel," he roared, struggling to keep his balance on the slope. "If I have to come in there and get you it's going to be ten times worse than it already is."

The smell of gas was growing steadily stronger. The floorboards creaked and creaked again. It sounded as if Maggie and Maurice were circling the room like voracious beasts of prey. Catweazle sat in his battered armchair, a silent observer – *see no evil, hear no evil, speak no evil*. HC looked so pale I thought he was about to fall into a faint where he stood. Danno had the floorboard up. He dropped the penknife, reached into the gap, and shook the airgun free from the Fine Fayre bag.

"If we make a run for it now, we can help you get away," I said.

"Come on," urged HC. "Let's go."

Danno began hurriedly loading pellets into the airgun's clip. The shadow swirled around him once more. "You go," he said. "This is between me and my old man."

278

"Holy fuck," said HC. "You can't just shoot him."

Danno wiped away the tears that had been running down his cheek with the back of his hand. "You heard him. He said he'd swing for me. Maybe it's me that's going to swing for him."

The house shook to the sound of Danno's old man crashing into the kitchen.

"Where are you, Daniel? Come out a take your medicine."

HC pressed a trembling finger up to his lip. I sucked in a long breath and held it there. I reached for the shovel and grabbed it for protection. Danno just stood there, splay legged, gun held in both hands, aimed at the open bedroom doorway, looking like some detective from an American TV show.

"If you've run out the front door, I'll still find you," warned Danno's old man, stomping noisily along the downstairs corridor.

Let him think that Danno has ran straight through the house, I prayed. *Let him go right through too, and out to the street.*

Maggie, it seemed, had other ideas. We all cried out when the door to the big bedroom slammed violently shut. "There's no place to hide, Daniel," yelled Danno's old man. He began to take the stairs, thumping his foot down deliberately on each step and chanting in mocking tones as he came. "Fee-fo-fi-fucking-fum. I smell the blood of my worthless son."

HC backed himself into a corner of the room. I kind of hovered by the rear window, knuckles turning white around the shaft of the shovel. Danno held the airgun before him, one hand steadying the other. The smell of gas in had become so strong now it was making me dizzy.

Danno's old man appeared on the landing. He was hunched over, looking as monstrous as Oliver Reed in the Wolfman movie. The twin shadows fell around him. Before I could do anything, he snatched HC's dad's shovel roughly from my grip and held like a weapon before him. The tea towel around his wounded hand was dripping fat splats of blood onto the dusty floorboards. He laughed when he saw the airgun. "You stabbed me with your toy knife. Now you're going shoot me with your toy gun?"

"Just back off," said Danno. "Or I'll take your eye out."

Danno's old man flicked his hair defiantly back over his head. "Go on then. Which eye? Left, or right?" He began advancing into the room, shovel held at shoulder height. "You don't have the guts to pull the trigger."

"Don't you dare take one more step," warned Danno.

Grinning Danno's old man took one more deliberate step. Danno pulled the trigger. Nothing happened. The gun's cylinder had finally run out of air. Danno's old man didn't waste a second. He swung the shovel wildly and knocked the airgun out of Danno's hand. Danno howled and doubled up in pain, pressing his wrist to his chest. "You broke my arm. You broke my arm."

Danno's old man raised the shovel above his head. Blood from the tea towel streaked back along his wrist. "Wait till you see what else I'm going to break. Nobody stabs me and get away with it."

HC stepped in front of him. "Leave him alone."

"What the fuck?" said Danno's old man, seeming to finally realise in that instant that there was more than just Danno and himself in the room. I guessed he hadn't even seen me when he grabbed shovel. Just reached for the nearest thing to hand. Heart crashing in my chest I ran to HC's side. "You going to kill us all?" The words almost made me sick with fear.

Danno's old man lowered the shovel a little. It seemed to me that he was more likely to be weighing up which one of us to take down first than considering whether to back down. "The three little piggies facing off the Big Bad Wolf, huh?" he said.

"You already murdered two people in this house," said HC. "Are you planning to make the list longer?"

The shovel was lowered a little more.

"Maurice," said HC. "Remember Maurice Henderson? The guy who built this house? You killed him and stole his money. And then you came back for more and when Maggie came home from the hospital, you killed her. Made it look as if she hung herself."

"What are you talking about?" asked Danno, still pressing his wrist to his chest.

"Ask him about the ring," I said, taking HC's lead. "Ask your old man about that wheatsheaf ring he wears, and how he came by it."

Danno's old man lowered the shovel some more and glanced guiltily at the ring on the finger

281

that poked out from underneath the blood-soaked tea towel. It was then that he noticed Catweazle's body in the old armchair.

"What the fuck?" he cried again. "Is that a dead body?"

The shovel dropped to his side. He sniffed the air and screwed up his nose at what he was smelling. Then he leaned in closer to Catweazle, sniffing again to see it was emanating from him and shaking his head when he discovered it wasn't.

Suddenly Catweazle's mouldering corpse rose out of the chair, arms juddering limply around it. It was as if a set of unseen hands were hauling up by the shoulders, like some flaccid marionette. All of us cried out. Danno's old man stumbled backwards and crashed heavily against the doorframe.

Catweazle's body danced a momentary macabre jig and then thumped heavily back down into the chair. The chair spun on its casters, rotating rapidly around the centre of the room like a crazy fairground, so fast that Catweazle's arms rose and flapped around him. Danno's old man gripped the shaft of the shovel. His unshaven chin jutted out. "I don't know how you little bastards are doing this. But you're not scaring me."

The chair came to halt. Catweazle's head lolled against his shoulder. His mouth fell open, the interior still darkly died from the Blu Flush. Now Maurice and Maggie materialised eerily behind the chair. Maurice gushing streamers of gas from his mouth and nostrils, Maggie black-faced and bug-eyed from the pressure of the vacuum cleaner flex tied around her neck.

Danno's old man held the shovel defensively before him.

"*Confessssssss,*" hissed Maurice.

"*Do it,*" urged Maggie, bloodshot eyes full of hatred.

Danno's old man looked down at the ring.

"*Confessssssss.*"

"*Do it.*"

"Holy fuck," said HC. "Holy, holy fuck. I see them. I see them now."

Danno nursed his wrist and watched as the arrogance of his old man's stature began to wither before us. I put my arm around Danno's shoulder.

"What's all the noise?"

The unexpected voice from the corridor made us all jump.

When we looked Mr Renton and his dog were standing there. Captain could clearly see the terrible apparitions of Maurice and Maggie. He threw back his head and let out a long, strangulated howl. Then he fell to his belly and began to whine, covering his brown muzzle with his front paws. Either Mr Renton didn't see a thing, or he was in a state of denial. His attention was focused on Danno's old man. "Did you hurt that boy? What are you doing with that shovel?"

"He's my son," snarled Danno's old man. "Mind your own fucking business, you old bastard."

Now Maurice and Maggie came gliding round from either side of Catweazle's armchair, advancing doggedly toward Danno's old man.

"You want the ring?" he yelled at them. "You want the ring back? Is that it?"

283

Captain's whining rose to a crescendo. "There boy," said Mr Renton, leaning down to pat his head. "The man's clearly drunk, or on drugs."

Maurice advanced, gushing clouds of gas. Maggie advanced, rubber flex hanging down from her broken neck and trailing down her back like a gruesome black tentacle. Danno's old man dropped the shovel. It went clattering down onto the floorboards. He began walking backwards, struggling to twist the ring from his finger.

"Confessssss."

"Do it."

The ring jerked free. Danno's old man tossed it to the floor. It rolled across the room.

"I did it!" he yelled. "I did it. I killed Maurice Henderson. I broke into this house and snuck up behind him in the kitchen and suffocated him. Then I made it look as if he'd gassed himself in the oven. Then I did the same with his spoilt rich bitch of a wife."

"What's he saying?" asked Mr Renton. "What's he talking about?"

Danno's old man's hands dropped to his side in defeat. The blood from his wounded hand dripped splat-splat-splat to the floor. "Is that what you wanted to hear?"

"Yessssss."

"Yes."

Danno's old man took another step back. "Now let me be. I've told you what you wanted to hear. I've given you back your poxy ring."

Maurice and Maggie, advanced even more rapidly, seemingly unwilling to relent or afford him

284

the slightest respite. All it took was two more backward steps before his legs hit the window ledge. With a startled scream he toppled backwards and pitched out of the window, taking the last remaining shards of glass with him.

There came a dull thud as he hit the ground.

"Dad!" cried Danno.

I helped Danno to his feet. When we looked out of the window his old man was lying in the litter strewn driveway in such a horribly twisted mess that it wasn't possible that he was anything other than dead. There was a moment's silence that seemed to last for ever. Then Captain started barking. When I turned around Maurice and Maggie were gone. The smell of gas had been replaced by the smell of dust and damp and mildew, with the faint undertone of the last remnants of Catweazle's rot.

"You two run to the phone box on the housing scheme," said Mr Renton, taking charge of the situation and addressing HC and me. "Phone 999. Ask for an ambulance. I'll stay here with the boy and his father."

"Shouldn't we ask for the police as well?" asked HC, moving toward the door and beckoning to me.

Mr Renton looked at Catweazle's decayed body. "That would be a very good idea. It seems to me that there's going to be a lot of questions that need to be asked."

Chapter Twenty-Four

Of course, it didn't simply end there. In my experience there is never truly an end to anything. Everything that happens in our lives remains as a revenant echo. No one gets to live happily ever after. That's another lie that people tell. We certainly didn't. That's for sure.

There was a police investigation. Questions were indeed asked. Plenty of them. But never once honestly answered. Long before any of the three of us were interviewed we colluded like the unholy trinity of cowards that we were and decided the best strategy was simply to lie through our teeth. HC concocted the lie, with a little input here and there from Danno and me. HC rehearsed us it its delivery. He was the master of deception.

Here's how the lie went.

That day HC and me had decided we wanted to go fishing in the river. We knew the rain would have brought out plenty of worms, so we borrowed HC's dad's shovel to dig them up for bait. We thought the railway embankment was as good a place as any to go digging. Once we had a good supply of worms we were going to go back to HC's house and borrow his dad's rod and tackle as well.

We were about to make a start when Danno came running along the track. He told us what had happened with his old man and that he was after Danno's blood. So Danno was going to go and fetch his cousin's air gun that he'd hidden under the floorboards in Maggie's way back at Easter when he'd done the run. His intention was to defend himself. He wasn't planning to shoot his old man or nothing, just threaten him to save himself from another beating.

HC and me had his back. Why wouldn't we? He was our mate, wasn't he? We'd gone with him into the house and up to the bedroom to hide. We'd brought the shovel with us for protection. We were as surprised as anyone to find Catweazle's dead body in the armchair. We would have reported it had we not heard Danno's old man screaming and bawling from up on the railway track.

Danno fetched the airgun from under the floorboards. By that time Danno's old man was already halfway up the stairs. He grabbed the shovel from me and attacked Danno with it. That was as far as the lie had to go, because Mr Renton had witnessed everything else, and there nothing like third party corroboration to seal the deal on a damned good lie. Renton never said anything about Danno's old man's confession to double murder. Either the trauma was too much that he forgot that bit, or he was still in a state of denial about what else we had all witnessed in that room. We didn't mention it either.

HC said that justice had been delivered. He said that this was the outcome that Maggie and Maurice had wanted all along. Their souls would rest in peace now, and there was no point in digging up the past all over again. We worried that Gordon Aitken and his girlfriend might come forward and say that they'd seen HC and me in the house, outside that little room, the day before it all happened. They didn't. Who knows, maybe they were caught up in a web of lies of their own?

I've no idea if the police believed the story we spun. All I know is that they didn't pursue the matter further. The verdict on Danno's old man was death by misadventure. Danno went to juvenile court for stabbing his old man in the hand, but he got off with probation and suspended sentence based on the mitigating factors of the abuse he'd suffered as minor.

The verdict on Catweazle was death by natural causes. No one asked us any questions about the condition of his corpse. The blue flush stains in his mouth and beard, the Silvikin and Shake 'n' Vac we'd covered him in, and the remnants of bubble gum still left over where we'd stuck the fly papers all seemed to be completely ignored. I suppose if they'd asked too many questions about that aspect they would, in turn, have had to start questioning our version of events. Too much paperwork and police time involved digging any deeper. Easier to leave the lid on a can of worms than open it up. Three delinquents from a council housing scheme weren't worth the effort it would involve. Sometimes a convenient lie is much preferable to an inconvenient truth.

It turned out that Catweazle had been in the Kings Own Scottish Borderers, just like HC's uncle. He'd been a sergeant. His real name was James McAndrews. In his day he was a bit of hero, decorated for bravery in Aden and given an honourable discharge. That news hit HC hard, what with his uncle's situation and the disrespect we'd all shown to Catweazle's corpse. I think he blamed Danno and me far more than he blamed himself. We were the ones who'd pressurised him into making his *run*, and that was where the whole thing started.

They boarded up all the doors and windows in Maggie's house. A tall chicken wire fence was erected around the front and back. A sign went up saying it had been declared an unsafe structure and that entry was prohibited. A new myth grew up amongst the kids on the housing scheme that winter. Apparently if you walked past the front of the house after sunset, you'd see the ghost of Danno's old man staggering and juddering around, all mangled and twisted from his fall from the window, his hair still somehow sculpted into a neat Brylecreme quiff.

After the new school term HC drifted away from Danno and me. He joined the army cadets and made new friends. I hung out with Danno for a few weeks longer. But he gradually started spending more and more time with Clutch and his gang, seemingly holding no sort of grudge for the beating he'd endured. He'd strut around town with them, provoking fights with poorly outgunned groups of kids, and then retiring to mooch around the jukebox in the cafe on the High Street. None of them ever bothered me. I, in turn, kept well clear of them. If Danno passed me on the street, we barely manage to nod at each other.

Once, when I noticed he was brazenly wearing the stolen wheatsheaf motif ring, I was so riled that I was sorely tempted to go for him, even if that meant taking a severe beating. I've no idea if he'd managed to pick it up from the floor when no one

289

was looking, or whether the police had returned it to the family after gathering it as evidence.

Seeing it on his finger made me feel as if everything we'd been through had been a pointless waste of effort. After all the trouble that ring had caused. So much for righting the wrongs of the past. I held my temper though and just stared him down in a manner that I was pretty sure left him in no doubt about what I'd come to think of him.

It kind of suited me that the three of us no longer hung out. I didn't want to be reminded of what had happened that summer. I didn't want in any way to confront the possibility that there had been ghosts in that old house, or that I'd somehow travelled through time to witness two murders and the terrible aftermath caused by the deception of how they had been covered up.

I tried desperately to get back with Deb. My efforts were in vain. She wasn't having it. Said she wanted to knuckle down and start studying for her O levels. Said I'd just be a distraction. It worked out for her. She was the only one out of the old gang who used to hang out at the Youth Club who stayed on at school. And, consequently, the only one of us who went on to attend university. She emigrated to Australia. I heard she opened a chain of coffee shops and became quite a successful businesswoman.

HC didn't fare so well. At eighteen he joined the Kings Own Scottish Borderers and became a soldier like Catweazle and his legendary uncle. I've often wondered if it was an act of redemption for his part in what happened in that little bedroom in

Maggie's house. He saw active service in Northern Ireland. On April 10th 1979 he was on patrol near the Divis Flats in Belfast. A sniper fired a single shot. The bullet entered the back of his neck and killed him instantly.

I went to his funeral. His mum cried the same way she laughed, like something terrible was stuck in the back of her throat, cluck-cluck-cluck, cluck-cluck-cluck, big breasts jiggling to the rhythm of her sobs. I felt so ashamed that in some irrational notion of dark humour the temptation crossed my mind to offer my condolences in the style of Foghorn Leghorn.

I kept thinking of HC's corpse bloating and decaying inside his coffin, then contracting and shrivelling, the way we'd witnessed Catweazle's body deteriorate in that old armchair. The image stuck in my head for weeks. I was terrified I might start seeing his ghost.

The funeral was the last time Danno and me exchanged more than two words. By then Shona was pregnant and they were about to get married. Yes, Danno finally got together with Shona. Stranger things happen. Anyway, the marriage didn't last. Alcoholism and domestic violence put paid to any notions of matrimonial bliss either of them might have harboured.

Shona turfed him out of their council flat just after their son's second birthday. But she'd become a heavy drinker too and the poor kid was already in care before he reached next birthday. Danno moved back in with his mum. She put up with him for a few years, but when she passed, he was evicted for failing to pay the rent.

He started sleeping rough and drinking heavier than ever. He'd hang around the town gardens, guzzling cans of Tennent's lager and mooching around in the bins for cigarette ends, just as Catweazle had done when we were kids. To all intents and purposes, he became *Malkie the Alci*, the character he'd created when we'd acted out *This Is Your Life* in Maggie's house. He died of liver failure when he was two weeks' shy of his 40th birthday.

I've no idea what happened to the ring and I've no intention of finding out.

That left me alone to carry the burden of the memories of that terrible summer. For a while I managed to make a bit of a career for myself from my repertoire of impersonations. Billed as Alan Rankin, Man of Many Voices, I played the Club circuit on both sides of the Border; CUI, British Legion, Ex Service, Labour, Liberal, Conservative, Constitutional, you name it, I gigged there.

By eighteen I had an agent. She got me a shot on New Faces, but I didn't make it past the auditions. I did a summer season as a red coat in a holiday camp and a terrible winter season on a cruise liner that toured the Norwegian Fjords and the Arctic Circle.

In the end though my material became dated and I kind of lost the knack for picking up current voices. I packed it all in when I started to get frequent hallucinations of Catweazle's bloated body slumped in a chair in the audience. I'd fluff my lines, forget who I was supposed to be doing, get booed of the stage.

I pursued an alternative and far less glamorous career path and started work at the old quarry as a dumper truck driver, progressed to an HGV license, which in turn led to career as a long-distance driver. I got married, had kids, and decided to track down my father.

It turned out he'd been living all those years in a little village only forty miles away. Mum knew where he was all along. She'd thrown him out because he was having an affair and forced him to agree as part of the divorce settlement to have no more contact with me or Libby.

He wasn't at all pleased to see me when I turned up on his doorstep. Not in the least interested in anything that had happened in my life. There was a picture of his two daughters in his sideboard. He kept looking nervously at his watch. "How can I help you, son?" he kept asking. "My wife will be home soon. I'd rather you weren't here."

His wife wasn't the same woman he'd had the affair with. She had no idea of his past life, or that he had other children. He too had built his life on a lie. "If it was me," I told him, "I'd have fought tooth and nail to keep in touch with my kids."

A sadness washed over him. He looked as shrunken and deflated as Danno's old man had looked that day in Maggie's house. Nothing like the picture of the athletic teenager HC and me had seen in the newspaper that time in the library. He just gave a pathetic shrug of his shoulders. "Different times, son."

"Don't you dare!" I yelled at him. "Don't you dare call me son!"

I confronted my mum about what had happened, and I made sure that Libby was there when I did. It caused a huge rift that didn't fully heal till my father died. His wife contacted the two of us. He'd told her everything when he'd been diagnosed with terminal lung cancer.

Both of us declined her invitation to attend the funeral. As HC would have said, there was no point in digging up the past all over again. But it did somehow mend the wounds with our mother. We meet up with Libby's clan every Christmas. Mum is in her late eighties now. Our kids have kids of their own. I usually try to entertain them with some of my old impersonations. They laugh politely, but most of the brood have no clue as to who the hell I am supposed to be taking off.

Mum and Libby usually last at least a couple of hours before they're predictably back at each other's throats. I've never told either of them the whole story of what happened that summer. My guess is they'd still refer to some of it as hippy-trippy shite.

I suppose that brings up the question of T. Lobsang Rampa and the so-called *'Wisdom of the Ancients'*. Was any of that true? I googled him once the grandkids had taught me to do more than just switch on a computer.

The T stands for Tuesday, which apparently has some mystical significance in Tibetan Buddhism. But it turns out he was probably just as much of a lair as the rest of us. His real name was

Cyril Henry Hoskin. He was a plumber from Devon. He was exposed as an alleged hoaxer by a private detective after he started publishing books and claiming to be an authentic Tibetan monk. Hoskin apparently justified his actions by asserting that as a boy he'd fallen out of a tree and his body was taken over by the metaphysical spirit of T. Lobsang Rampa.

Does that mean I never actually travelled back in time? That I never witnessed the murder of Maurice and Maggie Henderson by Danno's old man? That I never witnessed the horrific events on that rain drenched night when he cut the rubber flex from Maggie's vacuum cleaner, wrapped it coldly around her neck and hung her from the door to cover the fact that he'd just strangled her to death? All I know for sure is that Danno's old man confessed. He said in his own words that he'd murdered them both in the exact manner I'd witnessed in my dreams. So how the hell would I know that if there wasn't something in it?

There are still many nights when I fall asleep and find myself rising out of my body on my *silver chord*. I travel back through the *astral plane* to that hot summer fortnight in 1973. I usually find myself right back at the day we all fell asleep while HC was reading out the cheesy dialogue from the comic strips on the Bazooka Joe wrappers. Catweazle sits in his armchair, bloated and blistered, teeming with flies, and seething with maggots. Like a ghost observing a ghost I watch Maggie's malevolent spirit prowling about us, paying particular attention to Danno, as if she can somehow scent the blood ties between him and his murderous old man.

There are other nights when there is a grotesque tea party going on downstairs in the old dining room. Maggie presides at the head of the table. Maurice is to the left of her, hissing gas through his nostrils. Catweazle is to her right, stroking a fat, slimy toad that sits on his outreached palm. Danno and HC are there too, as their fourteen-year-old selves, shoulder length hair cut to emulate Rod and Ronnie from The Faces. And Danno's old man is there, moody and brooding, hair slicked back, long Teddy-Boy sideburns, looking like he will erupt into violence at any minute. Worst of all is the empty seat. I know for certain it's for me. They're all waiting for the day that I take my rightful place.

The old railway line is always there in those fevered dreams. It truly has become a dark scar that slashes through all the days of my life. It always leads me back to Maggie's house. The one dreadful truth that has remained constant throughout my life. Are these memories, or perhaps the effects of some sort of post-traumatic stress? Or do the ghosts of my past come back to haunt me? Who knows? My wife has a name for them. When I jerk awake, wide eyed, trembling and delirious, drenched in cold sweat, she calls them the night terrors.

THE END